"WHO ARE YOU?" BLISS ASKED.

"Who do you want me to be?" His head dipped to her throat, his silky hair teasing her cheek as he inhaled slowly. "Flowers and fruit. Roses, orange, a hint of vanilla. And heat. Why are you so hot?" The question was spoken in a husky whisper that turned her inside out.

"Because it's very warm in here."

"No, it's not. In fact, the breeze coming off the ocean is cool."

All Bliss felt was him, encompassing her without having laid a finger on her. "Your name. What is it?"

"If I tell you, will you let me kiss you?"

"No."

"Then I'll kiss you anyway."

The Pleasure Seekers

"Melanie George writes hot, steamy historicals with characters that leap off the page with spunk and spitfire."
—*Bridges Magazine*

"A treasure, a triumph, a treat for the heart! [T]ender, witty, and utterly charming. . . . Ms. George just keeps getting better and better."
—*Old Book Barn Gazette*

"[P]aradise found!"
—*Midwest Book Review*

"Sparkling wit and charming characters."
—*Affaire de Coeur*

Also by Melanie George

A Very Gothic Christmas
by Christine Feehan and Melanie George

The Art of Seduction

Melanie George

The PLEASURE SEEKERS

POCKET BOOKS

New York   London   Toronto   Sydney   Singapore

An *Original* Publication of POCKET BOOKS

 POCKET BOOKS, a division of Simon & Schuster, Inc.
1230 Avenue of the Americas, New York, NY 10020

ISBN: 0-7434-4273-3

First Pocket Books printing November 2003

10 9 8 7 6 5 4 3 2 1

POCKET and colophon are registered trademarks of
Simon & Schuster, Inc.

Cover design and illustration by Min Choi; photo credit: Andrea
Sperling/Taxi/Getty Images

Printed in the U.S.A.

For information regarding special discounts for bulk purchases,
please contact Simon & Schuster Special Sales at 1-800-456-6798
or business@simonandschuster.com

PART ONE

England

*"Cautious, very cautious," thought Emma;
"he advances inch by inch, and will hazard
nothing till he believes himself secure."*
Jane Austen

Prologue

There were things a man sometimes had to do that he wasn't particularly proud of. The day Caine Ballinger sold his soul to a woman for her pleasure, he'd taken the final step in his descent into hell.

One

The sleepless soul that perished in his
pride . . .
William Wordsworth

"*C*ome on, damn it." Sweat beaded on Caine's back as he thrust into the woman beneath him, her customary mewling sounds making bile rise in his throat. He wanted to be done with her so she would leave.

She was always ravenous for sex when she woke up, which was why he normally made himself scarce, but she had caught him unawares, climbing into his bed late last night after he had drunk himself into a stupor. He had come awake abruptly when she mounted his morning erection, for which he very nearly throttled her as he pushed her to her back.

"Oh, yes, Caine . . . that's it," she panted, her face wreathed in ecstasy. Olivia Hamilton, widow of the late Marquis of Buxton, and now Caine's patroness, was building toward her climax. "Now, Caine. Now."

Her legs gripped his flanks like an industrial clamp,

urging every ounce from him, whether he wished to give it or not.

She tossed her head back and moaned. A stream of bright sunlight slanted across her neck, showing the fine lines of her advancing age, which she claimed to be forty, but which he suspected was closer to forty-five. But she could have been twenty-five and it wouldn't have made his duty any easier. Fitting punishment for a man who had once been so immersed in a world of sin that he'd earned the nickname Vice from his comrades-in-debauchery. What a perversion of fate, to have been trapped by his own immorality.

Outside, the crisp snap of a gunshot signaled the start of the morning's fox hunt and the beginning of yet another weeklong house party, where he would hang on the fringes while England's most dissolute peers descended upon Northcote Hall. People he had once ignorantly called friends, in a home he had, in another lifetime, called his own.

Northcote had belonged to Ballingers since the fourteenth century, surviving sieges, the uncompromising elements of the Devon coastline, and a fire that had nearly gutted it a hundred years earlier. But it hadn't survived Henry Ballinger. His father.

The earl had been a good man, but distracted, the death of his wife pushing him deeper into his own world, his business ventures faltering until debt covered his head, and his son's head upon his death. Caine had barely escaped with the shirt on his back when he had learned how far-reaching the devastation. The entail on Northcote had lapsed. There had been no way to save it from the auction block, leaving an empty title as his sole inheritance.

Two years his father had been dead, his broken body found upon the rocks at the base of the cliffs. The last step in Henry Ballinger's march toward self-destruction was his inability to pay back the money loaned to him by the wealthiest nobleman in the region, Edward Ashton, Duke of Exmoor. There were many defeats the earl could accept, but not when it concerned a debt of honor. In that, his fall from grace had been absolute.

And so began Caine's own descent, his mind increasingly consumed with a growing hate, certain that his father would still be alive if the duke had given him more time to pay. Exmoor had pushed his father to his death as though the duke's hand had been on his father's back.

Since then, Caine's life had become a hellish purgatory, turning him into a man without a soul, without a conscience. He had nothing—nothing but the silent, impotent rage that kept him rising day after day, instead of taking his gun and putting a bullet through his brain.

Olivia whimpered beneath him, conveying that he was being too rough with her. But even that wouldn't make her leave. It wouldn't end this insanity, or change his circumstances. Or bring back the life he had once taken for granted.

"No, Caine," she begged when he began to pull out of her, his timing a near science.

She cursed his cruelty in tormenting her, which gave him a perverse sense of satisfaction. She may have a hold over him, but he had something she wanted badly. Eight inches of it.

His lack of cooperation was only a momentary annoyance, however, as she arched her hips up to draw him in and stroked her sex until she came, her muscles convulsing around his shaft, trying to wring his seed from him. But he wasn't taking any chances. He always wore the rubberized French letter to protect himself from impregnating her. One seed swimming upstream, and she'd have him in a choke hold for the rest of his life.

His duty complete, Caine rolled off her, letting the breeze from the open window cool his anger and his overheated body. Summer had finally settled in, banishing spring's chill to the hours before dawn.

The smell of the white jasmine that grew in abundance around the house drifted into the room, bringing with it the only vivid recollection Caine had of his mother. She had died when he was four years old, but the haunting fragrance taunted him with brief flashes of memory, of an ethereal figure with a sad smile.

"Caine," came the impatient voice of the new lady of the manor. "Untie me." She tugged on the red silk scarves securing her wrists to the bed posts.

Caine didn't bother to look at her. "No."

"Blast you, Caine! Untie me now."

He had tied her up for his pleasure, not hers. It kept her from touching him. "I think I'll ring for the maid," he said, reaching for the bellpull.

"Don't!"

Caine's hand hovered around the black silk cord. "Why not? The girl might discover a whole new appreciation for you, especially after you docked her a day's wage for spilling a cup of tea." Olivia reveled in her petty cruelties; it was the only thing that gave purpose to her life.

"She deserved it, the clumsy twit. I should have fired her on the spot."

"Your constant belittling made her nervous."

"Stop making excuses for these incompetent servants. You're always taking their side. One would think you cared about them."

Caine didn't want to think his actions were motivated by anything other than a desire to prod Olivia. She needed these little doses of humility, though it rarely took the edge off the bitch she was when not lying flat on her back.

"I don't care about anyone," he drawled. "You of all people should know that only too well."

"That's because you have no heart."

"True. But it's not my heart you want, is it? Now, you might want to close your thighs." His fingers wrapped around the bellpull.

"Someday, Caine, you're going to push me too far . . . and then I'm going to burn your beloved house to the ground."

Caine's hand curled into a fist. He had already been the recipient of her spite, as one by one she systematically destroyed the paintings of his ancestors that had hung in the portrait gallery for centuries. The few that remained now moldered in the attic.

"I see I have your attention," she said. "Good. Now untie me."

With a snarl, he loosened her bonds. Rolling away from her, he clasped his hands behind his head and stared up at the ceiling, thinking about the depths to which he had fallen; the single, fatal character flaw that had caused him to barter his body and soul.

"That was not well done of you, my lord," his unwanted bed partner chided as she rubbed feeling back into her arms, the pampered, spoiled princess of doting parents and a moronic husband who'd had the good sense to die.

"You got what you wanted, Olivia. Now leave me in peace, for Christ's sake."

"You're a mean brute, Caine, but utterly delicious." She slid her palm down over his stomach, the tip of her forefinger circling the head of his penis, now free of the condom.

He gripped her wrist and brought it down hard on the mattress. "Leave off," he growled.

"Don't be angry with me."

"I told you not to come to my bedroom."

"But you didn't come to me, and I needed you."

"So find another bedmate for the night."

"You're the only one I want."

Caine snorted. "You don't actually believe that delusion, do you?"

"Please, Caine. Stop barking at me." She sidled closer to him, her gaze running over his naked body. "Let me make it up to you."

Caine knew what she was going to do and told himself to stop her. He couldn't stand her, yet his body blared for some kind of fulfillment.

Her warm breath whispered across his rigid flesh a moment before she took him into her mouth, her blond hair teasing his groin. She was mocking him, knowing how bitterly he resented it when she did this.

She cupped him, massaging with expert fingers as her wet mouth slid further down his shaft, sucking hard, increasing its dimension as much as he tried to hold back the stirrings of his treasonous body.

Her lips closed tighter around him, her tongue toying with the crest, nursing just the head before going deep, her hand pumping the base as her mouth took in as much of him as she could manage, the suction building along with the speed, the pressure expanding in his loins.

On the verge of spewing his seed, she mounted him, her moan a husky contralto as she took the fully aroused, unprotected length of him inside her body.

Caine immediately wrenched her off him. "Damn you!"

Anger flared in her eyes as she leaned back against the pillows, her rouged nipples showing dark against the pale outline of her body and the blue satin sheets behind her. She looked like she wanted to hack him into little bits. But knowing she would get nowhere by inciting him further, she switched tactics, her lips curving into a pout, which for some godforsaken reason she thought worked on him.

"Why must you deny me? You know how much I want a child, yet you hold on to your precious seed like it's gold. I have money. I could give a babe all it desired: a governess to tend its dirty nappies, a wet nurse to offer up a tit when it's hungry."

"But no last name—unless you're suggesting marriage, and of course there is the fact that you don't possess an ounce of moral fiber."

"As though you do," she retorted. "Vice is your virtue. You're as conscienceless as they come."

She was right, of course. Vice had always been his stock-in-trade. "Don't you have guests to entertain?" he remarked pointedly, rising from the bed and grabbing his trousers from the floor. Shoving his legs into them, he stalked to the window.

Not surprisingly, she ignored his cue to depart. "Give me a child, Caine. Alfred was unable to do his husbandly duty. It's unfair, I tell you. Who shall take care of me when I'm old?"

"I don't give a damn."

"Every woman should have a child of her own."

"We've been through this before. The answer is still no. You may hold my finances, but you won't hold my future."

"How horrible of you to say such a thing. Haven't I given you everything you want? The finest clothes, pin money for your gambling, the cellar stocked with your favorite liquors, and my body to warm your bed. What else could you want?"

The one thing he seemed destined to live without, Caine thought bitterly.

"I try to be understanding of what prompts you to behave so cruelly. I know things have not been easy for you."

"Do not patronize me," he warned.

"Fine. Since you wish to be frank, and have raised the issue of your circumstances, let's discuss them, then. The cold truth is, I do hold your future in my hand."

His gaze snapped over his shoulder, the fury on his face making her flinch. "Don't doubt that I could find another patroness."

"But could you find one who owns your ancestral home?" she said with a taunting lift of her eyebrows. "Northcote obsesses you, Caine. It runs through your veins like a drug and you can't exorcise it. Now it belongs to me. I will get what I want eventually. I always do. So why not stop fighting it?"

Caine shut her out, knowing he was trapped by his own demons and unable to break free. Damn her for a soulless bitch, for tossing his weakness in his face.

His gaze centered on the sea beyond the cliffs. The turbulent blue-green water of the Bristol Channel mirrored his mood, waves cresting with white foam as they crashed thunderously against the jagged rocks that rose hundreds of feet high.

Despite the ghosts left to haunt him, this was home, his solitary link to the world he had once known. Northcote was his identity, his safe harbor, and without it he felt unanchored, adrift. Olivia had called it his obsession, and it was. He couldn't just walk away, no matter how much it ripped at his pride to submit to her sexual demands. He couldn't relinquish this last piece of his life.

Caine heard her rise from the bed and move toward him. "Though you deserve to be banished for your less-than-lover-like behavior," she said in a sultry voice, "I can't seem to send you away. You're very hard to resist, my lord." She wrapped her arms around his waist, her breasts flattening against his back as she purred, "And so very well endowed." Her hands slid over the front of his trousers.

His fingers closed around her wrist with just enough force to make her whimper. "Don't make me tell you again."

She pulled her hand away. "Please try to be civil today. You'll scare off my guests with that black scowl."

"As if I give a damn. You know how I feel about having those barracudas here." He hated being paraded about as her stud.

"I enjoy these gatherings. This place is as lifeless as a graveyard, otherwise."

"If you don't like it here, then why did you make your dearly departed, cuckolded husband buy it?"

"Because I found a wicked sort of pleasure in its tragic history. People throwing themselves off cliffs in despair. How very dramatic."

Caine tensed, her intended barb striking true. "Shut up."

"Oh, dear. I'm sorry. That was your father, wasn't it? I had forgotten."

"You're a vicious bitch, and you damn well know it." Christ, he had to get out. He was suffocating.

As he turned from the window, he caught a glimpse of two riders. The duo burst from the woods at breakneck speed, performing the most reckless of maneuvers as they raced toward the house.

When the lead horse attempted a perilous leap over a crevice, Caine's attention focused on the rider. Female. An idiotic female who was taking unbelievable risks with her life and that of her mount.

She was beating her male counterpart by a good two leagues as they thundered into the courtyard in front of the house, her husky laughter ringing in Caine's ears as she came to a dust-raising halt.

With a light hop, she dismounted, not waiting for assistance. With her feet now touching the earth, Caine was surprised to discover how petite she was.

She shook her hair away from her face; it had become unbound during her mad dash to the finish. The dark cinnamon tresses were lush and reached just beyond the middle of her back.

Beneath the straight, silky veil was a face of the most striking features. Piquancy battled with classic beauty.

Incredibly high cheekbones melded with a mouth so dazzlingly wide as to affect the whole aspect of her face when she smiled. Dark brows slanted above eyes whose color he could not discern, but which instinct told him were as blue as the water behind her.

"I've beaten you, Court," she said to the other rider in a breathless, laughing voice, pressing a light kiss to her horse's muzzle. "Do you yield?"

From his mounted position, the man offered her an exaggerated bow. His sandy brown hair, cropped close to his head, gleamed in the mid-morning sun. "I do, my lady. I submit to your greater horsemanship. You may count me as another man who has fallen victim to your superior skill."

She tapped his knee with her crop in a playful gesture. "Remember that when next you challenge me."

"Only a very foolish man would challenge you," he returned in the same light vein. His attention was then diverted, directing Caine's gaze to what he had spotted. Or rather to whom.

Lady Rebecca St. Claire, Olivia's niece, was strolling along the garden wall, her maid a few paces behind. The lady cast coy glances over her shoulder toward the man.

"If you'll excuse me, Cousin?" he said in a distracted tone. "There's a matter that requires my prompt attention."

Her amused gaze traveled in the same direction. "Oh, yes. I can see that 'matter' requires immediate attention," she returned in a teasing voice, her eyes alight.

With a conspiratorial grin, he saluted her with his crop and cantered off toward his quarry. She stood for a moment, watching him, sunlight glinting off the gold buttons of her riding outfit, a hunter green confection with a daring neckline and a clever split skirt that allowed her to sit her mount astride.

Unexpectedly, she glanced up and caught Caine watching her from the window. Her unflinching regard conveyed that she knew he had been eavesdropping. That didn't bother him. He had never claimed to be a gentleman and wouldn't pretend to be one now.

The whinny of her restless mare ended the long moment of appraisal. She inclined her head, the gesture distinctly mocking, as she turned and led her horse away.

Impudent baggage. She didn't know whom she taunted, and he was of a mind to educate her. Images ran rampant through his brain as his gaze followed the provocative swing of her backside, which held his undivided attention until she disappeared from sight.

"Don't drool, darling," Olivia chided in a proprietary tone. "I might take offense."

Caine reluctantly turned to look at her, forcing a bored expression to his face. "Jealous, Lady Buxton?"

She lightly fingered the ties of her dressing gown, her nipples showing clearly beneath the filmy material. "Don't be absurd, darling. I can have you whenever I want." As if to prove her point, she took the three steps separating them and pressed her body to his.

Caine stared down at her with disinterest. "The equipment needs a rest." He brushed past her and grabbed his shirt.

"She really affected you, didn't she?"

He tucked in his shirt, playing obtuse. "Since I've had the misfortune of knowing more than one 'she' in my life, perhaps you'd care to elaborate?"

"You know exactly who I'm speaking about. The little tart with all the hair." Envy rang in her words. Olivia's own hair was beginning to thin in spots, forcing her to wear hairpieces to enhance what nature had not given her.

Sitting on the edge of the bed, Caine shoved his foot into his boot. "And if she did?"

"Then I'd have to remind you that you can look but not touch."

Caine clenched his jaw and rose slowly from the bed. Closing the short distance between them, he stared down into Olivia's sly green eyes. "I give you certain liberties, but I'm not a man who takes well to women who attempt to control me. Remember that."

Her catlike smile told him she would humor him until it suited her to do otherwise. "This gathering has suddenly become far more interesting than I would have imagined."

"For you, maybe." Caine headed for the door, knowing full well where he was going. To the stables—questioning his motives the entire way for allowing a fiery bit of temptation to garner a reaction from him.

Olivia's words stopped him halfway out the door. "You don't know who she is, do you?"

Something about the way she framed the question unnerved him. He looked over his shoulder and noted the gleam in her eyes. "I assume you're referring to the hellbent-for-leather horsewoman?"

"I guess you wouldn't recognize her, would you? There really is no familial resemblance, and she does spend a great deal of her time in Paris, from what I understand."

"Get to the point."

"Does the name Edward Ashton mean anything to you?"

Everything inside Caine froze.

"Yes, I can see it does." She met him at the doorway. Caine stood immobile as she reached up to trace a finger along the jagged scar on his left cheek. "Does it still hurt?"

"No," he bit out, jerking his head away, his entire body suddenly feeling taut and explosive.

The scar was a reminder of his folly, compliments of one of the duke of Exmoor's henchmen. But Caine figured he deserved what he got for going to the man's London townhouse, drunk and wanting to avenge his father's death. He never made it past the front door. A burly footman had the advantage of sobriety, heft, and a broken bottle.

Caine remembered waking up in a charity hospital, where someone had deposited him, his brain feverish and his body awash in sweat as infection set in. Two months he had stayed, his world reduced to a solitary sphere of comprehension: revenge.

His gaze narrowed on Olivia's face. "Who is she?"

She reveled in her secret a moment longer, then replied, "Lady Bliss Ashton. Exmoor's darling daughter."

Caine felt as though someone had reached down his throat and divested him of his innards. "What is she doing here?" he demanded in a deceptively soft voice. "Did you invite her?" He took a menacing step toward her. "I swear, if you did—"

"No, blast you. I didn't invite her." For an instant she looked frightened, but then her hauteur surged back in full. "She must have come with her cousin."

"Well, get her the hell out of here."

She arched a brow. "And only five minutes ago you wanted to fuck her. How mercurial you are, my love."

Caine took another step forward, purposely crowding her. "Don't push me, Olivia."

"If you want her gone," she said, lifting her pointed chin and glaring at him, "then do it yourself. Certainly a big, bad man like you can drive away one little female. You do so excel at being a bastard."

"Remember that when you find her body washed up on the rocks," Caine snarled as he stalked from the room.

Two

She is Venus when she smiles;
But she's Juno when she walks,
And Minerva when she talks.
Ben Jonson

*B*liss meandered toward the stables, feeling oddly discomposed. She found herself replaying her silent confrontation with the half-naked, muscle-laden eavesdropper. An unexpected jolt had rocked her when her gaze locked with those brooding eyes, a total lack of contrition in the man's regard as he stared down at her with an expression both blatant and sexual.

She had come to Northcote at the invitation of her cousin, Court, who had shown up on her father's doorstep not three days after Bliss had arrived home from Paris for a visit. She soon discovered the reason. The lovely Lady Rebecca St. Claire and her mother—"the dragon," as Court referred to her—would be in attendance.

Clearly Bliss's presence at her cousin's side was intended to lend Court's interactions with Rebecca St.

Claire an air of propriety, which, had the lady's mother been more acquainted with Bliss's unconventional background, would have been comical.

Her upbringing had greatly differed from that of her peers. Her French mother was a restless spirit, always seeking new adventures, pushing the boundaries that threatened to restrain her freedom, teaching her daughter that all things were possible, even for a woman.

Her father, on the other hand, could be too serious-minded at times, stodgy, and occasionally rigid. But he was also a lovable bear of a man and a great political thinker with a heart as big as England.

Bliss had never really understood what had brought her parents together. Never had there been a more unlikely couple, though they always seemed so much in love. But six years ago, they had decided to live apart. Neither of them spoke of what had prompted the decision, and neither, to Bliss's knowledge, had taken lovers. In all the ways that counted, her parents remained faithful to each other.

Her father divided his time between their estate in Exmoor and their London townhouse, and her mother lived in Paris with Bliss. Bliss found England too restrictive to suit the artist in her, though she tried to come home as often as she could.

Stopping at a water barrel shaded beneath a gnarled beech tree, Bliss dipped her hands in, smoothing the liquid over her face and neck. Closing her eyes, she savored the coolness against her heated skin.

Images rose unbidden in her mind of a dark, handsome face, broad shoulders brushed by silky, ink-black hair, mussed, as though ravaged by female hands—which was undoubtedly the case as Bliss had glimpsed a woman's form obscured in the shadows behind him.

Bliss envied whoever she was. The brute was glorious. She would love to paint him, all those hard planes and eyes full of dire looks. He exuded danger, and everything inside her responded.

In Paris, she frequently painted nude male models, though her portraits were mostly of François, her dearest friend, who supported her art in a field dominated by men.

But artists were far more open to a woman in their midst than the rest of the domineering male world, in which women existed as brainless ninnies who were expected to do no more than look pretty and spend their days nurturing fragility.

Ciara nudged Bliss's shoulder, demanding attention. Patting her mare's neck, Bliss headed into the stables, where she was met by the stable master, a wizened old character who was quick with a joke and a smile. He took Ciara's reins and led her to the cross ties so Bliss could groom her.

The sound of running feet heralded the arrival of an out-of-breath young boy whom Bliss recognized as one of the grooms. "Come quick, Hap!" he urged. "Phantom's gone and jumped the fence!"

"Damn and blast that beast," the man muttered, then flashed an apologetic look Bliss's way. "Pardon my language, miss."

"Quite understandable." Bliss smiled. When he remained rooted to the spot, uncertainty etching his weather-beaten face, as though he thought he was deserting her in some foreign land riddled with scorpions, she prompted, "You'd best hurry."

He hesitated another moment, a slight frown pulling his wiry brows together, as if trying to catch hold of an elusive thought. He gave up the pursuit and promised to return in a matter of minutes, his bandy legs hastening out the door.

Shaking her head in amusement, Bliss turned toward the tack room to search for a curry comb and bristle brush to rub Ciara down.

Then a loud crash rent the air.

Whirling around, she found a huge black stallion in the far stall rearing on its hind legs and tossing its head, nostrils flared, eyes glazed and slightly wild. Its forelegs came down again and splintered the wooden slats on the stall door, trying to break free. The sight of the magnificent beast held Bliss immobile for a heartbeat, until she realized what was happening.

Ciara was in heat, and the stallion was primed for stud.

Bliss raced over to untie her mare, but the black had now forced its massive body through the shattered door. He swiftly headed down the center aisle, straight for Bliss, who barely managed to get out of the way to avoid being trampled.

As she stumbled to safety, the stud mounted Ciara. Bliss was powerless to do more than watch; only a fool would try to separate them now. Just seeing the damage the horse had done to himself trying to get to Ciara was proof of his lust. Blood seeped from the cuts on his legs and sides.

"Khan, down!" an enraged male voice suddenly bellowed.

Bliss turned to see the man from the window running into the stables, but he was too late. The deed had been done, even though the black responded instantly to his master's command.

Eyes sharp as flint slashed in her direction. "Damn you! What have you done here?"

For a moment Bliss could do no more than stare, startled not only by his imposing physical presence, but by the anger he directed at her.

Holding his glare, she rose to her feet. "What have *I* done?"

"Do you have a bloody brain in your head? Your mare is in heat! Did you take one second to think that there might be animals in here who would respond to her scent?"

"What I expected," Bliss countered, her own anger building, "was that any studs would be in the corral, safely away from temptation. As a guest, am I supposed to anticipate a problem such as this?"

He glowered at her, the light scar on his cheek showing the tic in his jaw, emphasizing the extent of his fury. The man was as superb as his stallion. Big, beautiful, and infinitely dangerous. He emanated barely controlled energy; there was no softness at all in his tall, solid frame. It was quite an experience to be the sole focus of all that restless, churning power.

"Where's the damned stable master?" he growled. "He should be drawn and quartered."

Bliss brushed away the hay clinging to her skirt. "This is not Mr. Rigby's fault. One of the horses jumped the fence. He didn't want to leave, but I told him to go."

Those black-flint eyes narrowed once more, as though calculating the benefits of her demise. "And who anointed you overseer here?"

Bliss sighed. "How you do go on. Perhaps if you took a few deep breaths or chanted a mantra, you might feel a bit more rational."

"You wouldn't like what I chanted."

The man was truly insufferable. "Has anyone told you that you have the manners of a grave digger? If I were not a lady"—a stretch, but he didn't know that—"I might feel inclined to take my crop to your hide."

"Then I'd put you over my knee and blister your backside."

"I suspect you'd try."

His gaze moved slowly down her body, as if mocking her worth as an opponent, and just as leisurely skimmed upward before his eyes locked with hers. Something besides anger now simmered in that intent regard.

"Hell," he swore fiercely as Ciara, now intolerant of the stud's presence, began to kick her back legs out at him. "Get your horse into a stall!"

Pushing past him, Bliss took hold of Ciara's reins and led her to the nearest unoccupied stall, silently fuming as she began to clean her mare up.

Out of the corner of her eye, she watched the despicable brute run his hands over his horse's flanks, the stallion's magnificent coat speckled with blood and several ugly gashes.

The churl caught her looking and glared at her, a gesture she returned. Undoubtedly he thought she would be cowed by those intimidating looks.

Never had she come across so disagreeable a person. He wore menace like an unholy aura, his black hair a banner of defiance as the silky strands caressed the collar of his wrinkled white shirt, the sleeves rolled up to his elbows, revealing large hands and a dusting of dark hair on his corded forearms.

The stable master dashed in then, a look of horror dawning over the poor man's face as he discerned what had happened.

"Where the devil have you been?" the oaf demanded.

Incensed, Bliss answered, "Out chasing down one of the horses, as I've already told you."

Eyes as cold as the Bering Sea slashed her way. "Stay out of this." Before she could retort, he refocused that diabolical regard on the stable master. "Get some salve and towels. *Now.*"

"Yes, m'lord." Like a frightened jackrabbit, the man hastened away.

Bliss watched him go, her body taut with indignation. "You're a bully, do you know that?"

That wholly unpleasant stare focused on her face as he stalked toward Ciara's stall, leading his stallion with lethal grace in his stride. He stopped in front of the door, the stud's nearness upsetting her mare, as he said, "You have no idea." His voice warned that she would find out before long. Then he guided his horse to the end stall, growling at Mr. Rigby as they tended the animal's wounds.

Bliss muttered words most young women didn't know, let alone speak aloud, about the man's origins and how utterly contemptible he was.

Once she was finished tending to Ciara, she dug out a sugar cube from her skirt pocket. Ciara's soft nose tickled her palm as she ate the treat.

"You'll be fine now," Bliss crooned, rubbing her mare's neck. "I won't let that beast come near you again."

She let herself out of the stall, her gaze shifting to the

far corner where only the stallion and the stable master now stood. Khan's master had departed. Good riddance.

Bliss turned to leave before the prince of darkness returned and she succumbed to the temptation to skewer him with the nearest pitchfork, but she ran up against an object as solid as a brick wall, which, to her misfortune, turned out to be Mephistopheles himself.

Bliss looked up to find fierce blue eyes glowering down at her, the expression on his chiseled face as dark and turbulent as a coming thunderstorm.

"Going somewhere?" he asked in a whisky-dark voice.

"Yes," she managed, his nearness wreaking havoc on her balance. "Wherever *you* are not." She made to move around him, but he sidestepped her, blocking her path. "Get out of my way."

"Your damn mare ruined Khan for stud."

The infuriating clod! "I beg to differ. Your damn stallion ruined Ciara for mating. I vow she'll never want to do so again, after what he did to her."

A muscle worked in his jaw, and he looked as though he was about to throttle her. "I don't think you grasp the concept of what has happened here."

"Well, let me see if my pitiful female brain can figure it out," she said with feigned sweetness. "Your stallion mounted my mare, two minutes of heavenly rapture followed, and now we're in a quagmire according to you, the master of all things, whose head is so bloated with self-importance I can only hope its prodigious weight topples you into the gaping maw of a bottomless pit."

The tic in his jaw increased in tempo. "You do know how to push a man."

"So I've been told. It's a blight on an otherwise exem-

plary record of feminine accomplishments, if one over-
looks the occasional discordant note on the pianoforte
and my haphazard attempts at a quadrille."

His face never changed; if he possessed any humor, it
was buried so deep as to be nonexistent. "You owe me a
stud fee for the privilege your mare has just been
afforded."

"Privilege?" Bliss gaped at him. "Surely you jest."

The look on his face told her he never jested. "Khan is
from the Anazah, a pure desert-bred Arabian, with a lineage that can be traced back to the Abbas Pasha."

She could tell the stallion was from the finest stock;
every line of its body conveyed this: from his graceful
head, tapering from the eyes to the muzzle; the sharply
cut cheekbones; the gentle arch from the poll to the with-
ers; the powerful loins, high croup, and fine haunches;
the well-set tail and short dock; the gaskins full and muscular without being heavy.

All and all, a truly spectacular animal. Any foal Ciara
might have would not only be beautiful, but would race
like the wind. Still, that didn't give the man the right to
make demands on her as if she were at fault.

"Ciara's dame was a wild Devonshire pony," Bliss
returned, "and her sire a Dongola Arab, straight from
Knight's Folly."

He stood unflinching, vastly unimpressed. "You'll still
pay the fee."

"I'll do no such thing." If she were a man, she would
punch his arrogant nose. That once patrician appendage
already sported a small cant, as though someone had
beaten her to it.

He closed the scant foot's worth of space that separated them, and Bliss had to stop herself from taking a step back, even though he stood so close that barely a breeze could whisper between their bodies. An incredible heat assaulted her, and she realized it was coming from him.

"You'll pay the fee," he said in a silky voice, "or pay the consequences."

She met his gaze unblinkingly. "Are you threatening me?"

"Yes."

Bliss could only stare, momentarily stunned by the sheer scope of his audacity. Then she laughed. "Does this barbaric manner of yours work on most people? Because it won't work on me. You can stomp about and tower over me and pound on your chest until you turn blue, and it will still change nothing. Good day."

Tension crackled in the air as Bliss brushed passed him. She could feel his dark, penetrating gaze boring into her back.

How dare he ask her to pay him! He acted as though her mare had pranced into the stables and lured the stallion to her with a siren's song, rather than his unruly beast being unable to keep his lust in check.

Had he even inquired as to Ciara's welfare? Or her own, for that matter? His blasted horse could have killed her, but all he was concerned about was his stud fee.

Suddenly, she was jerked up short. Something was holding her back. Or, she thought with mounting fury, some*one*. She whirled around to find the oaf's big-booted foot on the hem of her skirt, trapping her firmly in place.

"Are you mad?" she fumed. "Release me at once."

Surprisingly, he did, but only to grasp her upper arm and yank her forward, bringing her flush against his chest. Her nose barely reached the V in his shirt where taut, bronzed skin lay bare to her direct line of vision. A hint of sandalwood teased her nostrils. Very pleasing. Very masculine.

A curious thrill shot through Bliss as she tossed her head back, returning the glare of those frosty blue eyes that made her think of glacial streams.

His silky hair tumbled forward as his mouth, sensuous and full, came perilously close to hers. "This isn't over," he said, the words a vow.

Foreign sensations sizzled through Bliss's veins, and her heart missed a beat. "Unhand me. Or shall I scream down the rafters?"

His gaze dipped to her lips, as though thinking to stifle her that way, which very nearly tempted Bliss to test him. He was so maddening, he deserved his comeuppance, the irritating lout.

His grip eased, but his fingers trailed down her arm, leaving a warm path in their wake.

Far too affected by that simple touch, Bliss slapped him, then pivoted on her heel and marched away.

Caine watched her go, his hand pressed to his face like a bloody half-wit. He had seen the slap coming and let it happen. Hell, he deserved a cudgeling for allowing the sight of her to distract him.

Even now his gaze tracked her, drifting downward to the seductive sway of her hips, the slow melting heat in his loins proving again that brain and body don't always work in harmony.

The duke's precious daughter had just ruined his chance to make some additional blunt, which left him that much more at Olivia's mercy.

Like father, like daughter, Caine thought bitterly, his hands clenching at his sides. But he'd be damned if anyone would get the better of him this time. Fate, which had always held him in contempt, had seen fit to drop one hundred and ten pounds of retribution in his lap—and he would exploit this boon wherever, whenever, or however the opportunity arose.

Three

Careless she is, with artful care,
Affecting to seem unaffected.
William Congreve

*B*liss studied her reflection in the mirror, running a critical eye over her ball gown, which was fashioned in the latest Parisian style with a daringly low, square-cut bodice and high waist, which accentuated her ample bosom.

The dress was truly scandalous. Her nipples were covered by only the barest wisp of material. A single deep breath could very well expose her to all, but she enjoyed pushing the boundaries; life was too dull otherwise.

At first, she told herself that her choice of attire was arbitrary, but she knew better than to delude herself. Should a certain vile horse owner be in attendance tonight, she would give him the cut direct, while floating by on a cloud of satin decadence.

A knock sounded at her door. "Come," she called as her maid secured a delicate sapphire necklace around her throat to match the earrings she wore.

She turned to find Court leaning a shoulder against the doorframe, his golden brown hair tamed, his jaw freshly shaven, and his smile disarming. "You look lovely, Cousin." His gaze was warm and appreciative.

"Thank you." Bliss ran a hand over her satin skirt. The dark blue material shimmered with hidden threads of silver, which deceived the eye at every turn.

Court held out his arm to her. "Shall we go?"

"Yes." Unexpected nerves tightened her stomach as she linked her arm with her cousin's, but she forced down the unfamiliar sensation.

From the landing, the long gallery gleamed. The glass and brass sconces lining the walls cast a golden glow on the highly polished floors, making the wood look like still, dark water.

It was not so much the size of Northcote that impressed Bliss, as she had seen larger estates, but rather the combination of elements: the Turkish carpet in shades of crimson, emerald, and gold running the length of the stairs; the entranceway done in rose-hued granite cut from the cliffs; the numerous embrasures and niches lined in rococo paneling of rich cherry that housed Sèvres bowls brimming with hyacinths and ornate silver candelabras. An arched portal of Italian marble led into the ballroom, and an unusual chandelier glittered from a recessed dome, reflecting pinpoints of light that looked like diamonds in a midnight sky.

The house seemed to possess its own personality, or perhaps it was just her artist's eye romanticizing the elegant lines and graceful curves.

"It has been refurbished to its former glory by the marchioness," Court told her when she inquired about the house's history. "But it has a somewhat checkered past. The previous owner, the tenth Earl of Hartland, threw himself from the cliffs when he lost everything to debt."

Bliss's steps faltered. She had stood at the edge of those cliffs today, dwarfed by their sheer scope, yet strangely fascinated by their deadly beauty. What kind of suffering must the man have been going through to take his own life, and in such a brutal fashion?

"Tragic, I know," Court said, reading her expression. "But perhaps more tragic is that the earl's son haunts this place."

Bliss's eyes widened. "You mean there's a ghost?"

"No, the eleventh Earl of Hartland is very much alive. He was left virtually penniless when his father died, and the house was sold to the Marquis of Buxton, who passed away not quite a year ago. Soon after that, the earl's son returned. Now he's living here."

"Is he related to Lady Buxton?"

The look Court sent her was decidedly uncomfortable. "It seems my tongue has gotten the better of me. I have raised a topic that is not meant for polite company."

"Polite company?" Bliss laughed softly. "Good Lord, Court, you aren't going to start treating me like some harebrained female whose sensibilities will be outraged at the mere mention of impropriety? I thought you knew me better than that."

"I do," he replied with an endearingly boyish grin. "Sometimes I forget that you're not like other women."

"I'll take that as a compliment. Now, who is the earl's son?"

He hesitated. "His name is Caine Ballinger."

Bliss puzzled for a moment, tapping a finger on her chin. "Ballinger. I've heard that name before."

"I wouldn't be surprised. The man's exploits appeared frequently in the scandal sheets. Women, wine, and gambling were his life's calling, with women topping the list. But his success in the bedroom didn't extend to the gaming tables. He could have parlayed his money into quite a fortune, had Lady Luck not constantly frowned upon him. Apparently she was paying him back for his innumerable sins."

Bliss's interest was thoroughly piqued. "You will point him out to me, won't you?"

They had reached the gallery and were about to head down the stairs into the ballroom, when Court stopped and turned her to face him. "You're to stay away from him, Bliss. Do you hear me? Your reputation would be tarnished for all eternity if you were seen in his company."

Bliss couldn't help an amused smile. "My reputation, Court? Do you see my gown? Have you not admired my skill with a gun? Or remonstrated me for riding astride? Or come to Paris and viewed my paintings?" The last comment made him shift uncomfortably. "My reputation is what it is. I can't imagine it suffering further abuse."

"Being seen with Caine Ballinger will blacken it beyond all repair; the other things you've done will pale in comparison. Trust me."

Bliss looked down into the ballroom, searching the crowd for a man who epitomized vice. But what would such a man look like? "Is he here tonight?"

"Bliss," Court said in a warning tone.

"Is he in the ballroom? Do you see him?"

"Damnation, why did I open my mouth?" He raked a

hand through his hair. "Just once, couldn't you heed my advice?"

"You're beginning to sound like my father."

"The poor man's beleaguered. Between you and your mother . . ." He grimaced.

"I know." She smiled gently at him. "We Ashton women are a vexation to men."

He treated her to a crooked grin. "It's that French blood."

"*Oui,* blame it on the French blood." In a sisterly fashion, she brushed a lock of hair from his forehead. "Shall we go in?"

He took hold of her elbow, his expression sobering. "Please tell me you're not going to do anything foolish?"

Bliss bestowed a look of guileless innocence on her cousin. "Foolish? Why, Court, when have I ever done anything foolish?"

His stare was pointed. "You want me to start listing them? We could be here all night."

"Rest assured, I will be a shining example of moral rectitude."

"I would pay good money to see that." Then he gave her a look that said he was about to impart more worldly male advice. "Before we go in, there's something else you should know about Caine Ballinger."

"More?" She was already intrigued beyond measure.

That strained expression settled over his face again. "He's . . ."

"Yes?" she prompted when he faltered.

"He's a kept man."

Bliss was certain she couldn't have heard correctly. "Kept?"

"By the marchioness."

Her cousin's implication sank in. "You mean he's Lady Buxton's lover?"

A terse nod was his reply. The topic clearly chafed at him, which was silly. "The man sounds very enterprising," she mused.

"Damnation, Bliss! Are you being purposely obtuse?"

"Why does this subject bother you so? If the situation were reversed, you wouldn't have thought it worth mentioning. Indeed, men rally around each other in such circumstances, patting themselves on the back and toasting their good fortune, openly flaunting their transgressions while laboring under the mistaken impression that women don't possess the mental acumen to know what they're doing.

"But should a woman want a man for the same purpose, then there are gasps heard 'round the world, outraged men collapsing in the street. Women burned in effigy and cast out like lepers. Doesn't anything about that strike you as one-sided?"

Not surprisingly, her cousin frowned at her, reminding Bliss that he was the owner of a male brain, and therefore unable to grasp the concept of an independent, self-sufficient woman.

"We're men," he said as if that explained everything. "It's different."

"How so? Because men believe they created the world? And that women are simply receptacles for their lust?"

"You read too many books."

"And that is never a good thing, is it? Not for the delicate female brain."

"Why do you twist everything I say?"

"Because you make no sense."

Before he could utter any more absurdities that would have her so incensed she would scream, Bliss descended the stairs, barely waiting for the footman to announce her arrival.

Gently, Court took hold of her arm, drawing her to a stop at the bottom of the steps. "Look, I'm sorry. I just don't want you to get hurt."

Her anger softened, yet the issue was still a sore point with her. When would men ever see women as partners they could talk to, instead of as birthing machines and ornaments?

"I promise I'll be careful," she said, indulging his need to protect her. "I do believe that's Lady Rebecca over there, surrounded by at least eight gentlemen. My, but she looks like an angel."

Her cousin scanned the room, his gaze stopping when he spotted his lady love, men on either side of her, and her mother keeping them from getting too close with a fire-and-brimstone look.

The scowl that gathered on Court's face told Bliss that the demure Lady Rebecca meant quite a bit to him. He was clearly torn between staying with Bliss as her escort, or ripping off the heads of his lady's admirers.

Wanting some time alone, Bliss said, "Go on, Court. I'll be fine."

His conflicted gaze slid to her. "Are you sure?"

"Positive. You'd best hurry. I see Lord Danridge moving in." That was all the prompting her cousin needed; he cut across the dance floor.

Bliss breathed a sigh of relief. Now she was free to search for the elusive Caine Ballinger. She accepted a glass of champagne from a passing servant and retreated to the edge of the ballroom to observe the crowd, endeavoring to conjure up an image of a man whose prowess was legendary.

Oddly, the face of the hulk who had accosted her in the stables came to mind; those dark eyes, hard as quartz, and hair that looked as thick and soft as a sable pelt.

And that wicked scar.

Where had he gotten it? No doubt from the sword of some cuckolded husband. The man was a boor, purposefully intimidating, without a speck of gentleman existing beneath that exquisite exterior—an impressive six-foot-four, she would estimate, and weighing no less than sixteen stone, all solid. She found herself searching for him, surprisingly disappointed when she didn't see him.

"There you are, my dear."

Bliss started at the sound of a female voice. She turned to find her hostess bearing down on her, the woman's expression masklike as she took in Bliss's outfit.

"How stunning you look."

"Thank you." Bliss made her own quick perusal of Olivia Hamilton. What must it be like to control a rogue so infamous that his name was bandied about in clubs and salons alike?

"Those Parisian styles are so very daring, aren't they?" her hostess added, assessing the bodice of Bliss's gown.

Having only met the woman briefly that morning when she had arrived, Bliss had been afforded little opportunity to discern Lady Buxton's character. Now that she'd been scrutinized, judged and labeled within a moment, Bliss knew she and the marchioness would not be friends.

"The French are more visceral in their appreciation of clothing," Bliss replied. "They believe it should drape, and mold, and enhance." Her pointed look took in the older woman's attire. The dark burgundy coloring did little to enliven Lady Buxton's pale skin or hide a thickening figure.

The marchioness's smile was a mere baring of teeth. "I hear from your cousin that you dabble in art."

Bliss doubted Court had used those words. "Yes. My most recently dabbling was Marie Amelie d'Orleans."

Her hostess gaped. "*Princess* Marie Amelie? The newborn daughter of King Louis? *That* Marie Amelie?"

Bliss nodded, feeling petty in allowing the woman to bring her down to her level. "Though I hold no fondness for the king, the fee helped several orphanages."

"Fee? You mean you were *paid?*" The stunned look on Lady Buxton's face clearly expressed her opinion on the subject.

Women were not supposed to make their own money. They were expected to be wholly dependent on whatever a man chose to give them. But since the Good Lord had kindly gifted Bliss with two arms, two legs, and a brain, she had no intention of letting any of that atrophy while waiting for a man to direct her life.

"Yes," Bliss admitted, "though there is work I do strictly for myself." Paintings no one wanted, because of the subject matter. People didn't want their own shame staring them in the face day after day; better to just ignore it and pretend it didn't exist.

"Certainly your family can't approve."

"Oh, yes. They approve." Her mother, mostly. Her father merely tolerated her passion for art, in the hopes that it would go away and she would settle down with some perfectly boring lord who possessed little in the way of intelligence, and who would expect her to pop out one child after the next like a dutiful wife.

Lady Buxton gave Bliss another looking-over, as if there was something she had missed on the first inspection. "Perhaps I will allow you to paint Horatio."

"Horatio?"

"My dog."

Bliss refrained from a very unladylike retort. Instead she smiled indulgently and glanced out over the crowd, more than ready to be quit of the woman. She would even welcome the heathen from the stables at that moment.

As though discerning her thoughts, the marchioness said, "I heard about the incident in the stables. How frightening for you. I hope you weren't hurt."

"I was in no danger, as long as I did not stand in the way of true love."

"Khan is a brute, I admit, but quite a splendid stud."

As was Khan's owner.

"He only required a few stitches and should be good as new in a week or so."

The reminder of the stallion's injuries made Bliss feel thoughtless for not having been more concerned about his condition. She loved horses and had practically lived in the Exmoor's stables as a little girl.

Guilt settled on her shoulders. She was not generally so careless, but her mind had been preoccupied with images of turbulent eyes and tousled hair. Then she had been accosted by the owner of those eyes and that hair, and all thoughts other than anger, and an unsettling warmth low in her belly, had filled her.

"Excuse me, won't you?"

The marchioness inclined her head. "Certainly."

Bliss made a quick exit, stepping out onto the balcony for a breath of fresh air. She had never much liked balls; no wonder she had been such an abysmal failure during her first Season. She had refrained from repeating the debacle the following year. She simply didn't fit in with these people: the things that interested them didn't interest her. She needed stimulation, adventure. A challenge.

Dark eyes and a harsh, forbidding mouth intruded into her thoughts. Now there was a challenge, a man who refused to be tamed.

The memory of the stranger's large hand on her arm brought a shiver to Bliss's skin despite the warmth of the night, and her gaze was drawn down the slope of the hill leading away from the house toward the stables. Suddenly she very much wanted to see Ciara and Khan.

Suddenly she wanted to be anywhere but here.

Four

My Lady, tempted by a private whim,
To his extreme annoyance, tempted him.
Hilaire Belloc

Ciara whickered as Bliss entered the stables. She had pilfered two apples and a few sugar cubes before slipping out undetected, hoisting her skirts, and hurrying down the slope.

She was slightly out of breath and her hair had come free in a few places, the silky strands tickling her neck and upper chest. A trace of humidity lingered in the air and clung to her skin.

A cool night breeze blew in through the open stable doors, scented with the salt tang of the Bristol Channel and the heady smell of damp earth from a light afternoon rain. Just above the faint sounds of the crickets rose the distant boom of the surf crashing against the rocks.

Bliss felt at peace here. She could understand why the earl's son was compelled to "haunt" this place; she would be greatly tempted to haunt it herself. It was as though the world began and ended at these very cliffs, as if God had conspired to make the grass greener and the air sweeter.

Ciara nudged her hand, bringing Bliss back down to earth. She rubbed her mare between the ears and fed her one of the sugar cubes. "I know. I'm getting whimsical. But you're not one to pass judgment, considering your behavior this afternoon. Shame on you for allowing the first stud that comes along to have his way with you. Don't you know men don't like women who are too eager?"

"Only men who are fools, you mean."

Bliss whirled around at the sound of the deep, male voice that had plagued her thoughts for most of the day. She found the great, muscled titan leaning against Khan's stall, the door now reinforced, an additional partition raised.

Most of the man's body was in shadow, which was why she hadn't spotted him upon entering. But she could see his eyes, and they put her to mind of a wolf just rousing from his slumber as he glowered faintly at her from the darkness.

"It's not nice to sneak up on people," she said reprovingly, trying not to notice the deep V of his shirt, which brazenly displayed an indecent amount of tanned flesh, or the snug, buff-colored breeches that gloved his muscular legs.

A bottle of brandy dangled from his long, lean fingers. He tapped it rhythmically against his left thigh, the only outward sign that anything disturbed him. Was it simply her presence that unbalanced his equilibrium? Or was he still harboring resentment from that morning?

"There wasn't any sneaking involved," he finally

deigned to reply, his voice a deep thrum. "I've been here the whole time."

"Well, you should have alerted me to your presence. It would have been the polite thing to do."

"Ah." He nodded. "Well, I never do the polite thing. Life would not be nearly as enjoyable. If I didn't behave in such a deviant manner, I would have missed your little speech and subsequent fidgeting."

His remark made Bliss realize her fingers were clutching at her skirt. She immediately dropped the material, cursing his perception. "I'm not fidgeting."

"You're a bundle of nerves, and valiantly trying to quell the impulse to flee. What's the matter, my lady? Worried I'll begin foaming at the mouth?"

Bliss scoffed. "You, sir, worry me not a whit." *Liar.* "If you knew me at all, you'd realize how far off the mark you are."

His brow notched up in a skeptical taunt as he lifted the bottle to his lips, his gaze rolling over her in a brief appraisal, trying to make her uneasy. Which he did, but she would go to her grave with that truth.

Wiping the back of his hand across his mouth, he held the bottle out to her, the look in his eyes clearly challenging. "Come on. I won't tell."

"No, thank you."

"Not as much of a tiger as you appear to be, hmm?"

It annoyed her that his prodding very nearly had her snatching up the bottle to prove him wrong. "Not as much of a drunkard as you appear to be."

Something that might have passed as a smile briefly tipped up the corner of his lips. "So you decided to return to the scene of the crime, did you?"

Discomfited by his accurate assessment, Bliss averted her gaze. "I'm simply getting a breath of fresh air."

"Well, we have plenty of that here, so inhale as much as you like. I'll just watch."

Bliss hated that his penetrating gaze unnerved her even the smallest bit. "What are you doing here at this time of night?"

"I could ask you the same thing. Do you make a habit of spending time in stables dressed like a tart?"

His purposely taunting remark and manner infuriated her. "You despicable wretch! I'm tired of your snide comments and wounded mien. If you don't like how I'm dressed, then don't look at me."

"I didn't say I didn't like how you were dressed." Once more, that brooding gaze moved slowly over her, lingering long enough on her breasts to make her want to squirm, before resuming the torture all the way down to her slippered feet. "In fact," he drawled, once more meeting her eyes, "I like it quite a bit."

A shiver chased over Bliss's skin. "I'm delighted. How could I possibly have lived another day without your approval?"

A glitter of amusement sparked in his eyes before the shadows obscured his face. "The sapphires are a nice touch, too, Your Highness."

The jibe pushed her temper over the edge, and she flung the apple at him. He caught it cleanly, taking a big bite and treating her to a mocking grin.

"It's for your horse, you odious man."

"Ah, the lady's prodded by a guilty conscience," he taunted, offering the remaining apple to Khan, who inhaled it from his palm. "What do you think, lad? Her

Royal Highness deigns to feel compassion for you after Her Royal Horse spread her thighs and ruined you. This should be written down in the annals of history as a miraculous event."

Bliss ached to hit him. Never had a man been so outright belligerent toward her, or spoken to her so rudely. He didn't make a single pretense of treating her like a lady. But worse, she wasn't sure if what she was feeling was entirely anger.

"You're insane," she told him. "Completely uncivilized, like some wilderness animal."

"Did you hear that, Khan? The lady thinks we're barbarians. Maybe she'd like to find out for sure." His eyes glinted with wicked intent as he started toward her.

Bliss grabbed her riding crop from the peg outside Ciara's stall, thrusting it toward him as though it were a sword. "If you think I won't use this to bash your stupid head, think again."

He could overpower her. They both knew it, and yet he stopped, though not far enough away for Bliss's peace of mind. One lunge and he would be on her.

He inclined his head, then put the brandy bottle to his lips for another swig. Boozing cur. Why couldn't he look like the others of his ilk, who hunkered down in alleyways waiting for the tavern to open so they could resume their life of dissipation?

Instead he had to be all dark and glorious, a layer of stubble roughening his chin, adding to the aura of danger that radiated from him in waves.

With his head tipped back, Bliss took the opportunity to absorb the full length of his body, the shirt that strained across his well-defined chest and emphasized his enormous arms, the waist that showed not an ounce of fat . . . and the breeches sheathing his loins in the most distracting way.

The sound of him clearing his throat brought her gaze snapping up. He regarded her with a raised eyebrow, an ironic lift to the corner of his mouth. "Like what you see?"

Bliss prayed he couldn't make out her flushed cheeks in the dim light. "Not in the least. In fact, I was thinking that you look like an inmate from the asylum."

A moment of silence descended, then his booming laugh shook the rafters, the seductive timbre vibrating along her nerves disconcertingly.

When his humor abated, he said through that maddening half-grin, "You are the most aggravating female I've ever had the misfortune to meet." His tone and the look in his eyes told her that he didn't entirely hate her, which she shouldn't give a fig about, but she did nonetheless—a completely irrational reaction. "You think I'm a rude, arrogant boor, don't you?"

"Among other things. Is bathing outside your sphere of experience?"

"Ah, so you like your gentlemen well groomed, their hair neatly combed, their cologne an exotic blend of spices rather than that of hay and dirt. My apologies, Your Highness." He sketched a mocking bow. "Had I known you'd condescend to visit us poor wretches here in the lower realms, I would have donned my finery and engaged an orchestra."

"Stop calling me Your Highness!"

"My most profound apologies. Certainly I don't want to upset your delicate constitution. So do you have a name? Or should we commoners simply bow and scrape and call you 'milady' in the most reverent undertones?"

"Bliss," she snapped. "My name is Bliss."

"Bliss." The way he said her name sounded like a caress, before he added, "Certainly a misnomer."

"Go to blazes." She spun on her heel, needing to leave before she did something that she might regret.

"There she goes, running away again," he taunted. "I have to say I'm surprised, Khan. I thought she had more backbone than that. But wait. She's stopping. Now she's turning. I think she intends to do us harm, lad. Is that it, Lady Bliss? Do you plan to whip us into submission with your crop?"

At least ten different retorts rose to Bliss's lips, none of them remotely ladylike, and he would be expecting that. So she returned his unflappability with her own.

"Why *are* you out here malingering in the stables? Afraid to step into the light? Don't know how to dance, perhaps? Or is it that you don't want people seeing you eat with your hands?"

That worked. His jaw knotted and his eyes narrowed. "You really are a bitch, aren't you?"

"As often as you are a bastard. Now, if we're through exchanging barbs, I'll bid you good night."

She had barely turned when he demanded, "So what's the real reason you came out here?"

Bliss told herself to simply walk away, and yet some form of insanity took hold of her brain whenever she was near this man. "As the apple already suggested, I wanted to see how your horse fared. Believe it or not, I am not completely devoid of compassion. My only mistake lay in the assumption that your odious self would not be here."

"I guess I should feel hurt that you don't desire my company."

"I'm sure you prefer it that way."

"You don't have a clue what I'd prefer."

Bliss wondered at what point in this man's stunted evolution he had devoted himself to being an ass. "Well, let me set your mind at ease and tell you that I have no intention of tying myself into Gordian knots trying to unravel the complicated mystery you present. I suspect it would be a feat not even a mystic could accomplish."

"You're unmarried, aren't you? Can't find a man who enjoys being flayed alive by your rapier wit?"

"I can't find a man who possesses enough intellect to keep me interested."

"With a name like Bliss, one might wonder where your interests lie." He sent a pointed look at the bodice of her gown. Cad. "Dare I ask how you got that name?"

"In the usual fashion: my parents. More specifically, my mother, who rarely bends to conformity. She blames it on her French heritage. When I was born, she said she had never known such bliss."

"Ah, that explains your irrationality. You're partly French."

"And what nomadic tribe do you hail from?" She hated to think it, but she might actually be enjoying sparring with this aggravating cretin.

"Mother England, I'm afraid. Didn't the cultured tones give it away?"

A splendid retort was on the tip of Bliss's tongue, but he suddenly shouldered away from the post he was leaning against and closed the distance between them.

The crop lay against her leg. He slipped it from her

loose grip and tossed it behind him. He towered over her. She should be afraid, yet she was curious more than anything else.

"No more quips?" he said in a prodding tone, heat blazing from him as though he carried the sun's rays beneath his skin.

Her gaze roamed the breadth of his shoulders, the thick, corded strength of his neck, the harsh jut of his jaw, up to eyes that warned her away, yet dared her to try something.

"What is it that you want from me?" she murmured.

The way he looked at her told her she should know. "So did the glorified jackasses inside find your attire— what little there is of it—to their liking? Were they fawning over you like a pack of slavering idiots? Or did you shun them all with a wave of your regal hand?"

Bliss studied his mouth as he spoke. It was so firm and full, so capable of the most disarming of smiles, when he chose to bestow it upon mere mortals. What would that mouth feel like against hers?

"You should have been there to find out," she replied, a breathless quality to her voice that had not been present a moment before.

His warm breath fanned her cheek as he leaned down. "You forget, I like to malinger in dark places."

Bliss wet her suddenly dry lips. "Why is that, I wonder?"

"You never know what you might discover. Patience, I'm coming to see, can be a virtue. Perhaps the only virtue I possess at this moment."

"Who are you?"

"Who do you want me to be?" His head dipped to her

throat, his silky hair teasing her cheek as he inhaled slowly. "Flowers and fruit. Roses, orange, a hint of vanilla. And heat. Why are you so hot?" The question was spoken in a husky whisper that turned her inside out.

"B-because it's very warm in here."

"No, it's not. In fact, the breeze coming off the ocean is rather cool."

All Bliss felt was him, encompassing her without having laid a finger on her. "Your name. What is it?"

"If I tell you, will you let me kiss you?"

"No."

"Then I'll kiss you anyway."

"Why? You don't like me."

"You're right." He pulled her flush against his hard, unyielding chest. "And now you've forced me to prove it." His mouth came down on hers, annihilating any thought but of what he was doing to her.

His kiss was not soft or gentle or careful of her inexperience, but harsh and punishing and electric, forcing her to keep up or get swept away. Her hands moved restlessly at her sides, desperately searching for something to touch that wasn't him. But he was everywhere.

She couldn't begin to fathom what moved this man, or what moved her to allow him such liberties—his tongue teasing hers, his big hands running slowly up and down her sides before coming to rest on the outer swell of her breasts, his thumbs sliding underneath them as his thigh insinuated itself between her legs.

Bliss felt as though she were on fire. The things he could do with his mouth, the exquisite pressure he created as his lips slanted over hers, wrung soft moans from deep in her throat. She felt strange, like a foreigner in her own body.

It wasn't in her to deny her passions. She had kissed men before, quite a few, in fact. But none of those kisses had compared to this one. The man was an arrogant, infuriating devil, but he had the most deliciously sinful mouth.

It wasn't until Bliss felt the cool breeze against her nipples that she realized he had pushed down the scant fabric covering her breasts. A sharp jolt of desire sizzled straight to the heart of her as his thumbs flicked across the hardened points. Reality blazed across her skin like wildfire.

She tore her mouth from his and pushed at his chest. "Don't!"

Through passion-glazed eyes, he stared down at her, a flicker of ice glinting in the depths of his gaze. "Please tell me you're not going to act the outraged maiden. It's a wearisome ploy."

"No, my lord; it's much simpler than that. I don't want you."

A muscle worked in his jaw. "You're in heat, my lady. Just like your mare. I'd be happy to solve the problem for you, but not if you persist in playing games." His thumbs flicked her nipples again, and pleasure spiraled straight to her toes. He was toying with her, assuring a victory over her, if not in one form than in another.

"I may be in heat," she replied as calmly as her thudding heart would allow, yanking up her bodice, "but you are not the stud for the job."

Anger flashed in his eyes. "I guess you'll never know, will you?" He took a step back, giving her a parody of a bow. "Perhaps it's best if you heed your own words and not look so eager to rut." He extracted a cheroot from his pocket and lit it, regarding her through a thin veil of smoke as he added, "You never know who might oblige."

His coarse words sank bone deep. "Stay away from me. Do you hear? Don't come near me again, whoever you are."

"Ah, that's right. You don't know who I am, do you? Well, let me remedy that." He took hold of her hand, his grip unrelenting as he lifted it to his lips. "Caine Ballinger, my lady, late removed Earl of Hartland, at your service."

Caine Ballinger. The man who intrigued and intimidated her, who was both vile and tantalizing, was Olivia Hamilton's lover. She should have known—yet knowing didn't make the hurt she felt any less painful.

Bliss shoved at his chest. With a dark laugh, he released her, and she turned and fled.

Five

I stood
Among them, but not of them; in a shroud
Of thoughts which were not their thoughts.
Lord Byron

For the second time that day, Caine watched her go, his body in the throes of a lust so strong he very nearly chased her down like some puling adolescent flushed and panting with his first erection. But he had never run after any woman, and he'd be damned if he would start today.

Christ, of all the females in the world, why did it have to be the bloody Duke of Exmoor's daughter that he wanted to bed? Whose soft blue eyes could annihilate a man, butcher him down to that small place inside that he held remote from everyone, while still managing to make him hot as hellfire?

It was beyond comprehension how so black-hearted a man could have created such a vibrant, exotic daughter. And bloody damned smart, besides. No matter what angle he came at her, she deflected him. Both her looks and her intelligence had thrown him.

His name had garnered a very definite reaction. Did she know what her father had done to his? How the man's greed had cost Henry Ballinger his life? Even if she didn't know, it wouldn't make a difference. She hated him one way or the other, and that was fine with him. The feeling was mutual.

Caine exited the stables and closed the doors. Glancing toward the house, he saw the outline of people dancing in *his* ballroom, being served by *his* servants, many of them sleeping under *his* roof.

He would avoid them all for the next week, even if it meant spending his nights out in the stable. His horse was the only thing he cared about, anyway. Khan was all he had left of his former life—all he had left of his father, who had given him the black colt three years ago.

Caine dragged a hand through his hair and headed for the back entrance of the house. He would take the servant's stairs up to his bedroom, which was at the farthest reaches of the west wing, away from the buffoons and their ladies who might stumble into any room they came upon.

Northcote was unique in that it contained an elaborate system of hidden passageways, having been erected by a Saxon ancestor to prevent the Danes from sailing up the river to Exeter. Once a person knew the layout of the tunnels, he could go just about anywhere on the estate undetected.

Those dark corridors were Caine's only salvation during Olivia's interminable gatherings. She hated when he disappeared; she liked showing off her new plaything.

He used to enjoy being intimate with women, reveled in the power he held over them when they were in sexual thrall, needing what he could give them. But any pleasure he had once found in the act had left him the moment he had agreed to Olivia's offer. He'd never imagined he would know what it felt like to be an object, a female's whim, but he knew now and he hated the very sight of himself.

His bedroom was dark as a tomb as he entered it. Once upon a time, there would have been a maid to light his lamps and turn down his sheets, a valet to help him dress and undress.

Olivia didn't believe such things were necessary. If he needed dressing and undressing, he could come to her. He had never done so, but that didn't mean she wouldn't come to him.

Caine struck a match and lit the oil lamp on his bureau, the faint, burnished glow reflecting dully off the dark furniture and heavy drapes. His bedroom was vastly different from those he had occupied in his youth, with satin sheets and decadent splendor to heighten an experience that rarely included sleep. Now he had solitude and a view of the stark cliffs and churning waters, which better suited his mood.

He peeled off his shirt, remembering the way Bliss had stared at his chest, creating the first genuine stirring of desire that he had experienced in years.

God, how he'd wanted her to touch him. There was something about her that had temporarily made him forget who she was. For the first time in a long while, he had been consumed with something other than bitterness and rage.

"Where have you been, darling?"

Caine's body tensed as he glanced at his reflection in the mirror and found Olivia sitting in a wing chair across the room, one leg draped over the arm, only a diaphanous wisp of lingerie veiling her body. Dear God, not tonight. Not when another woman occupied his thoughts and fired his body.

"What are you doing here?" he bit out, sorry he had removed his shirt as her gaze trailed down his back and lingered on his ass.

"Waiting for you, of course."

"I told you not to come to my room."

"Yes, I know, it's your sanctuary from the world. Really, Caine, this obsession you have with protecting what's yours grows tiresome. It's only a room, for heaven's sake."

"What do you want?"

"For you to stop skulking about. Your absence this evening was sorely felt. My guests expect to see you. How do you think I feel when they ask for you and I don't know where you are?"

"I'm not your bloody toy," he growled, swiping his shirt from the floor.

"Leave it off," she insisted in a purr. "And please turn around."

Gritting his teeth, Caine faced her, his hand fisting around his shirt as her gaze stripped him.

"You are glorious, my lord. You have a body that was made to give a woman pleasure. How lovely that you're mine—and as long as I pay your way, darling, you do belong to me. I wonder if you're sufficiently appreciative of our arrangement."

"Don't push me, Olivia. It's not a wise move."

"Come here, Caine." She beckoned him with a finger. "And leave the shirt where it was."

He wanted her to get out and leave him the hell alone,

and there was only one way to accomplish that now, short of murder.

Fury a heavy knot in his stomach, Caine threw the shirt to the floor and crossed the room, coming to a stop several feet from her chair.

"Don't glower so, my love." She peered up at him through her lashes, the tip of her tongue wetting her lips. "You know what I want."

"Don't you ever sleep?"

"Sleep is a waste of time when I have you." Her sultry gaze ran over him, stopping at his groin and finding no evidence of arousal, which put a moue of displeasure on her face. "You are so delicious to look at when you're angry, and so very wicked with me in bed."

"So you purposely prod me, is that it?"

She lifted one shoulder. "Sometimes, yes. Watching you brood is no fun." She leaned forward and ran her finger over the front of his trousers. "I think you've been a bad boy tonight." She cocked her head, giving him a sideways glance. "Were you?"

Caine's jaw tightened. "You've been spying on me again, haven't you?"

"I have to keep an eye on my property," she said, her hand slipping beneath his waistband to take hold of him. "Or else someone might steal you. And this," she purred low in her throat, "is worth its weight in gold. I can't have anything happen to it now, can I?"

"This," he growled, gripping her wrist, "comes with me if I leave, and the next time you refer to me as property will be the last."

A childish pout puckered her lips. "Don't be angry with me."

"Stop bloody spying on me. I'm sick of it."

"I don't actually do the spying; that would be beneath me. Chadwick does it."

Chadwick. Her personal secretary, who Caine was sure was giving Olivia more than administrative services on the side. Had the man seen the kiss Caine had given Bliss? Had the maggot-ridden leper watched him ease down her bodice without her being the wiser? Watched him toy with her until he hadn't known which one of them was actually being seduced?

"I'd advise you to keep the bastard well away from me, or next time I'll strangle the little prick."

"He said he saw you with Exmoor's whore of a daughter. I thought I told you to stay away from her."

"And I told you that I'll do whatever I damn well please outside the bedroom."

She took hold of his waistband, trying to pull him down to his knees. Acid seared the back of his throat as he lowered himself to the floor.

"As long as you're not fucking her," she said fiercely.

"Good Christ," Caine choked out, derision lacing his tone. "How many erections do you think I can manage? You're constantly on me, hard or not. My cock doesn't even want to rise anymore. But of course, I must be giving it to any woman with breasts and a pulse. The milkmaid, the vicar's daughter. The vicar's wife. Your niece. Your sister. Half the female population of Northern England. Anyone I've missed?"

"Chadwick said you kissed her. Did you?"

"Yes." Chadwick was a dead man. "So what?"

"I thought you hated her."

"I do."

"Then why?"

"To punish her." But he had only tormented himself, his ardor slugging him like a prizefighter's jab to the solar plexus.

Olivia sat back in the chair, eyeing him. "I see this is going to be a problem."

"I told you to get rid of her."

"She's a guest. Besides, my niece seems to have developed a *tendre* for the lady's cousin. Court Wyndham is quite a catch, and I do not want to discourage the match." A look that Caine had seen far too many times came into her eyes. She traced his jaw with her finger and skimmed it down his neck. "Do you still desire me, Caine?"

"What do you want, Olivia? Blood?"

She studied him for a moment. "I can tell you're getting bored, and I want to make things enjoyable again."

That was a feat she would never accomplish. "I won't perform any of your perversions, if that's what you're thinking."

"Actually, I was thinking about Lady Bliss. I spoke to her tonight."

Caine stiffened. Olivia had a special fondness for telling other women details about his sexual performance, and consequently, they did whatever they could to entice him into bed.

Whether it was purely curiosity about his skill that drove them to proposition him, or if they were testing his willpower, or if they simply wanted what Olivia had, he wasn't sure. He hadn't been sure of any woman's intentions toward him in a long time.

"Do I need to worry about her trying to get me into bed, like those vultures you call friends?" he asked.

Olivia stared at him, first blankly and then with fury, as if she had never anticipated this possibility. "My friends have tried to seduce you?"

"What did you expect?"

She took hold of his waistband again and tugged him forward, between her thighs. "What did you do when they asked?"

"What do you think I did?"

"Damn you, Caine. Tell me!"

"Nothing, for the love of Christ!"

"Good. Because I don't like sharing." She dropped her shoulders and the silky material of her robe slid down her arms, exposing her breasts, her nipples rouged as usual, which made his stomach turn. "Do you think Lady Bliss is prettier than I am?"

Bliss was stunning; one of the most beautiful women he had ever seen. Her petite size made him feel like a giant. He had actually felt a moment of nervousness when he touched her, thinking how fragile she was, how easily he could crush her.

When she had forced him to stop, he had felt unwanted for the first time in his life, thinking she had seen straight through to the hole where his heart had once been, and found him lacking.

"Yes," he told Olivia bluntly.

"Why are you so cruel?" she asked in a stricken voice.

"Don't ask questions if you don't want the answers."

A speculative gleam suddenly came into her eyes. "I have a wager for you."

Caine tensed, his guard going up. "What kind of wager?"

"We need a bit of excitement, so I've come up with something that I think will make us both happy." A calculated look glinted in her eyes as she added, "I want you to seduce Lady Bliss."

"*What?*"

"It will be the perfect revenge for your father's death."

Caine couldn't believe what he was hearing. "Have you already forgotten your anger at my being with her tonight?"

"That was before I gave you my blessing."

Caine's hands fisted at his sides. "So now it's all right if I bed her?"

"Not exactly. I expect you to save your passion for me—unless she is a virgin. Your breaching that sanctimonious maidenhead would destroy her dear papa. His precious child, defiled by a notorious rake. What a coup de grâce!"

Revenge. The word reverberated through Caine's head. For a long time, he'd thought that if he could avenge his father's death he would be free of this obsession that drove him. Free to move on and find some new meaning in his life.

And here was an opportunity to strike at Exmoor's very heart: a woman's reputation for his father's life. Not an equal trade-off by any means, but a powerful blow nonetheless.

"I can see you're wrestling with your demons," she said, brushing aside the filmy silk covering her mound and placing his hand there, wriggling impatiently until he slipped a finger between her folds. "So I will give you additional incentive." She guided his finger over her swollen flesh, moaning low, as she finished. "This house."

Every muscle in Caine's body stilled. "What are you saying?"

"Keep going." Once his finger resumed moving, she continued, "If you seduce Lady Bliss and get her to fall in love with you, then I will give you back Northcote."

His home, returned to him. The dream that had consumed him for two long years. He could almost taste the victory. But he couldn't allow himself to be drawn in, to feel the surging hunger for something just out of reach. He knew Olivia too well. She had sprung her trap with a purpose in mind.

"You get something in return," he countered. "What is it?"

"Now, that was the hard part of this brilliant plan. What should be my reward, should you—the master of seduction—fail? Alfred, as you know, left me well provided for. I really don't need this house, but it came with such a delicious perk, how could I resist?" She hooked her left leg over the other chair arm and moved his hand down.

"Spit it out. What the hell do you want?"

"Can't you guess?"

"Leave off with the games."

She leaned forward and whispered in his ear, "I want a baby, Caine. *Your* baby."

Caine saw his dream wither and die. "No."

She stared at him, incredulous. "You won't give me a child, even for the chance to win back your home?"

"Not even if you promised me salvation. Besides, you're not about to bear the shame of having a bastard—and I won't let any child of mine grow up as one."

"God, you are so sickeningly sentimental sometimes. It's one of your more aggravating qualities."

"But it doesn't overshadow my other qualities, does it?" He purposely increased the tempo against her slick peak.

She tipped back her head and released an excited whimper. "No . . . it doesn't overshadow your many, umm . . . exquisite talents."

Caine eased back, not wanting her to come just yet. He needed to keep her exactly where he wanted her. She was placing something he desperately desired within his reach.

"Your plan won't work, anyway."

She moved in opposing friction to his strokes. "And why is that?"

"Because I said some things to the girl I don't think she'll forget."

"Oh dear. You behaved like a barbarian, didn't you?" She sighed and shook her head. "You were rather unhappy to see her, if I recall. Well, you are quite persuasive, darling. And your technique is . . . mmm, divine." Her body quivered as her hand covered his, trying to make him increase his pace.

"So we're at an impasse."

"Not necessarily."

"I won't give you a baby."

"Oh, but just think about it, Caine. If we married we could still go our separate ways, and your child can grow up here, in this house. Continue the family legacy. We can be . . . a family."

A family she controlled with detailed contracts and a monthly allowance, all structured to keep him under her thumb. Marriage to her would not change his circumstances; he would simply be a permanent stud rather than a temporary one. God, how he longed for peace.

Peace of heart. Peace of soul.

The need to find that peace was a wrenching ache

inside him, forcing the words from his mouth. "If I agree, you would put this all down in writing?"

The gleam of impending victory tipped up the corners of her lips. "I'll have my solicitor draw up the papers. Mr. Carlton is very discreet. No one need ever know."

Caine was caught between the emptiness inside him that he knew his home could fill, and the cruelty of what he was about to do.

He would win, of course. He had to. Too much was at stake. There was no way he would marry Olivia and give her a child to control. That left him with only one option: to succeed, no matter the cost.

"Fine," he said. "Draw up the papers."

Either way, he was damned.

Six

He lay great and greatly fallen,
Forgetful of his chivalry.
Homer

*C*aine stood in the shadows of the semicircular Doric porch, thinking about what he had agreed to the previous night. He had been reduced to the final depths of disgrace and sold whatever small part of his soul that yet remained to Olivia.

After he'd brought her to orgasm three times, she had fallen asleep—in his damn bed. Taking her back to her own room risked the chance of rousing her and having to pleasure her again, so he had shrugged into his discarded shirt and gone up to the roof. A walkway traversed the entire length of the house, and he could see the sky from any angle.

He had leaned back against the cool stones and stared up into the darkness, in the company of a sliver of moon and a handful of stars, the sound of the surf's continual ebb and flow familiar and soothing, sweeping in a tide of painful memories of a home that was once full of life and love.

The roof had been his private place as a lad. He would sneak off to avoid his chores and pretend an armada of pirate ships, flags of skull and crossbones flapping in the breeze, was heading straight for the cove, ready to cannonade the cliffs and loot the village, he alone able to save them all.

Grandiose visions for an eight-year-old boy who had once believed he would be knighted by the queen for his valiant efforts, a thundering roar of cheers and applause ringing in his ears as a chorus of angels sang "Hail Britannia" to the conquering hero.

Last night, he had watched the sun rise over the horizon, its red and gold rays spreading across the water, reaching inevitably toward land.

He remained motionless until the first beam of light touched his skin, waiting, as he always did, for it to warm him, to seep beneath the coldness that gripped him and bring something back to life inside his heart. To make him into the hero he had once so desperately wanted to be. But it hadn't happened before. And it didn't happen today.

So he had made a bargain with the devil and sealed it with his lips, his tongue, and his hands. Now he had to follow through, to seduce a woman he needed to hate. To utilize every weapon in his sexual arsenal to lure Bliss to him, every ounce of charm he possessed to fool her into believing he was someone worth loving.

His body craved hers; that was undeniable. And yet something gnawed at him. Had he not been entirely certain he had eradicated all signs of a conscience, he would have thought it was guilt that settled on his shoulders.

Not possible. He was merely feeling the anticipation of the hunt, the thrill of ultimate victory. Seducing women was a sport he understood down to his bone and sinew. He'd have his home back, his life back, or some semblance of it, at least. He had to do this for his father, for what Northcote had meant to him, and the generations of Ballingers before him.

Caine saw Bliss exit the house and head across the lawn. Stepping out of the shelter of the porch, he followed her. He hadn't yet been able to decipher her weaknesses, her desires, but he would.

She disappeared around the edge of the garden, past a small copse of trees. She was following the path that headed toward the sea, just east of the Point—the outcropping of jagged rocks that jutted out over the quay.

Caine had not been to the Point since his father died; he couldn't bring himself to get close to the cliffs. Memories would invade, threatening to tear down the wall that protected him from things he didn't want to acknowledge.

So he stood at a distance, hidden behind a scrub oak, around him a self-sown wood where all the trees had trunks like corkscrews and the branches were shorn from the west, pointing away from the wind.

Closer to the cliffs, the woods gave way to ling, bracken, and gorse. Motionless buzzards hovered in updrafts of air, while the gulls, returning from the ploughland, arrowed toward the sea.

He lit a cheroot, tension stiffening his body as he watched how close Bliss came to the edge of the precipice. One slip would send her tumbling down the side. He started toward her, but then she stepped back, wholly absorbed in the view.

For a long moment, she lifted her face to the sky. The sun's rays washed over her, encircling her in a golden hue, a chestnut-haired angel sent to earth to tempt and torment. The sight sent an unexpected surge of dark hunger sluicing through Caine.

Finally, she sat down in the grass. Arranging her skirts, she opened a sketchpad. He hadn't paid the slightest attention to what she had been carrying. His attention had been focused on the slender curve of her back, the indentation that marked a waist he could span with both hands, the way her backside moved with a hypnotic rhythm, and how the breeze wreaked havoc on her hair, dislodging the silky strands one pin at a time until most of the heavy mass had cascaded down her back.

Her hair was beautiful and he wanted to grab a fistful of it like he had done last night, to feel the cool, luxurious silk burn his palm as he pulled her head back and pressed his mouth to her neck. He could envision that thick mane spread out around her as he eased her to her back in the grass and came over her, their fingers laced together above her head.

Christ, he had to pull himself together. Seduce and destroy was his mission. And as he started toward her, Caine knew he would thoroughly enjoy the task.

A shadow fell over Bliss, one with a distinctly human shape: that of a man, with shoulders big enough to block out the sun. She didn't need to look to know who it was. The prickling of her skin told her.

She glanced up and was struck by the very sight of Caine, those velvet-blue eyes more intense than a storm-tossed sea, his raven hair streaked with gold, an aura of light limning his body, giving him the appearance of a fallen angel, reborn in darkness and come to earth to entice mortals into sensual realms.

Images of his face, of that scar that had fascinated her, his mouth upon hers, her breasts in his large hands, had kept her up most of the night, torn between the desire to bury a knife in his back and the desire to lay beneath him. Sheer exhaustion had finally pulled her down into dark, disturbing dreams, where he remained to taunt her. But she vowed he would not bother her today.

"You're blocking my light," she told him, looking away. She didn't like what she saw when she stared into his eyes. Ridicule, arrogance. Pain. The barest hint of vulnerability. Impossible—he was as vulnerable as a rattlesnake.

He startled her by kneeling down beside her, saying nothing, which was perhaps more unnerving than anything he had done thus far.

"What do you want?" she asked shortly. "Is this your personal section of grass? Is my dress the wrong color? What, pray tell, has disturbed your fragile sensibilities today?"

"Not my grass," he replied in a measured drawl. "And your dress . . ." His gaze drifted over her, his perusal more than thorough before meeting her eyes again. "Your dress is perfect. It makes your breasts look incredibly lush. They're surprisingly big for such a petite frame."

An unwanted blush prickled Bliss's cheeks. Never had a man possessed such an uncanny ability to shock her, when very little ever did. Caine clearly reveled in his wicked behavior, which made her body's uncharacteristic responses so maddening.

"Are you foxed?" she asked. From his haggard

appearance, his chin dusted with morning whiskers, his shoulder-length hair loose and wild, and his clothes slightly disheveled, she wouldn't doubt that he had continued indulging in spirits after she left him in the stables.

His smile was crooked as he replied, "Perhaps a little."

Bliss turned away from him. "Well, don't expect me to save you when you fall and break your fool neck."

"Are you always so cruel to men who leer at your rather remarkable attributes?"

"You're the only one who leers."

"Now, I find that hard to believe. Aren't those Parisian fops drooling over you?"

"Some of us are too busy with pursuits outside the bedroom to concern ourselves with such things."

His eyes narrowed a fraction and she knew she had made a direct hit. "If you're searching for some insight into my bedroom activities," he said in a silky tone, "why not just ask? I'd be happy to oblige your curiosity."

"You really do believe you're an amazing blessing upon the female population, don't you?"

He shrugged, his shoulders a massive slab of hard muscle and incredible width. "I've had no complaints."

Bliss didn't doubt that was the truth. Hadn't he managed to get his hands on her breasts with near blinding speed? Far worse, she had practically sighed into those large hands.

Something in her face must have given her away, because he said, "I see you remember. Good. I hope it haunts you. Lord knows it haunted me."

That revelation surprised her. She would have sworn he had forgotten about her in less than five seconds. But the smoldering look in his eyes told her he had forgotten nothing.

"Does your mind only travel down one road?" she asked tartly. "Perhaps if you broadened your horizons, you might have more on which to speak."

A glint of amusement lit his eyes. "Broaden my horizons, hmm? The idea sounds intriguing. Yes, let's broaden my horizons. What is it you wish to speak of? Plato? Aristotle? Or should we simply contemplate the sky and wonder how it all began?"

"Equality. That is what I wish to speak of, though I doubt it's a topic with which *you* are familiar."

He lifted a dark brow, pretending insult. "And whose equality are we referring to?"

"Women's."

"Ah." He nodded. "I suspected you were a dreaded reformer, out to change the male population with your incendiary war cry."

"And I suspected you wouldn't have the slightest clue about the idea of a woman being your equal. Beneath you, in bed and out, is where you prefer them."

"It does make the prospect of having to deal with your sex much more pleasurable, I admit." The crooked grin he suddenly leveled on her was thoroughly disarming. "But confess, you like me anyway, don't you?"

The man defined infuriating. "Go. Away."

He crossed his ankles. "The prospect of tussling with you in this grass is greatly appealing to me."

"Then I'll go." Bliss made to rise, but he caught her around the waist and pulled her back down, bringing them face to face, her hands braced outside his thighs, the heat from his body enveloping her.

"I was right," he murmured, his mouth dangerously close to hers.

Bliss swallowed. "About what?"

"Your eyes. They're as blue as the ocean, and just as deep." He gently swept a lock of her hair away from her face, his knuckles brushing her cheek, bringing a slight shiver to her skin. "Don't go. I promise I'll behave."

"You don't know how to behave."

"True," he said, his expression endearingly boyish. "But we can pretend, can't we?"

Bliss had to repress a smile. He could charm when he wanted to, and she suspected very few females, if any, had not succumbed. But why was he attempting to charm her?

Seduction—that had to be it. The man epitomized persistence. Well, he would have a long wait if he thought a smile—masterpiece of sensuality though it was— would melt her.

She realized with a start that she was still hovering over him and he was not holding her. She quickly moved away and sat back down.

He plucked a bluebell and held it out to her. The sight of that small flower moved Bliss more than she expected; something told her this man did not make such gestures. But she still couldn't trust him.

She returned her attention to the vista before her, doing her best to ignore him, a feat she couldn't even hope to accomplish.

She opened her sketchpad to a fresh sheet, intending to try; then he placed the bluebell on top of the paper, foiling her efforts. She nearly picked up the tiny flower, but caught herself at the last moment and brushed it away onto the grass. He put a hand over his heart, as though mortally wounded by her rebuff.

Getting out her charcoals, she studied the magnificent landscape stretched out before her. Massive headlands ran the entire coastline. Furze-clad projections fell away abruptly to the bay. Masses of low, dark rock girded a basin of turf, which drifted eastward, passing from one shape to the next.

Her hand began to draw before her mind recognized it, which was always how she worked, letting the subject guide her without thought. For thought could ruin what she was trying to create.

She had managed to block out the man beside her until he murmured, "Carlyle."

Forgetting her vow to pay him no mind, Bliss glanced over at him, which was a mistake. His face in profile was as wickedly beautiful as Lucifer, and as dark and moving as the cliffs she drew. He was idly thumbing through her copy of *Sartor Resartus*.

"It's a book," she said. "Certainly you've heard of them? They contain words and can be rather enlightening at times. I recommend you try one."

"I've tried a few in my life. Would you like to know what they were?" Devilry danced in the sideways glance he threw her.

"No." Bliss suspected the only enlightenment they contained was in-depth detail of a woman's anatomy. "I'm sure I could not possibly comprehend the depths of your keen intellect."

A soft laugh, deep and oddly musical, rumbled from his chest. "Well, let me see if my 'keen intellect' can recall what Carlyle was trying to convey. If I remember correctly, he believes members of the aristocracy are no more than idle, game-preserving dilettantes and social parasites who while away their days shooting pheasant and lolling about during the fashionable London Season, oblivious to the realities of the world outside their illustrious social strata. Is that about right?"

Bliss didn't want to be impressed by his knowledge of Carlyle's work, but he had managed to surprise her. "You truly are a brain trust, my lord. Bravo."

"And you, my lady, are still a bitch. But a very beautiful one."

His barb, though sugar-coated, stung. "I don't have to listen to this." She snatched the book from his hands, but he gripped her wrist when she went to rise.

"Stay."

She would not fall for that again. "If you don't unhand me, I'll hit you over the head."

"And I'd deserve it. But if you stay, I'll tell you about the island out there, the one you're drawing. It has an interesting history."

Bliss told herself not to be led astray by his offer, intriguing as it was. She would only regret it. This man exuded trouble, and yet that was exactly what drew her to him.

If only Court hadn't told her about Caine, how he haunted his home, and how his father had been driven to kill himself, perhaps he would not hold so much fascination for her.

He didn't deserve any compassion. He reveled in tossing any kindness back in her face, yet beneath the cool appraisal that said apologies were beyond him lay a glimpse of susceptibility, as if her staying meant something to him.

She tugged her hand from his and turned away. "What about its history?"

He handed her back her sketchpad, which had spilled from her lap. "It was a favorite haunt of pirates," he replied.

"That's not so unusual." Devon had always been a haven for pirates and smugglers, its secluded coves and hidden caves perfect spots to store stolen booty.

"True," he said, "but that particular island was once inhabited by the Knights Templar. A token from King Henry II. Legend also has it that a race of giants once lived there."

"Giants?" she scoffed. "Now you're making things up."

"No, a group of islanders found a huge stone kist with skeletons measuring nearly eight feet tall."

"I suspect you're a descendant," Bliss said absently, her gaze skimming over his long, muscular legs stretched out in front of him, and up the well-defined torso that had been pressed tightly to hers the previous evening, before finally settling on his face, where his quirked eyebrow made her realize what she was doing. "I mean . . . you're tall. Taller than most men."

"Six-four probably just seems like a giant to you. You can't be more than what? Five-one?"

"Five-two."

"Baby-sized."

His assessment raised her hackles. "I may be small, my lord, but that is where the comparisons end."

As she should have guessed, those penetrating blue-black eyes dipped to her breasts, and Bliss was mortified to feel her nipples harden.

"No, not small," he countered in a husky murmur.

"Impressive, actually. Distracting, in fact. Far more than a handful, if I remember correctly."

The memory of his hands on her breasts made heat spiral inside her. "Is your mind perpetually in the gutter?"

"Acutely. I'm a shameless sinner, rarely taken with a noble intention. More so than usual, today. There's just something about you that stimulates my baser instincts."

"How flattering. But I doubt I'm the only female who manages that feat." Olivia Hamilton's cold, beautiful face came to mind, images of her and Caine in bed, their bodies merging, the warm lips and hands that had touched Bliss with such explosive power caressing the eager widow. "Perhaps I'd better leave if I'm such a distraction to you."

"I promise I won't touch you if you don't want me to." He leaned toward her, the sea breeze ruffling his silky hair as he murmured, "But I want to. Very much. I can't help myself. I'm fascinated by all those buttons on your dress."

Bliss followed his gaze. The tiny pearl buttons ran from her neck to her waist like luminescent beads of chastity, warding off libertines.

Glancing up, she found the king of libertines studying her. "You're trying to seduce me, aren't you?"

"Yes," he confessed, looking boyishly hopeful. "Is it working?"

His blunt, honest answer made her shake her head and smile, though she looked away so he wouldn't see it. She could see why he had been so successful a rake.

She started as his finger nudged her chin, turning her face toward him, forcing her to meet his gaze. "I lied about your name, you know." His breath stirred the hair at her temple. "It does fit you."

Bliss glimpsed the intention in his eyes and laid her hands against his chest. "Don't . . ."

"Don't what?"

"Don't kiss me."

"Just once." He edged nearer, his lips only a whisper away, his hand closing over one of hers and sliding it beneath his coat, his heart a steady thump beneath her palm.

"No."

She thought he would press on, despite her protests. Instead he murmured in her ear, "Do you remember my fingers on your nipples?" His sensual words sent a rivulet of warmth down her spine.

She wanted to scold him for his wickedness, and yet she whispered, "Yes."

"They were so tight and hot. I wanted to wrap my lips around them and find out how sweet they were." The finger beneath her jaw trailed slowly down her throat. "Have you ever had a man's mouth on your breasts, love? Or his shaft between your thighs, pleasuring you in ways you could only imagine?" The fine layer of whiskers on his jaw rasped lightly against her cheek. "Are you a virgin, sweet Bliss?"

The erotic web he had spun dissipated. "How dare you ask such a thing!" She shoved against his chest, but barely budged him.

"I have my answer." He took hold of her hand and smoothed his thumb over her palm. "How have you managed to stay chaste this long?"

She wrenched her hand from his. "By staying away from men like you!"

"It's unfair to lump me in with men who don't know

the first thing about giving a woman what she really wants. Such men are only concerned with their own pleasure. Though I've never bedded a virgin before, I assure you I would breach your maidenhead with the utmost care. You would be so ensnared in the force of your passion that you would only feel a slick heat when I entered you."

Bliss's traitorous body responded to his brazen words, though her voice gave nothing away. "Does this kind of love talk work on Lady Buxton? If so, the woman has even less taste than I had given her credit for."

His eyes hardened and his jaw tensed. "She has nothing to do with this."

"No? I would think she has a great deal to do with this. I doubt she would approve. You are her—"

In a second, Bliss was flat on her back with Caine lying half on top of her, his hands pinning hers to the ground, the fury in his eyes a tangible force.

"Don't," she whimpered, the feel of him on top of her, his solid weight, the rock-hard muscles she could see flexing beneath his shirt telling her how vulnerable she was.

They were far enough away from the house that no one would hear her should she scream. But she wanted to believe he wouldn't really hurt her, even though she knew full well how volatile his temper was.

"No one tells me what to do. Not Olivia, not anyone. Do you understand me?" When she didn't respond quickly enough, he barked, "Do you?"

"Yes!"

The muscle in his jaw worked. "Jesus . . . you make me crazy." The torment in his voice almost convinced her that she did, and that vulnerable look haunted his eyes again. "Please . . . just kiss me."

"Caine . . ." Bliss knew she should deny him, yet when he touched her, she forgot everything.

Tenuously, she slid her hands up over his shoulders, following the hard contours to his neck, where her fingers entwined in his thick, silky hair, sifting it through her fingers, unconsciously wetting her lips. His gaze drifted to her mouth and then back to her eyes as his head slowly descended.

The warm pressure of his lips against hers sent sensation everywhere. The ache that had been a dull throb between her thighs built with every sweep of his tongue against hers.

She loved the heavy, solid feel of him that made him real in a way he had not been before, even though she could tell he was keeping his full weight off her. He made her feel fragile, feminine. Protected.

The last thought was odd, considering he had pushed her down into the grass, yet she didn't want gentleness. She wanted someone vital and strong and magnificent. No man had ever been a match for the strength of her will, but this man was more than her equal.

He took hold of her wrists and manacled them above her head with one hand, leaving her powerless, completely at his mercy. She gasped into his mouth as his free hand cradled the swell of her breast, her nipples hard and sensitive.

Have you ever had a man's mouth on your nipples?

She never had, but she wanted to feel his mouth on her. She squirmed restlessly against him, her thigh brushing the hardness between his legs.

He groaned, a deep, primal sound, and squeezed her breast. His mouth found every sensitive spot on her neck as his thumb teased her nipple through her dress.

His hand rose to the first of the buttons at her throat. Her heart thumped wildly with each one he released, his lips tasting every piece of flesh revealed.

She whimpered as he worked his way down to the valley between her breasts. He raised his head then, and her heavy eyelids fluttered open to find him watching her as he undid the remaining buttons, slowly pushing the material aside, only her thin chemise separating her naked flesh from his blazing eyes.

Wantonly, she arched up to meet his mouth, her head tossing back as his tongue wet her nipple through the material, making the ache between her thighs redouble. Then his lips wrapped around the exquisitely sensitive peak and sucked with just the right pressure, as though he instinctively knew exactly what she wanted.

But hadn't he claimed she would be ensnared by passion when he took her? He was a master at seducing women, and only yesterday he had hated her, had wanted to teach her a lesson.

Perhaps he still did.

Wouldn't it be her supreme downfall if someone should happen along and find her writhing beneath this man? A man who tallied up his conquests in numbers Bliss couldn't even begin to imagine? And he belonged to the marchioness, his body meant for her sole and exclusive use. He was out to prove something, to conquer and claim her. And she was letting him.

"Stop!" When he didn't immediately respond, she tugged at his hair, her nipple slipping from his mouth.

She could see the wet spot on her chemise, her areola dark against the fabric, and shame washed over her.

Lazily, he rolled to his side. She scrambled out from underneath him and pushed to her feet. He stared up at her, his dark eyes filled with heat and a burgeoning anger at her dismissal.

"Did I suck too hard, your ladyship? If you would but lie back down, I can try again. I'm sure this time I can get it right."

Her chest was tight and her fingers clumsy as she did up the buttons on her dress. "Go to hell," she told him in a shaky voice, her legs threatening to buckle beneath her as she turned away and tried not to run back to the house.

Seven

∽◌∾

There, in the moonlight, dark with dew,
Asking not wherefore nor why, would
Brood like a ghost, and as still as a post . . .
Walter de la Mare

𝒯he last reflection of a dying sun coated the sea in an iridescent pool of red as it sank below the horizon, ushering in the night, which settled over the landscape in an inky blackness that was complete. Yet Caine could still make out the looming outline of the massive rocks rimming the quay, blue fingers of fog coiling around the jagged peaks as the cliffs worked their way out toward Morwenstow.

In the distance below, the whitewashed farmhouses and cottages of the village stood out like beacons. Down there they lived another life, far removed from the man who had once been destined to preside over the Hall—before his pleasure-seeking ways had made him oblivious to the world he once knew.

His father's tenants, now Olivia's tenants, were the only ones who treated him as though he was the same person who'd grown up among them. They had not acted differently because of what he'd become. And yet Caine felt as though he stood outside a wall a thousand feet high, the gates closed to him.

Perhaps it was the villagers' plight as much as his own that bound him to this place, adding one more tie that kept him from leaving. Olivia was an outsider. She didn't understand the way things worked.

Caine's weary gaze lifted to Bliss's window. Her drapes were drawn, but he knew she was in there. He had seen a shadow pass back and forth as though she were pacing, perhaps as coiled into knots as he was.

As much as he tried to congratulate himself for his victory that morning—and it had been a victory, for she had succumbed, and so sweetly he still burned from the imprint of her body—he couldn't seem to summon up much enthusiasm.

He hadn't handled things well, and that wasn't like him. But when he looked at Bliss, he didn't just see the Duke of Exmoor's daughter. He also saw . . . Bliss. But he couldn't allow himself to get diverted. He had to seduce her with the same single-minded ruthlessness he had employed in the past. Yet for one fleeting moment, he felt something he hadn't felt in a long time. The loss of his humanity.

"There you are, darling."

Caine stiffened as Olivia materialized from the darkness, a harlot swathed in a cream-colored gown, as polished and unappealing as a wax effigy, though she never failed to believe she looked youthful and innocent—a joke of monumental proportions. Any innocence Olivia had once possessed had eroded long ago.

She had confided to him once that she had seduced one of her father's closest friends, a lonely widower, when she was only eighteen. She had caught him looking at her and knew he wanted her.

Once she had gotten him in bed, she had driven him to the brink of death with her sexual antics and then taunted him afterwards by accusing him of being a dirty old bastard for defiling a young girl, and threatening to tell her father that he had raped her. She sank the final nail in his coffin when she vowed that soon all of London would know what he did.

The man shot himself that same night.

Caine turned away from her, the sight of her sickening him more than usual. He had touched something pure today, something he had never experienced before—a woman who was completely innocent in the ways of men, who had blossomed beneath his seeking fingers and eager mouth.

Just the image of Bliss's high, full breasts and those sweet, tight nipples made him hard. And it was that hardness that Olivia felt when her arms wrapped around his waist, her hand, inevitably, moving over his groin.

"You should have told me you were randy," she purred, massaging him. "You know I would have obliged."

Caine indulged in a fantasy, letting himself believe that it was Bliss touching him, Bliss undoing the buttons of his trousers and taking his erection into her hands, Bliss skillfully pumping him.

He imagined her as she had been that afternoon, lying beneath him, kittenish sounds falling from her lips, her desire a heady aphrodisiac, making his hands shake and sweat trickle down his back, a single feverish thought pounding relentlessly in his brain: to bring her to the heights of ecstasy and emblazon his touch in her memory.

Yet in the back of his mind, where a tiny speck of sanity still remained, he wanted Bliss to hurl every vile name she could think of at him and push him away, not allow him a single liberty. Christ, didn't she know he was no good? Couldn't she see what she risked?

And yet she had given in to him, surrendered to his seduction. Now, in his fantasy, he did to her what he wanted to do then: rucking her skirt up to her waist; her thighs, smooth and taut, opening for him to settle between them; her eyes telling him how much she wanted him.

He eased into her gloved warmth, felt the thin veil of her virginity impeding his process and hesitated. He had taken so many women that their images had become a single blur. But this was different. Bliss was different. He couldn't mess this up like everything else in his life.

But she saved him, arching up and bringing him inside her, deep, so damn deep and tight. His body was on fire for her. He wanted her to feel each stroke, ache for each erotic kiss, beg for more.

He wanted to be remembered.

And not simply as some stud to be used whenever a female needed his services, but as the man who had taken her virginity as though it was destined for him alone.

And with each deep thrust, each taunting glide, each taste of her pouting nipples, he tried to assure himself that what he was doing was sanctioned, his due, his long-awaited revenge, instead of simply thanking God that she had granted a craven bastard like him such a gift.

As her body bowed against his, her nipples thrust high for him to lave with his tongue, pushing her over the edge into sweet oblivion, the first convulsion rippled through her. Her muscles tightened around his shaft, pulling him into that wet heat. A groan welled up from deep inside his chest as he found his release, her arms twining around his neck and holding him close, as though she never wanted to let him go.

"Mmm, that was delicious," Olivia murmured against his back, the dream disappearing like a vapor trail. "I came furiously, imagining all that luscious cream inside me intead of wasted on my prized orchids, though I suspect they'll grow to twice their size now."

Caine wanted to howl. He opened his eyes, disgust boiling up inside him. Jesus, what was he thinking? They were outside, where anyone could have seen them. His gaze jerked to Bliss's window, relieved to find the drapes still closed.

He stepped away from Olivia and buttoned up his trousers, feeling nauseated and angry and bloody sick at heart. What had become of his life, his pride? He had been emasculated somewhere along the way and he couldn't find his way back.

Moving to the edge of the incline, he looked down. "What do you want?"

"A thank you, at the moment," Olivia replied, her tone self-satisfied. "You must admit, I have spectacular hands."

Caine didn't want to think about how images of Bliss

had led to his vulnerability with Olivia. "Why don't you go find your guests? They're probably missing their reigning queen."

"Yes," she mused, a smile in her voice, "they do adore me. And I must strive to keep them happy. They want to see you, you know."

"Forget it."

"Some of your old friends are here. They wish to know how you're faring."

Caine had spotted Clarendon, Lynford, and St. Giles when they arrived together earlier in the day. None of those bloody vipers had been his friends. The only true friends he'd ever had were the group of men who formed the Pleasure Seekers Club—all confirmed bachelors with a solitary goal: the pursuit of pleasure in whatever form it took, with himself leading the pack as the founding member.

He had avoided all of them since his father's death, and had even turned Lucien away a few days earlier when his friend had made a side trip to see him before continuing on to Cornwall to take charge of his ward, Lady Francine Fitz Hugh, whose brother had died serving his country.

Caine couldn't face them, not now that he had become a mockery of the very sport he had once pursued so vigorously. As for St. Giles and his lot, he'd see them dead before he spent a second in their presence.

"Entertain them yourself," he said tightly. "You always put on a good performance."

"Fine," she replied petulantly. "Do as you please. I will simply have to let St. Giles amuse Lady Bliss tonight."

Caine stiffened. St. Giles was a bigger reprobate than he was. Whereas a woman could tell Caine's intentions, St. Giles was a damn snake charmer, his golden good looks camouflaging the rot beneath. All he had to do was smile and a woman was his. None of them realized the depths of his depravity until they were in his bed and discovered that his idea of pleasure included a blindfold and a whip.

"He's taken quite a fancy to her," Olivia went on in her calculated assault. "Apparently he caught a glimpse of her this morning and claimed to be hopelessly infatuated. Lynford and Clarendon are more plebeian; they simply want to bed her—both at the same time, a delicious *ménage à trois*."

When Caine made no reply, she prodded, "Perhaps I'll invite St. Giles into our bedroom. I will confess to a certain eagerness to see if his endowments measure up to yours, though I suspect they'll fall short." She snickered, her pun amusing her. "It could be quite an enjoyable evening, don't you think?"

Slowly Caine turned to face her, his gut tightening. He couldn't allow any of those mongrels to have Bliss.

He intended that pleasure for himself.

"I see I finally have your attention," she murmured, spiteful satisfaction glittering in her eyes. "I knew you wouldn't want to ruin your chances with the lady, whom I saw hastening toward the house this afternoon. And less than a minute later, there you were, coming from the same direction, your expression not at all happy.

"So what happened, darling? Did you find the lady was immune to your exalted charm? I rather suspected she wouldn't be an easy conquest. You do have your work cut out for you, don't you?"

"Don't worry about my part of this bargain. I can handle her."

"Oh, I have no doubt. Who can resist you, after all?" Her gaze lingered below his waist before returning to his face. "Well, then, I'll expect to see you inside in five minutes." She turned to go, then paused to look over her shoulder. "I imagine you'll have something wicked in mind for me later, considering the lovely gift I just gave you?" She didn't wait for a reply.

All afternoon Bliss had contemplated the merits of sending a note to her hostess, telling her that she was unwell and unable to attend the supper party that evening.

But ultimately her stubborn streak, which was both a blessing and a curse, asserted itself. To not appear would have a certain overbearing earl thinking he had affected her, and he would gloat. That image goaded her into dressing.

She picked her attire with care, donning a gown made of delicate Chantilly lace and butter-soft Indian cashmere, which flattered her curves, giving her a soft, feminine appearance. Elegant decadence rather than overt.

Now, with Court's compliment on her appearance still warming her, Bliss strolled along on her cousin's arm, listening to glowing tales about Lady Rebecca. Bliss smiled and nodded, though her mind was focused on the grand dining salon and who would be within.

"I hope you aren't put out with me for abandoning you today?"

It took Bliss a moment to realize Court had addressed a question to her. "Don't be silly. You know I'm perfectly capable of entertaining myself."

He gave her an endearing grin. "I am properly chastened, my lady. So tell me, what did you do today?"

Images of Caine's lips fused to hers, and that glorious mouth trailing hot kisses down her throat before suckling her breasts made her breath catch.

"I did a bit of sketching down by the cliffs."

"They truly are remarkable, aren't they?"

"Yes." Bliss thought of Caine. "Very remarkable."

He was arrogant, infuriating, and vicious when thwarted, and yet he fascinated her. She told herself that his appeal was solely physical, a baser instinct, as he had referred to it. Reprobate or not, he was the most undeniably virile male she had ever encountered, and he wore his masculinity like a badge of honor.

She refused to be like every other woman he knew, wanting a piece of him to appease her curiosity. Yet when he set his sights on seduction, it was rather hard to concentrate on his innumerable faults and sins.

Bliss caught sight of the marchioness exiting the library and hastening toward the dining salon at the end of the hall, where her guests were gathering. As she and Court passed the library, Bliss glanced in. The room was dark and she wondered what the woman had been doing. Reading seemed an unlikely possibility.

Bliss's steps faltered as she caught sight of a dark figure lounging on the threshold of the open French doors, only the tip of his cheroot illuminating his face. Her eyes locked with Caine's as he watched her walk by. He had been with Olivia, alone in the dark. A woman and her lover.

Did they not get enough of each other at night, that they had to steal these moments together? Did Caine remain with Olivia not out of obligation, but because he had feelings for her? Had he bedded the woman only minutes after Bliss had denied him?

The unsettling thoughts stayed with her as she entered the dining salon, the room awash in a subtle hue of light. Instead of using the chandelier above, all the sconces were lit and every crevice held a candle, giving the room a fairy-tale quality.

The long mahogany table gleamed with wax and the crystal glasses glittered with gold, matching the silverware and the rim on the fine bone china. An eye-catching centerpiece, adorned with flowers cut fresh from the garden, graced the middle of the table.

"You've outdone yourself, Lady Buxton," one of the gentlemen remarked, lifting Olivia's hand in his and pressing a kiss to the back.

His thick hair gleamed molten gold in the light, his skin was tan and his teeth as white as the tablecloth. All in all, very handsome. Yet when his gaze settled on Bliss, his assessing look put her in mind of a hawk who had targeted his prey.

"And who is this enchanting creature?" he said, his bold gaze appraising her. "I don't believe we have been formally introduced."

Olivia stepped forward and put a hand on his forearm, guiding him toward Bliss. "Jeremy Lockhart, Earl of St. Giles, may I present Lady Bliss Ashton and her cousin, Court Wyndham, Marquis of Seaton."

"Seaton," the earl intoned with a brief incline of his head before turning those dove-gray eyes on Bliss. "Charmed, my lady." He lifted her hand and kissed the back, lingering a moment too long. Court stiffened beside her, ready to take exception, but then the man straightened, a hint of a roguish smile on his lips. "Ashton. Now, where have I heard that name before?"

"Exmoor, don't you know," muttered one of the other gentlemen, a pudgy fellow with wire-rimmed spectacles and a face of owlish proportions and sour expression. The marchioness introduced him as Lord Lynford.

"Are you related to the Duke of Exmoor?" a third gentleman, Lord Clarendon, queried. He was a bit taller than the other two men, his black hair lightly salted with gray at the temples.

"Yes," Bliss replied. "He's my father."

Lord Lynford harumphed. Loudly.

"Is something the matter, my lord?"

Clearly bursting at the seams to make his opinion known, he hesitated but a moment. "Your papa's always got the House of Lords in a stir. Just last week, he proposed a new version of Gresham's Law. Wasting time on nonsense, I daresay."

Bliss knew the law he spoke of, having had an animated discussion with her father about it at dinner her first night home. "By nonsense, do you mean the education of the lower classes?"

"I do," he responded with a disdainful sniff. "The Lords have more important issues to discuss."

"I believe we, as a society, have a responsibility to assist those who are not as fortunate as ourselves."

He frowned at her. "What we need is to keep them

where they belong. What good is teaching them anything? It's not going to change their lot in life."

"So your opposition is based on the belief that any rudimentary education might cause them to be dissatisfied with what they have? And that literacy could make them susceptible to the inflammations of radical and atheistic propaganda?"

He raised a quizzing glass to his eye, one beady orb narrowing disagreeably on her. "We don't need any revolts on our hands. The more they know, the more they expect."

Bliss's ire rose at this all-too-common train of thought, owned almost exclusively by the upper class. "I find that a very small-minded view, my lord."

The quizzing glass popped from his eye and his jaw dropped like a drawbridge. "Small-minded?"

"Yes. You cannot imagine a world beyond the one in which you exist. The enfranchisement of the common mind will enrich ordinary men's tastes and perhaps enhance our own, through the perceptions they derive from experiences we don't have. Society could benefit from an infusion of new intellectual blood. Sheer humanitarianism demands that something be done to help those who cannot help themselves."

"Here is the very reason I am thankful that women have no say in the affairs and politics of men," he intoned self-righteously. "It would be the ruination of a fair country. You'd be wise, young lady, to concern yourself with matters more suitable to your gender."

Before Bliss could tell him what she thought of his pompous opinion, the marchioness interjected, "Let us all sit, shall we?" then guided him away.

A warm hand gently cupped Bliss's elbow. Startled, she looked up to find Lord St. Giles smiling down at her. He led her to her seat and took the chair beside her. Thinking it was a mistake, for certainly she should sit next to Court, Bliss darted a glance at the place cards in front of the plates. The earl's card was indeed there, her cousin relegated to sit two seats down, beside Lady Drayton, who immediately engaged him in a conversation.

Bliss's gaze was drawn to the vacant chair directly across from her. Caine's seat, she suspected, at the left hand of his lover, deposed from the head of the table, where he would have sat if fate hadn't intervened.

Bliss couldn't blame him for not appearing; it had to pain him to be a guest in his own home. Why did he stay? And where was he now? Still in the library, mocking them all?

The thought had no more than crossed her mind when she sensed a change in the air, the voices around her growing hushed, the skin on her arms prickling.

She lifted her head and looked toward the doorway. And there, leaning indolently against a marble pillar, resplendent in black evening attire that fit his muscular frame perfectly, his jaw freshly shaven and his hair tamed, was Caine, his gaze focused on her.

"Darling!" Olivia chirped. "Do come in and sit down. I was just about to tell Lady Bliss that I had the chef prepare several French dishes just for her."

"Ah, Hartland!" St. Giles intoned. "At last we've been honored by the phantom of the hall. How've you been, old boy?"

Caine didn't respond. Instead his gaze ran over each

person in attendance, making a few of them squirm in their seats. Then he stalked to the sideboard and poured himself a drink. When he turned around, he held two glasses in his hand.

He started toward the head of the table. Bliss studied her wineglass, her body tensing with each step he took until he was standing directly behind her chair.

She didn't want to look, but as the moments ticked by and he didn't move on, she felt compelled. Glancing over her shoulder, she found him staring down at her, his gaze hooded.

Then he held out the glass that Bliss had thought he'd poured for Olivia. "Drink up. You'll need it."

She took the glass without thought and watched him as he moved around the table and took his seat, slouching negligently and quaffing a hearty swig of liquor, defiance radiating in every line of his body.

He was completely oblivious to the woman beside him, who openly ogled him. According to Court, the generously endowed Lady Fairfax was barely twenty-six but already twice widowed.

The lady's carnal appetites were apparently well known, and her gaze traveled leisurely from the crown of Caine's head, down his body to linger pointedly in his lap. Bliss was surprised the woman didn't lick her lips.

But Caine was staring intently at Bliss, as though he were angry with her. He had not been granted free liberty with her body and he was vexed. But she was not one of his conquests. When she gave herself to a man, it would be on her terms. Not his.

The tension in the room mounted until Lord

Clarendon broke the silence. Turning to Bliss, he asked, "You're French, my lady?"

"I'm part French, my lord," she replied, taking a sip of her drink, seeking its fortifying properties. "On my mother's side."

"And she's an artist," Olivia added, her voice holding that sweetly condescending tone.

"An artist?" Lord St. Giles said, giving her another appraising glance. "What do you paint, my lady?"

Bliss absently fingered the rim of her glass. "People conducting their daily lives, mostly. The flower girl, the fish hawker, the prostitutes."

"Prostitutes!" Lady Fairfax exclaimed. "Why, that's scandalous!"

That comment coming from such a woman was laughable. "And why is it scandalous?"

"Because no respectable lady should look at them, let alone paint them."

Bliss gave a mental sigh. Most days she could deal with such sanctimonious views, but tonight her patience was rapidly ebbing. "And this makes them any less important than you or I?" she asked calmly. "Perhaps if we took a harder look at the conditions that might cause a woman to sell her body, we would learn something."

"Well, I would never do it," Lady Drayton said in a haughty tone, the rich adornments gracing her wrists, neck, and earlobes conveying she had known no other life besides that of being pampered and cosseted. "I don't care what the reasons."

"Even if you were starving and had three hungry children to feed?" Bliss had met such a woman—many, in fact. Lisette was not much older than Bliss had been at the time, and yet her eyes were aged, worn down.

She had been huddled with her children on the steps of the *Mont de Piété*, where people went to pawn items in the hopes of surviving another day.

The girl had tried to get a job in one of the factories, she had confessed to Bliss, but none were hiring. Then a fancy-looking gentleman had offered her two francs to service him in the alleyway. That was as much as she could make at the factory, working a sixteen-hour day. She had wanted his money badly, but had refused.

Bliss had not been able to bear the thought of another woman being used for a man's sexual gratification, and she had vowed to find Lisette a job. The next day, a friend hired Lisette as a maid. But Bliss knew she could not save everyone. Each week, new faces dotted the boulevard between the Gymnase and the Madeleine.

Lord St. Giles scoffed, "No person of any self-worth would considering bartering their body for payment." His gaze focused on Caine, his words clearly meant as an insult.

Caine remained impassive, steadily draining his glass. Only the glint in his eyes gave away the murderous feelings going on inside him.

"What do you think, Hartland?" the earl prodded. "I'm sure you have an opinion on this particular subject."

The room grew hushed, and Bliss realized her mistake in introducing the topic. As much as Caine angered her, she did not want to see him ridiculed.

His gaze elevated only minimally over the rim of his glass as he eyed the earl. "I would think you'd know better than I, St. Giles. Isn't the Comte du Lac still looking to garrote you because of your indiscretion with his comtesse?"

"That's right," Lord Lynford remarked, peering at the earl. "You cannot return to Paris because of that little incident, can you, St. Giles?"

"Shut up, imbecile," the earl hissed, his gaze never wavering from Caine, bad blood clearly simmering between the two men.

A handful of servants entered then, silencing everyone while the dishes were being served.

As soon as the servants departed, the earl said, "I seem to recall you lost quite a hefty sum to me in a game of hazard about the same time, Hartland. You always were the unluckiest bastard at cards. Pissed away every shilling your father sent you. What a shame."

Only Caine's hand tightening around his glass gave away his mounting fury.

Seeking to deflect the conversation, Bliss remarked, "The food looks delicious."

Her hostess beamed as though she had prepared the meal herself. "I hope the French delicacies make you feel at home."

"How kind of you."

"What do you call this?" Lady Buxton asked, scooping up a bit of the food she referred to.

"*Laitance de Carpe au Xérès.*"

"My, how exotic that sounds. What is it?"

"Fish sperm," Bliss replied, smiling around her spoon as Olivia gagged, her fork clattering to her plate as she reached for her wineglass. Bliss thought she saw a faint smile curling Caine's lips before disappearing behind his drink.

"I find it quite tasty," Lady Fairfax remarked in a husky

contralto, her gaze sliding to Caine as she eased the spoon into her mouth and sucked in the delicacy.

Male jaws plummeted around the table.

At the far end, Lord Kingsley, who had been quiet until that point, asked Bliss, "Do you live in France, my lady? Or do you make your home here?"

"I share an apartment with my mother in Montmartre, but I visit my father as often as possible."

"Which is where I found her," Court said, giving her a warm smile, "hoping she would grace me with her delightful company."

"Someone must keep you in line," she replied, returning his smile and earning a few chuckles from the group.

"Montmartre." Lord Clarendon looked to her questioningly. "Mount of Martyrs, I believe is the translation."

"Yes. Some people believe the town was named after Saint Denis, the first bishop of Paris, and his deacons, Saints Rusticus and Eleutherius, in the third century. Others believe it has to do with the unknown martyrs buried at the summit of the hill."

"I thought only peasants and harlots lived in Montmartre," Lord Lynford said, his tone conversational, but the gleam in his eyes showing spite.

Bliss glimpsed the fury that stole over Court, but an unexpected champion spoke up before he could.

"Cork your mouth, Lynford," Caine warned, flicking a razor-edge glance at the man. "Or I'll shut it permanently."

Lynford sputtered, "Now listen here, Hartland—"

"Hush, fool," Clarendon ordered in an undertone. "He means it."

While Lynford muttered beneath his breath, Bliss stared at Caine, shocked not only that he had finally spoken, but that he had actually defended her.

Before she had a moment to marvel at this miracle, he reverted to form, blatantly eyeing Lady Fairfax's bountiful assets. Contemptible lecher.

Then his gaze cut in Bliss's direction, his brow lifting in a question mark. He raised his glass in a goading salute, and promptly drained the remainder of his drink.

Eight

True nobility is exempt from fear:
More can I bear than you dare execute.
William Shakespeare

*B*liss could barely contain her sigh of relief when the evening drew to a close. Court chuckled as she eagerly accepted his proffered arm and escorted her from the room. They were barely out of earshot before he began ribbing her about her verbal castigation of Lord Lynford.

"He had it coming," she said, her sense of conviction augmented by the amount of wine she had consumed. "He wouldn't understand the idea of equality if the Lord descended from heaven and trumpeted it in his ear."

Court chuckled. "You are a delight, cousin, and I'm very glad you came here with me."

"You were in need of a respectable token to keep Lady Rebecca's fire-breathing mother at bay." Bliss faltered a step, her legs unsteady beneath her. "Where were they tonight?"

A slight frown creased his brow. "Rebecca's mother does not like the people her sister chooses to associate with."

Bliss couldn't fault the woman for that, having now met the people in question. "Why is she here, then?"

"She is living off her sister's largesse," he explained. "Her husband gambled away all of their money before dying ignobly at Leighton Field, where he had been forced into a duel for cheating."

"I see." Another sad example of a woman's complete dependence on a man, which forced her to sit by helplessly as his ineptitude left her at the mercy of others.

They stopped in front of Bliss's bedroom door, and not a moment too soon. She needed to lie down. "I'll see you in the morning." She leaned forward and kissed his cheek, weaving slightly.

Court halted her with a hand on her forearm. "Are you all right?" Concern lit his eyes.

"Of course."

He didn't look convinced. "You drank quite a bit tonight, which is unlike you. I know Lynford is a cretin, but I've seen you hold your own against men far worse than him."

Lynford was the least of her worries. It was Caine and his brooding presence at dinner, watching her in that detached way of his, that kept the wineglass rising to her lips. He unnerved her effortlessly, which made Bliss angry with herself.

He was ruthless and determined. She could read her downfall in his eyes, and felt powerless to prevent it. He was like a rushing river, sweeping away everything in his path, and she could not get out of the way in time. If foolish stubbornness weren't keeping her from leaving, she would have departed the first time he touched her.

"Bliss?"

Bliss realized she was standing there mute. "I'm sorry, Court. My mind is preoccupied this evening."

"I know." He paused, studying her face before asking far too astutely, "Has something happened between you and Caine Ballinger?"

"Happened?" If Court had noticed the tension between her and Caine, who else might have?

"Something tells me you didn't heed my advice to stay away from him."

He was right, of course. He had warned her, but she had done as she pleased.

"Has he said anything to you? Done anything untoward?"

Would kissing her breasts be considered untoward, even though she had nearly begged him to do so?

"You're worrying for nothing," she finally replied. "The man is harmless." An exaggeration of epic proportions; Caine was as harmless as a powder keg in a ring of fire. "I can handle him." Another exaggeration, one she hated to admit even to herself.

Her cousin's expression was skeptical, but he capitulated. "You will tell me if he tries anything, won't you?"

"Of course. Now, I really need to get some sleep."

He nodded. "Good night."

"Good night." Turning, Bliss entered her room and slumped against the closed door, waiting for her balance to return and wondering just how far she would fall before this week was over.

*　　*　　*

Something was afoot.

Unease filled Caine as he drained the remainder of his drink, watching Olivia sidle up next to St. Giles, whose leering gaze had followed Bliss as her cousin led her from the room.

Their heads bent close, the pair spoke in low tones, a sly smile curling Olivia's lips as they separated. She gave St. Giles a suggestive wink before she left the room, her backside undulating in blatant invitation.

When St. Giles turned and found Caine watching him, he smirked, his expression one Caine had seen numerous times during their acquaintance and which always heralded trouble.

Caine slowly rose from his chair, the legs scraping ominously against the floor, his fists aching to rotate the bastard's nose to the back of his head.

He refused to believe his fury had anything to do with St. Giles's interest in Bliss—the way the swine had practically drooled over her shoulder all night, leaning close in that pretentious, confiding way of his so that he could get a glimpse down her bodice, or engaging her in conversation to the exclusion of everyone else, refilling her wineglass before it was half finished, or finding a way to make continual contact with her body—his hand brushing hers, his fingers on her forearm.

No, Caine's irritation had nothing to do with Bliss. He simply loathed the buggering whoreson. To his immense dissatisfaction, St. Giles gave him no further provocation. Instead, he inclined his head in a facetious taunt and exited the room.

Caine followed a moment later.

Something told him that St. Giles was not going to his

room or even Olivia's. He had set his sights on Bliss, and Caine couldn't allow anything to happen to her. She was his ticket to freedom, and he'd be damned if he'd let the bloody malfeasant ruin her before he had the chance to ruin her himself.

Once on the upper level, Caine stood in the shadows watching St. Giles, who also kept to the shadows, spying on Bliss and her cousin, who were talking in front of her bedroom door. Caine suspected he was waiting for Seaton to leave so he could sneak into Bliss's bedroom, taking her unawares and then forcing himself on her.

Caine's hands fisted at his sides, his brain calculating the most painful ways to castrate the little shit. The idea of incapacitating St. Giles by driving his head through the wall was also a pleasurable image.

The man denied Caine the opportunity, however, as he cautiously eased his way down the hall, coming almost parallel to where Caine stood and then slipping into Olivia's bedroom. Not a single sound of protest came from within.

Instead of returning to his own room, Caine moved closer to Bliss and her cousin, catching the last part of their conversation. So the lady thought him harmless, did she? A grave mistake in judgment—and one that would prove useful to his plans.

When she finally entered her bedroom, Caine ducked inside one of the hidden passageways, disappearing from sight just as her cousin passed where Caine had been standing.

Caine's steps were swift and sure as he made his way down the darkened tunnel to the hollow wall, where small holes had been bored through the panel to give the viewer access to the room's occupants.

He looked through, wanting only to make sure Bliss bolted her door. The interlude with Olivia might not be enough to quell St. Giles's lust, and Bliss was just drunk enough to be unable to fend the man off.

Caine found her leaning back against the door, her eyes closed, her body so still that she looked asleep standing up. A solitary oil lamp glowed on the table beside her, casting her silhouette against the wall and bathing her skin in a honeyed hue.

She swayed lightly and opened her eyes, blinking as if to clear the fog before them. She shook her head and rubbed her temples. Obviously the alcohol had affected her more than he thought. She'd had several drinks, and the brandy he had given her was well-aged and potent.

With an unsteady gait, she pushed away from the door, haphazardly divesting herself of one slipper, then the other. She moved to stand in front of the mirror, surveying herself.

Caine wondered if she saw what he saw: the full breasts and tiny waist, the silky skin and delicate features, the curtain of thick, mahogany hair that tumbled free, riveting his gaze as she ran her fingers through its long length.

Her hands then slipped to the hidden clasps cleverly concealed in the front of her gown, revealing herself bit by bit until she stood before the mirror garbed in nothing more than a demure, lace-trimmed shift.

Damn, but she confused him. Sometimes she seemed like two women. One, a lady of grace and poise, who didn't know the meaning of backing down and who fought for women's rights with a strength and self-confidence he had never before encountered in a female. The other woman was a bit uncertain, slightly vulnerable, and innocent in a way that aroused every protective instinct he possessed.

She stood for a long moment regarding her reflection in the mirror, and he remained like a voyeur, unable to retreat, to save himself. She had ensorcelled him.

Breathing became difficult as he watched her small hands with their long, tapering fingers smooth across her stomach before stunning him by sliding up to cup her breasts, her forefingers skimming over the pointed tips that thrust against the material, her body shivering in response.

His hands fisted against the hard, cold wall, a groan welling up inside his throat as a surge of heat blasted him from the inside out.

As if shamed by her actions, she abruptly turned from the mirror and sat down on the settee, raising the hem of her chemise to the middle of her thighs so that she could roll down her stockings. She paused midway, pressing a hand to her head and weaving a bit.

Leaning back, she closed her eyes, her face pale enough to concern him as her hand slipped down to the cushion where it lay palm up, fingers still.

She had passed out.

Caine remained rooted to the spot, telling himself that the only reason he had not yet left was because her door was still unlocked. He had no choice but to bolt it. She wouldn't remember come the morning if she had done it herself or not. Tomorrow he would find a way to make sure she kept it locked, but tonight he was stuck with the duty.

He pushed at the panel, which gave way with only a slight displacement of air, and entered her room. He moved soundlessly across the floor toward the door, but came to a stop when she stirred in her sleep, a strap on her chemise sliding off her shoulder, causing the material over her left breast to droop. The light from the oil lamp shimmered over the thin lawn, revealing the high swell of her breasts and the faint outline of her nipples.

She lay there like temptation; ripe for the plucking, primed for seduction. He could take her now, own her body tonight, begin her ruination.

Instead he bent down and blew out the wick on the lamp, cloaking the room in darkness but for the slim beam of moonlight shining between the drapes, the ray slanting over her face and rippling down her body like a runnel of white gold, tormenting him with the places it touched.

He forgot about the door as he came to stand before her. A length of hair draped her shoulder, hugging the curve of her breast. He picked up the silky strands and absently fanned them through his fingers.

He still couldn't reconcile the fact that no man had claimed her body. Why? What was she waiting for? True love didn't exist, if that was what she was hoping to find. That emotion was only a sop for romantic hearts and fools. And he didn't take her as either.

Unwittingly, she had given him the ammunition he needed to use against her. He had discovered her weakness, the weakness all women possessed: the lure of unconditional love. The solitary overriding goal of suckering some poor sod into poetic declarations of unending devotion and heroic acts of gallantry and glorified beds of roses. And fidelity. Always fidelity.

It was a communal flaw, an inbred female need to own a man's heart fully, to be his one and only. And now that Caine recognized what he'd been overlooking, he had gained the upper hand. To win back his life, he would take whatever advantage he was given. He had no other choice.

He let go of her hair, but her pale, smooth cheek became another enticement, beckoning him. He could not resist. He trailed a finger along her jaw, down her throat, along the tender curve of her collarbone, stopping where the chaste white ribbon held her bodice together.

His hand dropped away, his fingers curling into his palm. *Lock the door and go, you bloody fool.* What the hell had come over him tonight? Too much liquor. Not enough liquor. Weariness, self-disgust, apathy.

He stared down at Bliss, waiting for the anger to steal over him, for the hatred to come, but only a dull ache settled in the bottom of his gut.

Why deny himself? Why not look at her, touch her, do whatever the hell he pleased? He lived by no moral code. He was not a gentleman, and no one would expect him to be.

He knelt down, his hands settling on either side of her thighs, and yet he did not touch her. Instead he studied the embroidered pattern on the garters holding up her silky stockings, which smoothed over legs that were taut, the muscles lightly defined.

He had never really looked at a garter before; he'd just blindly removed them with impatient haste. Bliss's garters had cherry red rosebuds and dark green vines. Very feminine. Surprisingly erotic.

He trailed a finger over one, memorizing the pattern

before sliding to the soft skin exposed above her stocking. The shift had ridden higher, only a wisp of material covering the feminine delta between her thighs. His hand ached to slip beneath the lacy edge and find her heat.

He pulled back, hooking a finger under the garter and slowly easing it down her leg, the filmy stocking following suit.

Caine held the silky garment in his hand. It felt as insubstantial as light, and was still warm from her skin. He closed his eyes and breathed in that arousing scent of flowers and innocence, a dark hunger stirring to life inside him.

He didn't stop to think why he tucked it in his pocket. He simply moved on to the other garter and stocking, until her legs lay bare before him.

He wondered what the hell he was doing, even as he pressed his palms lightly to her thighs, her skin silkier than the stockings and far more tantalizing.

His thumbs pushed against the hem of her chemise, raising it by damning degrees, until his hands began to shake. An effect of the alcohol, he told himself, and yet he could not go any further.

He caught a glimpse of something on her right inner thigh. He gently nudged her legs apart with one hand and reached for the curtain with the other, allowing a sliver of moonlight to wash over them, illuminating what he had not been able to make out.

A small, perfectly round beauty mark.

Dangerously close to the dark apex that enticed him.

Caine sucked in a deep breath, teetering on the border between sinner and saint, before forcing his hands from her thighs and easing away from her. He remained on his haunches for long moments, trying to understand what madness was stealing over him. He felt hot and cold, his gut tight, his throat dry.

He had to get out.

He stood, ready to go. But for some reason, he reached down and lifted Bliss into his arms, turning toward the bed and laying her down. He wasn't sure what he intended to do with her, or to her, until he pulled the coverlet over her, deciding to do nothing. Revenge would be far sweeter with her willing and wanton beneath him.

The slight click of the doorknob brought Caine to attention, his body stiffening as his gaze jerked over his shoulder, the barest creak of a floorboard alerting him to an intruder. He melded into the shadows as the door slowly opened. A faint light from the hallway spilled into the room, revealing the person's face.

St. Giles.

Caine knew the lecherous maggot hadn't given up. He had marked his territory the minute he set eyes on Bliss, and now he intended to follow through.

The door closed with a faint snap, and the bolt Caine had come to lock slid home. He could make out St. Giles's dark form as he came to stand beside the bed. He wore black trousers and a black and burgundy dressing gown, his intentions clear.

He stared down at Bliss, a faint, sadistic smile on his face as he trailed his knuckles along the curve of her throat. "You are a morsel," he murmured, hooking a finger around the strap of her shift and easing it down. "Now let's see those luscious tits."

Caine lunged out of the corner, his fist impacting with St. Giles's jaw with a resounding crack of bone against bone, sending the son of a bitch spinning to the ground unconscious, the thick Aubusson carpet muffling the sound, a thin line of blood trickling from St. Giles's lip.

Caine glanced over his shoulder at the creak of the mattress, thinking to see Bliss awake and ready to take the fire poker to his groin. But she had only rolled to her side.

None too gently, Caine heaved St. Giles over his shoulder, exiting Bliss's room and heading away from the man's suite, situated two doors down from Bliss—which Caine now knew had been intentional.

Stopping at the last door on the left, he raised his booted foot and kicked the door open, startling the occupant, who was primping in front of her vanity table.

Olivia whirled around at the sound of his entrance. "My God!" she exclaimed. "Have you gone mad?"

Caine unceremoniously dumped St. Giles at her feet. A large knot was forming on the man's jaw, which would be thoroughly black and blue come morning.

"What have you done to him?" she demanded, staring wide-eyed at St. Giles's prone form. "Oh, Lord, you haven't killed him, have you?"

"No. But I should have." Caine's gaze skewered her when she raised her eyes to his, and she noted the volatility simmering inside him. "He was in Bliss's bedroom. But you know all about that, don't you?"

Nervousness replaced the stunned look in her eyes. "I have no idea what you're talking about."

"I saw the two of you huddled together earlier. You know St. Giles's tastes in women. You said something to him to make him think Bliss would welcome him in bed, didn't you?"

"Good Lord, no! Why would I do such a thing?"

"Because you enjoy manipulating people and don't give a damn about the consequences."

Her abrupt laugh was mirthless. "This, coming from you? A man who drifts through life without feeling a single thing?"

"I don't send others to do my dirty work."

"You're a man; you don't have to. We women have to employ whatever means are at our disposal."

"Deceit, treachery, and pretense?"

"If necessary." She canted her head to the side to give him a view of the faint bruise on her neck. St. Giles's mark. "I'm simply making things a bit more interesting."

Caine's jaw knotted. "That wasn't part of the bargain."

"No one said there wouldn't be any competition. I couldn't make this too easy for you, could I?"

"You go too far. You know St. Giles's reputation."

"Firsthand." A baiting smile curled up the corners of her lips. "Jealous?" When he didn't answer, she grew sullen. "So he's a little rough—some of us like it rough."

"Bliss isn't like you."

Anger sparked in her eyes. "The chit's so bloody self-righteous. All her sanctimonious preaching of that women's equality nonsense. There's only one way to be a man's equal: conquer him in bed."

"She has opinions. Maybe you should form a few that deal with matters above the waist."

"Oh my, now there's a laugh. The conscienceless Earl of Hartland cares about women's issues. What's next, I wonder? Will you grow a heart, too?"

"Don't count on it. All I care about is you keeping the hell out of my way so I can get this farce over with."

She toyed with the sash on her dressing gown. "You

were in the lady's boudoir, I suppose, and that's how you came about being her knight errant?"

The image of him as a protector of a woman's virtue, and that woman being Exmoor's daughter, churned acid in Caine's stomach. "I was in her room. And if you hadn't interfered, I might have begun to lay the foundation for her downfall."

"By bedding her, you mean?"

"Precisely."

"You've already ascertained that she's a virgin?"

"Yes."

She eyed him with begrudging admiration. "You work fast, my lord."

"I have ample motivation."

"Indeed." She gazed up at him through her lashes, her expression blatantly sexual. "Well, now that you have been thwarted and you find me to blame, I would be willing to take the lady's place as punishment."

"Ask St. Giles," he told her as he pivoted on his heel and headed for the door. "He enjoys dirty work."

The sound of a vase crashing against the closed door echoed through the hall.

Nine

Man is an embodied paradox,
A bundle of contradictions.
Charles Caleb Colton

$\mathscr{B}$liss followed the path that wound along the edge of the cliff, feeling as though she dangled high above the sea, the perception of overhanging the water a frightening but oddly thrilling sensation.

Below, the turquoise water sparkled like a glittering gem in the late morning sun, foam splashing against the jagged rocks as headland after headland rose to the east, creating long shadows that shifted in alien shapes amid the rugged landscape, harsh edges softened by a transparent gray haze, earth and sea and sky all veiled in a flush of pale rose pink, clouds of foliage blurring the craggy peaks of distant promontories.

She breathed the sea-scented air deeply, the cool wind like silk against her skin, stirring her senses, life gradually seeping back into her hazy brain and leaden limbs, the punishment for her overindulgence.

What had come over her last night, that she imbibed so much?

A single word answered the question: Caine.

His unwavering regard had set her nerves on edge. No matter how hard she tried, she could not seem to force him from her mind.

Even in her dreams, she garnered no peace. She had vivid images of him touching her, a hand on her cheek, a large, warm palm resting against her thigh, her body craving more, wanting to arch up against him, but unable to because her limbs were unresponsive.

The lone cry of a solitary falcon pierced the stillness around her, the bird an obsidian speck against the pale blue sky, hanging suspended on invisible gusts of air, its long, curved wings buffeted against the breeze.

The western side of the valley beckoned her—its steep inclines covered with short grass, sea-pinks and thyme, and crowned by a great mass of boulders—to the inland where barren ridges gave way to a profusion of copses and thickets, several deeply cleft combes brimming with trees and purple-crimson flowers.

And in the middle of all this emerged a church spire, reaching a long, tapered finger toward the flawless heavens. Bliss headed in that direction, perhaps thinking to find answers to the questions plaguing her.

A slight movement over the top of the rise caught her eye. A lone figure stood perilously close to the rim of the precipice, wholly absorbed in staring down at the churning fury below.

Bliss slowed her pace as she neared Caine, afraid a sudden movement would startle him and send him over the side. He seemed oblivious, distant. Perhaps it was the desolation of his pose, or the solitude of his surrounding, but something about him was different.

His profile, limned by the morning sun, was bleak, anguished. He was jacketless, his shirtsleeves rolled up, his fawn-colored breeches molding his thighs, his dark brown riding boots scuffed.

His ebony hair was whipped by the breeze and painted with fiery streaks. A virile man in every way, yet never had she seen him look more like a boy, lost and alone.

Stones skittered at her feet, alerting him to her presence.

His head jerked, his gaze slashing in her direction. "What the hell do you want?" His expression was unwelcoming, an edge of desperation sharpening his features.

She returned his gaze steadily, her heart beating an erratic tattoo. He was a man of breathtaking beauty, as wild in this untamed and dangerous place as he was frightening. He seemed to balance on the edge of destruction. It was there in his eyes, as tumultuous as the crashing waves against the shoreline.

He didn't want her there. And in that moment, Bliss could truly believe he hated her. She knew she should go, leave him to whatever thoughts were troubling him, but the torment etched on his face held her immobile.

"I didn't mean to intrude."

He turned away from her, staring back out over the turbulent water. The sea mirrored his mood, imperiling anyone foolish enough to get too close. But what was truly foolish was for her to believe he was capable of any emotions besides those that were self-serving. He had proven countless times that he acted only in his own interest, and would do whatever was necessary to get what he wanted.

Still she moved toward him.

"What is it you want?" he growled when she stepped up beside him.

Bliss looked out over the horizon. The faint glow of early morning light gave way to the sizzling hue of a warm, lemony sun that spread across the landscape like molten gold. "It's beautiful, isn't it?"

"You fancy the view, do you?" His words were sharp as ice picks. "Perhaps the real reason you're here is for a repeat performance of yesterday's skirmish in the grass. Is that it, my lady? Have you decided you like the feel of my mouth on your—"

"Stop it." She whirled to face him. "Why must you make everything sexual? Not all women desire that you bed them."

"Oh?" He raised a sardonic brow. "And what is it that you desire? Friendship? Companionship? A man who wouldn't think of laying a finger on you? Who wouldn't dare defile the holy vessel you are by shoving his rod between your virginal thighs? Do you even have any desires? Or have you always been frigid?"

The barb stung as had been his intention, but it seemed as though he was purposely trying to push her away, hating the fact that anyone, but her most especially, had come upon him at a vulnerable moment.

"There are many things I desire, my lord," Bliss replied in a hushed voice. "Perhaps if you took a moment to actually speak to me, rather than abuse me, you would know."

"I know more than you think."

"And what is it that you think you know? That I'm a frigid, horse-hating witch out to crucify any male who doesn't subscribe to my way of thinking?"

"No. That you're opinionated, troublesome, and bloody brazen." He gritted his teeth, adding, "Strong, self-confident, and brave," as though the words were torn from him.

The unexpected compliment warmed her. Then he turned abruptly from her. "Get the hell out of here, will you?"

Bliss hesitated and wondered why. He had made his wishes plain enough. She would be foolish to believe Caine needed anyone, especially her.

She turned to leave, but he reached out and grabbed her arm to pull her back. "What are you—"

"Stay." Frustration glinted in his eyes, and something else. Something dark and speculative. Bliss told herself to refuse him, that he could not be trusted. Yet he compelled her.

"What do you want from me?" she asked.

"I don't know."

"Are you always so difficult?"

"Yes."

His honest answer softened her, a reluctant smile tugging at her lips. His gaze dropped to her mouth, but for the first time, no ulterior designs marred his handsome face, but rather an expression that was almost . . . yearning.

"Do I frighten you?" he asked, searching her eyes for the truth.

"Sometimes."

He paused, then said, "Perhaps you should be more wary."

"Are you warning me away, my lord?"

"Are you warned?"

"No."

That response garnered her a slight, begrudging grin. "You really aren't like other women, are you?"

"I'm afraid not," she said, wondering if the truth repelled him as it did most men. "My father despairs over that fact. He tries, but he just can't figure me out. He often regards me as though I'm a baffling problem for which no solution is forthcoming."

Caine's face suddenly clouded over, his eyes growing sharp again, angry. "Let's go," he said brusquely, taking hold of her hand and pulling her along.

"Where?"

He gave no response, just kept walking, his stride eating up the ground, forcing her to take two steps to his one. Bliss had to dig in her heels to get his attention.

"Stop. Please."

That penetrating stare settled on her in its usual disconcerting fashion. "What is it?"

Her heart was pounding wildly, but it had little to do with their rapid pace. "Where are we going?"

"Does it matter?"

At that moment, Bliss wasn't sure it did. She liked the way Caine's hand felt in hers, and the possessive glint in his eyes. And she liked his rugged, unapologetic ways, how he held nothing back. Much like her.

She knew spending time with him was wrong. There was another woman to consider, and Bliss had never been one who shared well. Perhaps it was due to being an only child. When something was hers, it was hers alone.

But Caine would never belong to any woman. It wasn't

in him to be faithful. Even when a man of his sort married, usually only to beget an heir, he kept a mistress on the side.

But it didn't matter. She had a full life and didn't expect that being a wife and mother would ever be a part of it. She existed outside the boundaries, which intimidated most men. Yet a small voice inside her head told her that Caine was not a man who was easily intimidated, if ever.

"I think it's best if I go on alone from here." She tried to tug her hand from his, but he held firm, refusing to let go.

"You're hot."

"Excuse me?"

He pulled a handkerchief from his pocket and closed the distance between them. Her heart sputtered to a halt as she stared up into his eyes. "You're perspiring," he murmured.

"Oh." She flushed. "Well, I had to practically run—"

"Ssh." He stepped closer and began to gently dab at her face, which only grew hotter under his scrutiny, the small scrap of material no barrier to the touch of his hand, the warmth of his fingers, the heat of his palm.

All of which slid down to her throat.

Then to her chest.

There he lingered, his gaze almost studious in his observation of her, his ministrations a caress, making breathing difficult.

Finally, she took a shaky step back. "I had best be going."

His arm slowly lowered. "Why? Do you dislike me that much?"

She should say yes; perhaps that would ward him off. But the words would not come. "This isn't right."

"We're simply taking a walk." He paused, then said, "Do you think I would force you to do something you didn't want to do?"

Bliss wished she could honestly say yes. Tell him he was despicable enough to force himself on her. But when he had touched her before, she had instantly responded, her body blossoming under his lips, every fiber of her being desiring more. He had by no means coerced her into doing anything she didn't want to do.

"No," she replied softly.

"Then what is there to worry about?"

More things than she could even begin to name. "Perhaps I just wish to be alone." To salvage whatever pride and virtue she had left before he demolished both.

"I see." His jaw tightened. "Well, I feel it's my duty to make sure you arrive at your destination unscathed. These cliffs are dangerous. One slip and you would be fodder for the sharks. I would certainly be stricken were that to happen."

His sarcasm in the face of her honesty incited her temper. "Really? One would think you'd hasten my departure from this earth."

"How little you think of me."

"Forgive my impertinence. I had forgotten you were to be canonized. Caine Ballinger, Patron Saint of the Boorish and Misguided."

The amused smile that touched the corners of his mouth did not reach his eyes. "You should be a man, my girl. You hold grudges as well as any of us."

"Not grudges, my lord. Observations."

"You have plenty of those, too. Was your purpose last night to skin Lynford alive with your tongue? If so, you did an admirable job."

"I'm surprised you noticed, considering how preoccupied you were." Blast her rash tongue! Now he would think she cared that he had leered at Lady Fairfax.

He slanted an eyebrow, devilish provocation in the twist of his sensuous lips. "Paying attention, were you? Why is that, I wonder?"

"Perhaps because you were sitting directly across from me. One tends to notice a man with his eyes down a woman's bodice. One would think you'd be more circumspect."

"Truly? And why is that?"

"Respect, perhaps?"

"Ah, so now begins my lecture on the rights of women. I was wondering when I would be treated to a lengthy dissertation on the subject. Well, I'm prepared. Slay me, my lady."

"If I thought it might make a difference, perhaps I'd attempt such a Herculean endeavor."

"Oh, but it will make a difference. I'm thoroughly infatuated with your brain, you see. It works in such intriguing ways. I specifically enjoy your views on prostitution." The glint in his dark eyes mocked her as he said, "So tell me, love, would you spread your thighs for me were I to pay you?"

The cutting remark came out of nowhere, and before Bliss could think, she raised her hand to slap him. Caine gripped her wrist, stopping her just short of his face and yanking her up hard against his body, her breasts crushed against the muscled planes of his chest.

"I've already been treated to that particular remedy. I'd prefer something more original this time around."

Bliss's body thrummed with fury even as a curious thrill shot through her at being so close to him. How could she dislike him and yet want to be held by him?

She wrenched her hand from his. "Whatever made me think you had a redeemable bone in your body?"

Something sparked in his eyes before the emotion was banked. "Redeemable, am I? I think I should be flattered you find me worthy. I'm not, however." Before Bliss could summon a retort, he said, "Now enlighten me, if you will, about what riles you so about men. I find myself reluctantly fascinated by you. Under the spell of this strange infatuation, I'm experiencing an unexpected desire to get to know you better." He grazed her cheek with his thumb, the gesture feeling like a mark of impending possession, and a fleeting impulse to lean into the warmth of his palm coursed through her.

"I'm a challenge to you. Nothing more."

"You are a challenge, that's true. As to being nothing more, you assume too much." The heat reflected in his gaze scored her. "So tell me, how do you feel about marriage?"

Bliss made no reply, certain he was merely amusing himself at her expense.

"Come now," he coaxed. "You must have an opinion on this particular subject. You are so outspoken, after all."

"If you must know," she said, lifting of her chin, "I find the concept flawed, the institution biased, and the expectations suffocating."

"Already we are seeing eye to eye. Go on."

It was an invitation Bliss could not resist. "Marriage

has no benefits for women, as long as men are governed by the idea of subservience as a supreme value. Their wives' very existence is made useless as they are encouraged to spend their days being decoratively futile. Women are expected to live under a glass dome rather than lead any sort of meaningful life."

Caine's lips formed into a semblance of a smile. "An impressive recital." Then he quoted, " 'Women are to be either drudges or toys beneath man, or a sort of angel above him.' Thomas Henry Huxley, I believe."

"And is that what you think, my lord?"

"I think such a statement leaves out one essential element."

"And what is that?"

He leaned forward, his warm breath caressing her cheek. "Passion."

Bliss tried not to think of the images that word evoked or how odd his nearness made her feel. "Women are not supposed to be passionate, my lord. Indeed, our lack of passion is an idea that is universally accepted as a fact. To assume otherwise is indecent."

"Then I guess you would be excluded from that assumption."

Bliss didn't want to respond to his unexpected compliment or the look in his eyes, yet her knees felt decidedly weak as she said, "I thought you found me frigid?"

He seemed to find the curve of her neck fascinating. "Perhaps I simply think you possess far more passion than you allow yourself to express. Maybe you're not as free as you believe yourself to be."

"Nonsense," she scoffed, and yet his remark struck a chord. Was she afraid to give her desire free rein? "Just because I allowed you to seduce me—marginally—does not mean I would have held back had I been interested in . . ."

"In?" he prompted when she hesitated.

She forced herself to meet his gaze squarely. "In making love to you," she replied.

"Let me clarify one thing," he said in a disturbingly husky tone. "You didn't *allow* me to seduce you; you were willing to be seduced. There's a difference. And you haven't even been properly seduced yet. But not for lack of trying, I assure you." Before she could take issue with his arrogant assumption, he went on. "So with this dim view you have of the male population, should I assume you intend never to marry?"

"I've resigned myself to being unmarried."

"Cleverly worded, love. But it doesn't answer the question."

"Why would any intelligent woman want marriage?" she countered, watching a curlew as it rose up from the trees in the distance, thinking about all the dreams she had once had about the man she would someday marry, and how those dreams began to crumble when she realized that she did not possess the qualities a man would want in a wife.

Caine cupped her chin, making her look at him, his fingers warm against her skin. "For the same reasons a man might want marriage," he murmured, his thumb caressing her cheek. "Love, companionship. Children."

Children. The very thought made Bliss's heart ache. She stepped away from him. "A husband has all the rights. He can take away the children if he likes. He can withhold money and property, openly keep a mistress.

But should his wife prove unruly, or worse, unfaithful, a divorce is readily granted him. So 'wife' is simply another word for 'chattel.' "

"Not all men are as you describe. But you skirt the issue," he pressed, relentless for an answer.

Bliss glanced away from him, watching the breeze stir the tall grass. "Perhaps I'd marry if I found the right man. But I doubt he exists."

"Such cynicism for such a young woman. But I suspect you're right; we men can be boors. And yet my curiosity needs appeasing. What kind of man would win your heart?"

Bliss bent down to pluck a wildflower, smoothing her fingers over the petals. "Someone who's kind, who cares for others. Someone I can talk to, who believes my opinions matter." She looked up at him then and was captured by the intensity in his regard. "Most of all, I want a man who would never think of looking to another woman for comfort. And I desire honesty, for without it, there is nothing."

He regarded her for a long moment beneath those thick lashes, the wind ruffling his silky dark hair, and she found herself strangely impatient to hear his reply.

"It would appear you require all the things I'm not. I guess I wouldn't be considered a favorable suitor." A moment of silence enveloped them before he said in a surprisingly gentle tone, "Would you believe me if I said I was disappointed?"

She wanted to. How she wanted to. "No. I wouldn't."

He dug his hands into his pocket, watching her with unreadable eyes. Bliss didn't understand why his silence hurt. But it did.

She forced down the strange emotions and sought comfort in the familiar. "Is there some reason you're up so early this morning?" Perhaps wanting to strike out at him, she added, "I didn't take you for a man who rose before drinks were being served."

A faint, wry expression softened the harsh lines of his face. "Your tendency to speak your mind is refreshing, sweet, but my wounds might heal quicker if I was not so often on the receiving end of your verbal bullets."

"Perhaps you shouldn't incite my temper, then."

Amusement crinkled the corner of his eyes. "I will take that under advisement. Though I must confess to finding you quite a sight when your passions are aroused."

Bliss felt her face flame, images of his mouth pressed intimately to hers, and to other places, assailing her. "If that was some underhanded remark—"

The smile that suddenly lifted the corners of his lips was carnal as he took a step toward her. "Your mind was in the gutter, wasn't it?"

"No, I . . ." She stepped back, trying to put distance between them, but her foot hit a protruding rock and she stumbled.

Caine's arm shot out, snaking around her waist like an iron band as he hauled her forward, her skirts brushing his thighs. "Careful," he murmured, staring at her lips as though he wanted to kiss her. A shiver skittered over her skin, hoping he would, and knowing he shouldn't.

"Don't." She pressed her hands against his chest, her palms branded by his heat.

He didn't seem to hear her. His focus was too intent

on her mouth. His head lowered, and in the next instant, his lips brushed over hers like the touch of butterfly wings, soft and incredibly tender. Before she had a moment to savor the kiss, he pulled back and released her.

Bliss touched her fingers to her lips, trying to still the tingle caused by the warm pressure of his mouth. "Don't you ever think of asking first?"

"Not when I see something I want." His gaze caught and held hers as he said, "Did you want me to ask?"

She didn't know what she wanted. Never had a man so confused her, or caused her emotions to churn with such turmoil. "I don't think you should be kissing me."

"You don't think?"

"You shouldn't."

"Well, I'm glad one of us is sure." He slipped his hand around hers. The way he held onto her seemed proprietary, but she didn't mind. She didn't want to fight anymore.

They walked side by side, heading away from the house and farther into the lush countryside. The spire of the church she had glimpsed earlier came into view.

She paused at the top of the incline to stare down at the old Georgian vicarage, nestled at the base of the hill. It was covered in ivy, and tall trees peered over a crumbling wall that she suspected had once been used as a defense to keep out enemies. Now a profusion of vivid wildflowers softened its edges.

"It's lovely," she murmured. "What's it called?"

"St. Nectan's."

"Can we go down?" When he made no reply, she glanced up at him. His profile looked carved from stone as he stared down at the church, his grip on her hand tightening almost imperceptibly.

Finally, he gave an abrupt nod and they headed down the hill. A sense of unease settled over Bliss—a feeling that she was descending to a destination from which there would be no turning back.

Ten

Long is the way,
And hard, that out of Hell leads up to light.
John Milton

The church faced east with a garden plot in front; an
ancient wall separated it from the long slope of lush
green valley beyond. The western side of the building was
gabled, with a high archway built into the center of the
wall. Faint green lichen crept over the stones.

Her hand still clasped tightly within Caine's, Bliss let
him guide them toward the north side of the building,
where an Early Perpendicular window marked the
chapel. A central doorway opened into a cavernous
space.

The air was slightly musty as they entered, and a
peaceful hush encompassed them as they moved into the
interior. Prisms of sunlight pierced the stained glass win-
dows, dappling the floor in a kaleidoscope of colors.

They moved down the aisle quietly, stopping before
the altar as though they were about to confess their sins

to God—or pledge their troth to each other from this day forward.

It was an odd thought, and Bliss forced it back, concentrating instead on the square space sunk into the wall above the altar, where faint traces could still be seen of a fresco of Christ looking down upon his worshippers.

Her gaze shifted about the room, noting the newel staircase that led to the floor above, where she suspected the vicar resided. A little window with two cinquefoiled openings enabled the priest to look down into the chapel, the height of the sill from the floor suggesting that it might serve as a prie-dieu.

As though her thoughts had conjured him up, a side door opened, allowing a thick shaft of daylight to spill into the room, banishing the shadows, the breeze sending dust motes dancing in the air as the vicar stopped on the threshold.

His unruly mass of white hair was windblown, his cheeks ruddy from the sun. In his hand, he held a fresh cutting of flowers. A warm and welcoming smile spread across his face.

"Dear boy," he said in a hushed tone, coming toward them. "Is it really you?"

The transformation that came over Caine riveted Bliss; it was as if whatever inner turmoil he'd been carrying had been removed.

The vicar reached out and clasped Caine's hands in both of his. "It's been a long time."

"Two years."

The vicar's face grew somber. "Yes. Two years." Then his gaze lit on Bliss and he bestowed that warm smile on her. "And who is this lovely young woman, my lord?"

An uncomfortable expression filtered across Caine's face as he replied, "This is Lady Bliss Ashton."

The vicar's gaze suddenly jerked to Caine's, something akin to alarm on his face.

But Caine's gaze was intent on her, as though purposely avoiding the man's regard. "My lady, this is Vicar Meade. He's been here since before I was born."

Bliss dropped into a light curtsy. "How do you do, sir?"

The vicar's gaze slowly returned to her, the strange expression still on his face. He cleared his throat, darting a final glance at Caine, who had stepped away to study the altarpiece.

"A pleasure to meet you, my lady. May I ask what brings you to our quiet hamlet?"

"I'm attending a house party at Northcote with my cousin."

"I see." The vicar continued to regard her with unease. "I hope you are enjoying yourself?"

"Yes, thank you."

Again, the man shot a glance over his shoulder at Caine, who had turned away from his contemplation of the altarpiece and was now standing in an open side doorway.

Over his shoulder Bliss caught a glimpse of the graveyard outside, the headstones in neat rows, square gray monuments to the deceased. Caine could have been carved from the same granite, he stood so still.

"If you'll excuse me?" the vicar asked in a distracted tone.

"Certainly." Bliss watched the stout parson as he

moved toward Caine and laid a hand on his shoulder.

A moment later they exited out the door, the glare of the sun swallowing them as though they had disappeared through the gates of heaven.

Once more, a sense of disquiet settled over Bliss and she wondered what was going on. The moment she and Caine had started down the hill, she had felt him become more and more tense until he seemed so brittle, she thought he would shatter.

"Hello, there."

Startled, Bliss whirled around. Standing a few feet away was a portly, older woman with a round face and thin rimmed spectacles perched on the bridge of her nose, magnifying bright eyes that seemed to belie the woman's age.

"I frightened you," she said in an apologetic tone, reaching out to lightly touch Bliss's hand. "I thought you heard me come in. I'm Margaret, the vicar's wife."

"How do you do?"

"A pleasure to meet you, my dear. Lady Bliss, correct?"

"Yes, but—"

"I overheard your conversation with my husband. Please don't think I was eavesdropping; I was in the choir pit trying to tighten a loose pedal on the organ." She pointed to the stone structure positioned directly above the entrance to the church. "My husband is quite brilliant when it comes to his sermons, but he possesses no aptitude for fixing things, I'm afraid. Come, sit with me."

Bliss followed her and sat down in the first pew, her gaze drifting to the side door, hoping to catch a glimpse of Caine. Something was troubling him. More so now than when she had spied him standing at the edge of the cliff. In a moment of utter clarity, Bliss believed she understood perhaps part of what it was.

"Is Caine's father buried here?"

Margaret turned toward her, a hint of sadness in her eyes. "Yes. Interred two years now in the family plot, next to his wife, Lady Francis." Her gaze drifted to the old stone cross standing sentinel behind the altar. "I never thought I'd see that boy enter this church again. The day he stood alone beneath the tree where his father's buried, I saw all the goodness seep away. Something died inside his lordship when his father passed, and neither my husband nor I could help him."

She looked back at Bliss. "Henry was a wonderful man. Loved that lad with all his heart. No father could have cherished a son more."

Bliss hesitated, then asked the question that would no longer remain unspoken. "Is it true his father killed himself because of debt?"

The woman stared at her, a worried frown adding lines to her brow. "You don't know?"

"Know what?"

Margaret shook her head. "I thought perhaps . . . But no, that's not the way he is."

"I don't understand."

The woman took hold of Bliss's hands and gave a gentle squeeze. "Be patient with him. The lad's suffered a great deal of hurt and has turned into a man who lashes out at the world. He was never like that. I remember him as a bright, smiling boy who cared for his animals and was loved by the villagers."

It was hard for Bliss to picture the man Margaret

spoke of so fondly. She had only seen the darker side of Caine, except for brief glimpses of something beneath his harsh exterior, leaving her struggling to understand him. A deeply vulnerable man existed below the layers of subterfuge, and that was the man she desperately wanted to get to know.

"He's never brought anyone here," Margaret remarked, as if it was important for Bliss to know. "Even when his father died, he kept everyone away. I had hoped that when he returned . . ." Her words died away and she glanced toward the cross once more, perhaps seeking comfort. When she finally looked back at Bliss, a renewed determination lit her eyes. "Will you do something for me?"

"If I can."

"All I ask is that you try to understand Caine. Don't rush to judgment as so many other people have. I think he believes he failed his father, and the burden chips away at him a little more each day. He and his father were so much alike. After Lady Francis died, the earl worked even harder to give his son the life he thought he deserved, and when things fell apart . . ." She shook her head sadly.

A sound at the door brought both their heads up. The vicar stood on the threshold, his shoulders slumped forward, a hand braced against the frame, his face pale, and his breath coming in short pants as though he had been running. Alarm immediately rifled through Bliss's body.

She pushed to her feet, as his wife said, "What's happened, husband?"

"His lordship . . . he's out of control."

Bliss didn't wait to hear any more. She met the vicar at the door. "Where is he?"

"No, my lady. 'Tis too dangerous. His mood is black. I fear you might be hurt."

"He won't hurt me." How she knew, she couldn't say. But she felt it in her heart. "Where is he?"

He hesitated, looking to his wife, who nodded her head, before replying, "Near the north moor."

Bliss was out the door in the next second.

She found Caine standing amid a pile of rubble, rocks strewn about him, limbs broken from the trees nearby, the flowers planted next to a headstone torn from the ground. Bliss didn't need to look to know whose grave it was.

"Caine," she said softly.

His entire body stiffened. "Get the hell out of here," he snapped viciously, a warning that would send any sane person into retreat. And yet Bliss could not go, could not leave him with his despair.

She came up beside him and his gaze slashed in her direction. Never had she seen such pain in a man's eyes, such utter desolation.

"You just don't get it, do you?"

"I think I do," she murmured. "At least in part."

"Christ," he said, in a low, pained voice, "what am I doing here? I couldn't wait to get away from this place when I was younger. I was so damn eager to leave it all behind and find something else, something different. There was nothing here but the land and the sea, both stretching out before me like a yawning chasm. Everything I wanted was out there, just waiting for me to come and grab hold. I didn't want to spend the rest of my life being a glorified sheep farmer. I didn't want to become my father. I didn't want his legacy."

"There's nothing wrong with that. If there was, then I would be guilty, too. I rebelled against the life that had been mapped out for me merely because I was a female."

"It's not the same. Your parents . . ." His jaw clamped shut, a muscle working as he gritted his teeth.

"What?" Bliss gently asked.

An intense emotion carved his mouth. "Nothing."

"Caine, please . . . talk to me."

His head turned sharply, his eyes a glittering black. "Your parent weren't like mine! Now leave me the hell alone. Save your tender sentiments for someone who gives a damn. I didn't ask you to be my bloody savior."

"Maybe that's exactly what you need."

His laugh was short and bitter. "Not from you." He looked away, and repeated softly, "Not from you."

His words hurt more than Bliss would have ever imagined possible. He was like the tide, pushing her away and pulling her back, needing her but not wanting her, leaving her emotions in a constant state of upheaval.

"Caine . . ." She laid her hand on his forearm, but he jerked it away.

"Go," he bit out in an icy voice. "Now, before I do something I'll regret." He allowed her only a moment to comply, perhaps never really intending to give her the chance to elude him before his hands gripped her upper arms, his fingers digging into her flesh, dragging her forward.

His mouth came down hard on hers, brutal, wanting to punish her rather than allow her to see his pain. He did not care that they stood in the shadow of a church, or that the vicar and his wife might see them.

Bliss pushed at his shoulders, struggling to break free, but his arm wrapped around her waist, holding her immobile as he walked them backwards, shoving her up against a tree, his hard, heated frame molding tightly against her as his hand came up and squeezed her breast.

Even as she fought him, her body arched beneath his touch, her nipples hardening, pressing wantonly against his palm. His thumb scraped over the tight point, and a moan welled up in her throat.

She tore her mouth from his. "Caine ... please ... "

He kept up the torment for another moment, then with a muffled curse he shoved away from her, leaving the tree as her only support. Her legs were weak from the force of his assault—as well as the desire he had so easily stirred inside her.

He raked a hand through his hair and she saw it tremble, telling her that he was not as cold and unaffected as he wanted her to believe. The vicar's wife had bade Bliss to understand him, but at what cost? Whatever was brewing between them was growing into a madness that seemed to be spiraling out of control, and she didn't know how to stop it.

"Caine," she repeated softly, her appeal almost lost in the rise of the wind and roar of the waves below them. "Talk to me."

"'You can't even see your own destruction when it's standing right in front of you." He faced her, his eyes without emotion. "Come near me again, and I promise I'll give you what you're asking for."

"What are you saying?"

"Jesus, you really are a virgin. Fine. Let me spell it out for you. I'll screw you, your ladyship. Tempt me again with your false offers of kindness, and I'll give you all the gratitude your tight little body can take."

She could see in his eyes that he was purposely trying to hurt her, to push her away. "My offer is not false," she said in a shaky voice. "I want to help you."

"Help me?" A savage smile twisted his lips as his gaze crudely raked her form. "Then lie down in the grass and spread your legs." He walked toward her until he was towering over her, and leaned forward until his breath warmed the flesh beneath her ear. "They say I'm good. Would you like to find out?"

Bliss pushed him back. "What drives you to be so cruel?"

"Do you fancy me a cause, lady? A lost soul to be saved?" His mouth curved in a grim line. "I'm afraid you're too late."

"I don't believe you." He regarded her with so predatory a look, her face flushed. She forced herself to return his gaze. "No man whose countenance reflects such despair is without remorse. Should you need a friend, I'm here. Should you need a confidante, I'll listen."

"Is that what this is all about?" he said derisively. "Being my friend? Or is it simply that you want to hear the details of my father's cowardly demise? How he jumped from that cliff, his body so mangled when it was pulled up from the rocks below that his casket had to remain closed? Does that appease your insatiable curiosity?" His hands were fisted so tightly at his sides that his knuckles shone white.

"Let's move on to other matters now, shall we? Like how I'd feel between your silken thighs, my rod sliding in and out of you, your breasts quivering beneath my hands, my lips. Does that melt you, sweet? Do you find your body responding?"

The images his words evoked wrenched the breath from her lungs, and her body did respond. He was a master at this game, after all. But she would not give him the satisfaction he sought.

"No," she said, her voice barely audible.

"Liar." His gaze slid away from her, locking on some point behind her. He muttered a curse beneath his breath.

Bliss turned and found the vicar and his wife standing near the rectory, their faces pale and concerned. When Bliss looked back at Caine, something close to regret had settled over his face.

He grabbed her hand and pulled her away. "Where are we going?" she asked, struggling to keep up with him.

He didn't respond, but his pace slowed a bit and his hold on her hand eased. Yet she knew he would not let her go. There were forces at work within him that she could not begin to fathom.

Within moments, they were following a winding path behind the vicarage, enclosing them in silence and a sense of peace. They walked without speaking. The path opened into an enclosed valley. Within was a village made up of cob-walled, thatched cottages and little slate-roofed houses with their own gardens, all jumbled together as if they had been thrown down accidentally. It was quaint and lovely.

Bliss glanced up at Caine. The way he looked at that

moment, like a child who'd lost his way and come home at last, tugged at her heart.

An old woman waved to them then, her eyes alight, a warm smile wreathing her timeworn face as she beckoned them over.

"Stay here," Caine told her, his eyes warning Bliss not to disobey. Then he walked over to the old woman, who patted him on the hand in a motherly fashion.

The two of them stood together for a moment, the woman doing all the talking, and gesturing to something inside the house. Caine stepped into the cottage and Bliss, curious, moved closer. She caught a glimpse of an old man lying in bed, and a younger woman, possibly his daughter, sitting at his side.

The man smiled weakly up at Caine, his eyes, like that of the woman Bliss suspected was his wife, glowing with happiness at seeing him. A moment later, the man was besieged by a coughing fit, a hacking bark that wracked his entire spare frame with spasms.

The faces of both the man's wife and daughter blanched. His wife leaned over to try to get him to drink something when the episode subsided, while his daughter held his hand and dabbed his brow with a cold cloth.

Caine stood rigid by the man's bedside, yet when he thought no one was watching, he briefly closed his eyes, the anguish evident to Bliss.

The man on the bed drifted off to sleep, clearly too weary for lengthy discourse, the occasional cough jarring his body as Caine stepped to the side with the man's wife.

Though the shadows of the cottage's dim interior shrouded most of Caine's face and body, Bliss caught a glimpse of him pressing money into the woman's hands. She stood in stunned disbelief. She had not taken Caine for a man who cared about other people's troubles. His world seemed wrapped up in disillusionment and cynicism.

The woman shook her head and tried to put the money back in his hand, but he curled his fingers over hers, the gesture speaking volumes.

The woman's head slowly lifted and she wrapped her arms around Caine's neck, making him bend down so that she could press a kiss to his cheek. The stiffness of his bearing told Bliss that he was uncomfortable with the gratitude.

He gently disengaged himself from the woman's embrace, haltingly accepting a hug from her daughter before stalking out of the cottage, leaving Bliss to follow or get left behind.

They continued along the path, where the trees gave way to a fir wood. Bliss caught far-off glimpses of the ocean through the ruddy trunks and great dark fans of the branches. The scent of pine needles and the sea stirred around them.

At the end of the path was a clearing, and down a short slope lay a crystalline pool of water. Leaves shaded the glen from the sun's bright rays, dappling the ground with subdued, mysterious light.

Caine guided her down the incline to stand at the water's edge. Only the barest breeze shirred the surface, their reflections rippling on tiny waves. It was exactly the way she would have pictured the Garden of Eden.

Bliss glanced up at Caine and her breath caught in her throat at the intensity in his gaze as he stared down at her, branding her with heat. He appeared every inch the voluptuary, at home in his lushly wooded seraglio.

"Why did you bring me here?"

He took hold of her hand and tugged her forward, his voice a dark, husky rumble as he replied, "Because I intend to make love to you."

Eleven

'Tis a thing impossible to frame
Conceptions equal to the soul's desires;
And the most difficult of tasks to "keep"
Heights which the soul is competent to gain.
William Wordsworth

$\mathcal{C}$aine's words ignited a warmth inside Bliss that fanned out, and she realized what she was feeling, what she had forced to the background time and again.

Her own desire.

She couldn't deny the attraction anymore. But the need Caine aroused in her wasn't simply a response to his immense physical beauty, that smoldering virility that clung to every sinuous curve of his body, or the dark hunger in his eyes that made her think he could lose himself in her.

It was all of that and more. It was the glimpse of the man behind the walls he had built, awakening something fierce and heartrending inside her.

He haunted her. It was shameful and confounding. What she felt . . . it was nearly unbearable. But she couldn't allow any of that to matter, because it could not be like this.

"No," she said softly, backing away from him. "You won't make love to me."

He hunted her lazily, his eyes conveying who would emerge the victor. "Who's to stop me?"

"You won't force me."

"No?" The word was a taunt, as was the hand that skimmed up her side to boldly cup her breast, flooding her with sensations she prayed he didn't see. "You seem to forget that I take what I want."

"But you won't stoop to rape."

A humorless grin tipped up his lips. "It wouldn't be rape, my lady. I'd have you panting for it in short order."

Bliss raised a trembling chin. "You, sir, possess tremendous arrogance."

"Sometimes," he said in a low, dark drawl, "arrogance is all a man has. Now kiss me, damn you."

Bliss held her ground, pressing her hands against his shoulders. "What was the matter with the man back in the village?"

Caine's arm slid around her waist and tightened. "None of your business." He leaned forward to kiss her, but Bliss turned her head.

"Was he ill?"

Fury flickered in his eyes, but it seemed directed inward rather than at her. "He's dying. Now leave off." He pressed his mouth into her neck, nuzzling her.

"You gave his wife money," she said, trying not to respond to the overwhelming heat he was creating. "I saw you."

"Be quiet."

"This bothers you. Why can't you admit it?"

"Quiet, I said." He kneaded her breast. "I'm tired of this bloody cat-and-mouse game."

Bliss put her hand over his, trying to push it down, though the woman inside her demanded that she give in, that she wanted him as much as he wanted her. "Maybe you are tired of it, but you still won't force me."

"God damn it! Stop saying that."

"Why? Because it makes you see that you're not as dishonorable as you want everyone to believe?"

"I am dishonorable."

"Then take me. I dare you." Bliss knew she was playing a dangerous game, knew she could never hope to win if he overpowered her. She saw the dark glint in his eyes and recognized a moment too late that he was out to prove something.

"As you wish." His mouth came down on hers, his tongue forcing her lips open, slipping in to mate with hers as one hand slid over her buttocks, pulling her harder against his erection.

His other hand locked in her hair, tipping her face up. His kiss hurt; he meant it to. She could taste the anger in it, but hot need had surged up the moment he touched her, leaving only awareness, only piercing sensation, as the tips of her swollen breasts molded against his chest, craving the feel of his hand.

As though understanding what she wanted, he cupped her breast and caressed her nipple through her clothes, a growl building in his throat as the material impeded access to what he wanted.

He deftly freed the buttons on her bodice from their moorings and then untied the ribbon holding her chemise closed. His eyes were burning coals as he stared down at her, challenge in their depths as his hand slid across the exposed flesh before slipping under the lacy material to stroke her.

Bliss caught her lip between her teeth to keep from moaning as he toyed with her nipple, the few remaining buttons coming undone, her dress pooling at her waist, leaving her completely bare to his sexual regard.

"God," he said in a hoarse voice, "why did you have to be so damn beautiful?" The question seemed both compliment and curse, as though he didn't want to acknowledge his attraction for her.

He lowered her to the ground, his lips closing around her nipple and suckling. Bliss moaned low in her throat and tossed her head back. It felt so good.

He glanced up at her, a feverish light in his eyes. "Am I forcing you, my lady?"

Mute with desire, she shook her head and arched her back, ashamed as she silently begged him not to stop. With a gleam of satisfaction, his mouth closed over her nipple, pulling and then licking, over and over again. Her other nipple was tormented as his forefinger flicked back and forth, a throbbing ache centered between her thighs.

With no pretense of gentleness, he rucked up her skirts, gripped her thighs and dragged her forward against him, searing her with rough male heat.

He cupped a hand between her thighs, his fingers pressing against her as he found the opening in her pantalets, separating the moist folds of her most intimate place and finding her aching pleasure point.

He began to massage the nub slowly, then in circles, teasing her, his eyes burning into the very depths of her as he watched her face, holding her gaze captive.

"You're so wet," he said in a sensual rasp.

"Don't . . ." She shook her head, not wanting him to weave any more of a spell around her than he already had.

"Don't what?" The finger between her thighs feathered over her sensitive flesh, barely touching her, taunting her, her body yearning for him not to stop.

"Please, Caine . . . I . . ." Coherent thought left her as he leaned down and laved her nipple.

"Tell me what you want, love. I'll give it to you."

Bliss rocked her head back and forth, a groan spilling from her lips as he gently scraped his nail over her sensitive peak. Then he stopped, and she nearly cried out.

"Do you like what I'm doing?"

She felt like the most primitive of animals, writhing there in the grass, what remained of her rational mind telling her not to say anything, knowing with the uttering of the words that he would own some part of her soul. And yet she could not stop herself.

"Yes . . ."

He smiled to himself and kneaded her breast, pushing the tip high before drawing it into his mouth, wringing moans from deep inside her. Then he eased back and blew a warm breath across the turgid pebble, making it pucker and swell, his wicked mouth so close.

"Should I kiss the tip, like this . . . ?" He placed tender kisses on her nipple that were wicked and erotic. "Or suck, like this?" His beautiful mouth closed over a taut peak and tugged, sending a wave of heat spiraling downward.

Bliss knew he wanted her to beg for every seductive touch. And she would, if she must. "Suck."

"Hard or soft?"

"Soft."

"With my tongue?"

Mortified by how desperately she wanted him, she could only nod. His long, silky hair fell on her, an erotic caress across her heated flesh. Bliss threaded her fingers through it, holding him close as his hot mouth sweetly tortured her sensitive tips, creating ripples of ecstasy everywhere he touched.

He wanted something from her, something more than just her total surrender. But she was afraid to look too closely, afraid she'd realize that she was just another conquest.

She caught only the briefest glimpse of wickedness in his expression as he looked up at her . . . before sliding down her body, until his dark head was positioned between her thighs.

Her back arched as his tongue speared into the heart of her like a hot flame, pressing in and out, then skimming up her inner lips. The first touch of that dark fire on her engorged tip made her writhe against him and hold his head there. He chuckled darkly, enjoying the power he held over her as his arms pinned hers to the ground while he licked and sucked and stroked her over and over again, his fingers rolling her nipples.

A driving need for something, a fulfillment she didn't understand, clawed at her, and on the verge of her discovery, he stopped his sensual assault.

Bliss whimpered, her body shuddering as she opened her eyes and found him watching her, not allowing her to look away as his tongue flicked the very tip of her swollen sex, a bolt of heat making her moan.

"Watch," he gruffly ordered.

She understood his intentions a moment too late, her reactions slowed by the heavy languor he had created, an aborted plea whispering from her lips as she reached down to grab his hand, but not soon enough to stop him from inserting his finger inside her, invading her, bringing the intimacy to another level.

Bliss squirmed, hating the feel of that rough invasion and loving it at the same time, wanting him to stop but wishing he would go on.

"Christ." He closed his eyes and pressed further into her, his face ragged, a muscle working in his jaw as he slid another finger in, making slow circular motions inside her as his thumb massaged her tight bud, bringing her to the pinnacle again, her entire body balanced on the edge, and holding her there, just there, making her squirm before starting over.

Then he changed the rhythm, moving in and out of her, stretching her, a pressure building when he tried to push too far, his wet mouth sliding between her breasts, sucking her nipples until they were rigid points, whispering sexual words about how they felt in his mouth, how they responded to the caress of his tongue.

Then he inserted two more fingers into her drenched passage. "That's how it'll feel when I'm inside you," he said in a deep, passion-roughened voice. "Fuller, though. Farther in."

Bliss wanted to pull away as much as she wanted to push against his hand. "Caine . . ." She didn't know what she was asking him for.

"I know, love." He slowly eased out of her, spreading the moisture on his fingers over the sensitive peak he had loved with his mouth, before kissing the tip, then giving it a teasing lick, and another, and another, working her up all over again, bringing her to the precipice and finally, blessedly, ending the torment by drawing the hot point into his mouth.

When he gently bit down, Bliss's world unraveled, a wave of pleasure pouring in scalding rivulets through her veins and culminating beneath his questing tongue and lips, the pulses flowing from deep inside her.

Afterward, she lay sated, boneless, her limbs unable to move as the final ripples thrummed through her. She had never realized it could be like this between a man and a woman. Never understood exactly how much she had been missing.

Caine moved off her, rolling to his back and locking his hands behind his head, staring up at the sky through the canopy of leaves above.

He was so big, so solid. So very real. She wanted to hold him, to lay her head against his chest and listen to his heart beating beneath her ear.

But his posture, solitary and defiant, warned her away. He had gotten at least part of what he had wanted. She had writhed beneath him, as he had once said she would. And yet, he hadn't taken her.

His gaze slid sideways, those hot blue eyes spearing her as expertly as his tongue had moments before. "So was it as good as you hoped?"

Bliss tried not to flinch, unprepared for his abrupt reversion back to his usual scorn. She had been sure she sensed something tender in his kisses and the way he touched her, but what happened between them didn't mean anything to him.

Hating the hurt she felt, she struggled for composure. "Having no other man to whom I can compare your skills," she said, praying he didn't see her hands trembling as she adjusted her skirt and bodice, "I wouldn't have the foggiest notion if your lovemaking was all that it should be. But if it will put your fragile male pride to rest, I promise to give you a proper rating once I have sufficient information."

Hard fingers suddenly gripped her upper arm to pull her around. The look in Caine's eyes was feral. "What just happened between us was not lovemaking," he said, fury in each clipped word. "But since you feel equivocal about my performance thus far, I guess I'll have to give it another go."

"No, Caine . . ."

He stopped her protest with his mouth, gripping the back of her head and holding her tightly against him as he once more deftly undid the buttons she had just done up.

Sounds of protest rose in her throat as she tried to push him away, but her struggle was halfhearted. The moment his mouth had touched hers, anticipation had rocketed through her, the blood sluicing through her veins in growing excitement. She now knew what he could do, and her body yearned for the sensations he could evoke.

His large, warm hand slid in to cup her breast as he pulled her on top of him, making her straddle him, to feel his hardness pressing against her heat, burning her through her clothes.

He suckled one nipple and gently plucked the other. She whimpered, shivering as his hand skimmed up her calf and over her thigh, knowing where he was going, her body needing the fulfillment he could give her.

The first touch of his finger against the sensitized peak between her downy curls made her throw her head back wantonly, her thighs spreading boldly across his lap.

"Lift up your skirt," he commanded in a husky murmur.

Without thought, Bliss did as he asked.

"Higher. I want to see you."

Her entire body trembling, she pulled her skirt all the way up, not realizing that he had divested her of her pantalets, leaving her femininity completely bare to his view. She tried to cover herself, but he pushed her hands away and continued stroking her.

He gripped her buttocks, lifting her up, his gaze still riveted to hers as he raised his head and impaled the heart of her with his tongue, flicking just the tip, the most exquisite part.

Her back arched, words tumbling from her lips, encouragement, pleasure, demand. She didn't know who she was in those moments of ecstasy. She only knew that she needed what Caine was giving her.

As a second climax spiraled from the very depths of her being, Bliss felt replete and drugged, her body sagging against Caine's, his arms wrapping around her and holding her against his chest, something possessive and tender in his embrace.

She allowed herself to drift in that gauzy world for a few minutes, but reality flooded her senses all too soon. She had given herself over to Caine's complete mastery not once, but twice.

She expected to see a gloating expression on his face,

but he was staring at the leafy canvas above their heads, strain bracketing his eyes and mouth.

She didn't understand him. Here was a man infamous for his sexual appetites, and yet, once more, he had not taken her. In the throes of the passion he had so skillfully woven, she would have let him do what he pleased.

Her gaze shifted to the faint scar etching his cheek. Without thought, she reached up to run her finger over it. In the next instance, her wrist was gripped in Caine's viselike hand.

"Don't," he ground out.

Bliss wet her suddenly dry lips, trying to breathe past the constriction in her chest at the warning in his eyes. But she wanted answers, needed to know more about him.

"Where did you get it?" With trepidation, she raised her free hand, waiting for him to stop her again, his gaze following her arm's ascent until her fingers hovered only a scant inch away. Then, taking a breath, she touched him. His eyes clamped shut and his jaw worked, but he did not wrench her away this time. "Talk to me, Caine," she said softly.

He did not speak. His body lay rigid and unmoving beneath the questing probe of her fingertips.

"Does it still hurt?"

A moment of silence, then: "No."

"Did you get it in a fight?"

He expelled a sound, a muttered curse. She couldn't quite tell. "Yes."

"Was it terrible?"

"Jesus." He made a short, brittle sound. "What is it you want from me? Can't you ever just let it go?"

His rebuke brought a cold sense of reality back to

Bliss. She pushed away from the warmth of his body and sat up. "It's been a most edifying day, my lord. I thank you for your services. If you'll excuse me, I find I'm in need of different company."

She made to rise, but he grabbed a length of her hair. She let out a sharp cry of surprise as once more she found herself staring into his piercing eyes.

"Don't, God damn you."

"Don't what?" she returned in a brittle tone, equally angry.

"Don't you bloody thank me. Not now. Not ever. I won't take that shit from you. Not from you." His grip eased, but he wouldn't let her go.

"Then talk to me. Tell me what troubles you."

An expression that was half anguish and half fury washed over his face, and Bliss wanted to wrap her arms around his neck and hold him. But she knew he wouldn't let her.

"Does your pain have to do with your father? I know—"

"You know nothing," he cut her off, pushing to his feet and moving to the edge of the woods, his hands sunk into the pocket of his trousers. He was silent for so long, she thought he had forgotten she was there. Then he said in an emotionless tone, "The villagers think my father haunts these cliffs. They claim they've seen him down on the shore below the Point."

Bliss came to stand at his shoulder, staring down a sharp descent of ferns and heath, the ground falling away so abruptly that she could only see space. Caine looked as though he was leagues away from this place, his mind focused on memories.

"Others say they've seen him driving his carriage or riding over Challacombe Downs, followed by a pack of his hounds." He shook his head. "Christ, what people will actually believe."

"And what do you believe?" she quietly asked.

His gaze slid to her. "Death is death. And nothing can change it."

"No. Nothing can change it. But we can hold onto the memories we have. No one can take those away." She paused, debating the wisdom of what she was about to say. "What happened to your father wasn't your fault."

His jaw worked and he turned away from her. "Do you want to take a swim?"

Bliss shook her head as he moved past her. She heard him remove his clothes, each piece tumbling to the ground with the barest sound.

She kept her gaze averted until she knew he had entered the water, and then she turned. Only the slightest ripple in the glasslike surface marked his way.

The water looked cool and inviting, and Caine's beautiful body rose from it like some Dionysian god, his black hair wet and skimming his shoulders, his chest a bronze sheen, little rivulets sliding over the defined planes and dancing over the hard ridges of his stomach before disappearing beneath the unbroken surface that shielded the rest of his body from her view.

"Are you sure you don't want to come in?" he asked.

Bliss shook her head, unable to stop looking at him, feeling an undeniable pull that was so much more than physical.

His fierce curse brought her gaze up.

"What's the matter?" she asked.

"You."

"What did I do?"

"Don't you know not to look at a man like that? You're asking to be deflowered." He swore again and plunged beneath the water.

She blushed and felt ridiculous. She was a mature, world-wise woman, and yet Caine managed to expose feminine weaknesses she hadn't realized she possessed.

When he surfaced, she was determined to reclaim control. "Why didn't you make love to me?"

"Because you weren't ready," he said without missing a beat, the water swishing as he moved toward the bank, exposing more flesh with each step, a challenging light in his eyes as he drew closer, daring her to look away. Even if she wanted to, she couldn't have.

And then he was standing on solid ground, naked and glorious, beads of water caressing his muscular body as he stood in a patch of sun, the rays backlighting him.

She followed the path of a drop of water as it skirted his collarbone, then raced over one satiny brown nipple and curved along a beautifully sculpted stomach, before disappearing in the thatch of dark hair at his groin.

"Stop it, Bliss." The words were a growled warning, and as she watched, his shaft, thick even without an erection, began to swell and lengthen.

Her gaze lifted and met his. His eyes were so dark, so fierce, and yet she glimpsed the desire. All for her. The knowledge burned inside her.

"You could have made love to me," she heard herself confess, remembering how mindless he had made her the moment his hands and mouth began working their magic on her body. "Why didn't you? I thought you took what you wanted."

"I do."

"You didn't want me then?"

A muscle worked in his jaw. "You know I did."

She started toward him, watching each subtle inflection on that harsh countenance, the way his hands slowly curled into fists at his side. He wasn't so tough, so dangerous. Not at that moment. Not with the way he was looking at her.

"You wish I wasn't so bold, don't you? I can see it in your eyes."

"It'll get you in trouble."

"Will it?" She wasn't sure what devil prompted her to reach out and stroke her finger down the silky jut of his erection, but she felt satisfaction in his sharp intake of breath.

She'd always endeavored to overcome whatever intimidated her, and never had a man intimidated her more than this one. Caine threatened the very balance of her life.

Without warning, his hand wrapped painfully around her wrist. "Don't, for God's sake. I'm not some animal; I'm a man. Christ . . ." His voice was ragged. "I'm a man."

He pushed her hand away and turned from her. As he dragged his clothes from the ground, Bliss wondered what she had just done, and how she had unintentionally hurt him.

When he turned back to her, dressed, his stone-cold expression had returned. The look he sent her froze the apology on her lips. "Let's go," he bit out.

She followed him up the path. They were halfway to

the village when the young woman from the cottage ran up to them, her face pale.

"What's the matter, Sara?" Caine demanded, concern in his voice.

"Oh, m'lord," she cried, twisting her hands in the folds of her skirt. " 'Tis the mistress."

"Lady Buxton?"

She nodded. "She's thrown us out." Tears spilled over her cheeks.

"Thrown you out?"

"Aye, she says we've got two days to be gone. We gave her man the money y' gave us, but he said because Da is sick and can't work, we've got to get out." Her eyes, glassy with unshed tears, implored him. "What will we do? We have nowhere to go."

"You're not going anywhere."

"But the mistress—"

"The mistress can go hang. Don't pack a thing. I'll figure something out."

"Oh, but y've already done too much. I can't let y' put y'rself out anymore on account of us."

"I said I'd help, and I will."

Heart-wrenching tears trickled down Sara's young face, and Bliss saw the hero worship there. The girl launched herself against Caine's chest, wrapping her thin arms around his neck. He didn't seem to know what to do. He accepted her gratitude, but his body remained unyielding, his arms stiff at his sides.

"Thank y', m'lord. Y' are the most wonderful man in the world."

He gently dislodged himself from her embrace. "Go back and tell your mother something will be done."

"Yes, y'r lordship. And thank you." She hesitated, then kissed his cheek. Picking up her skirt, she fled back toward the village.

Bliss came up beside him, both of them watching Sara until she disappeared from view. "She loves you, you know."

"I know," he replied somberly and without satisfaction. "She doesn't realize her mistake." He started back toward the house.

Twelve

His madness was not of the head,
but heart . . .
Lord Byron

*T*he hall was quiet when Bliss entered with Caine. They had walked in silence, as if their time together in the woods had never happened. Once more Bliss had been shut out.

Thinking of Caine's role in the welfare of Sara's family, Bliss remembered the stud fee he had demanded from her for Khan. She had believed his reasons to be purely malicious; now she realized there might have been more to his request.

She had never considered how he might be forced to live, or how a man of such unflinching pride dealt with his lowered means. Relying on someone else would never sit well with him. Perhaps the drastic alteration in his life was part of the reason for his bitterness, what made him keep people at a distance. Living as a guest in a home that should have rightfully been his could not be easy.

Bliss didn't know what power kept Caine here, what invisible bond tethered him to this land, but she felt it. Perhaps it was simply that his father had died here. She believed his father's death was truly at the root of his disillusionment and anger, though she couldn't tell if his rage was directed at himself or his father.

A burst of laughter at the far end of the hall brought them to a momentary stop, and Bliss recognized Olivia's voice. The other voice was familiar as well: Lord St. Giles. She'd know that guffaw anywhere. The man had hung over her shoulder all through dinner the night before, his nearness bordering on suffocating.

Entering the morning salon with Caine, Bliss found Olivia and the earl deep in conversation, their heads bent close to one another. Bliss wondered how Caine felt about what he saw. Was he jealous? Could he have feelings for Olivia? Perhaps it was not simply the lure of his house that kept him here. Perhaps the true lure was the woman who glanced up at them, a sultry smile curving her lips upon spotting Caine, those catlike green eyes growing cooler when her gaze lit on Bliss.

"Where have you been, darling?" she asked in a sleepy, come-hither voice. "I was looking all over for you. St. Giles and I were just about to have a late breakfast. Won't you join us?"

The earl's gaze raked over Bliss, something mocking in those gray depths as he inclined his head. Bliss wondered if he could tell what had transpired between her and Caine. Did a woman's face take on a different light when recently pleasured? More so if the pleasure had been great?

Bliss noted the large knot on the earl's jaw, the bruise dark and quite nasty. Her brow furrowed as a faintly puzzling image came to mind: her bleary eyes flickering open in the dead of night to see two figures silhouetted in the shadows of her bedroom, scuffling. But it had just been a dream, she told herself. Like the one she'd had of Caine taking her tenderly in his arms and gently laying her down on her bed.

"I have to talk to you," Caine told Olivia in a clipped tone, adding with emphasis, "alone."

Olivia remained seated, her posture almost challenging. "You can speak in front of St. Giles. He's not a gossip-monger." Turning to the earl, she said, "Are you, my lord?"

"No, my lady. I am the very soul of discretion." Looking at Caine, he said mockingly, "Speak your piece, Hartland. We're all friends here."

His look chilled Bliss. She instinctively moved closer to Caine, wanting him to know she was there and on his side.

Caine's gaze speared the earl, his eyes black as they narrowed on the man's face. "How's your jaw this morning, St. Giles?"

The taunt was evident. *Had* Caine punched the earl? If so, why?

The smug expression disappeared from the earl's face as he dabbed his napkin to his lips. "A bit sore, but hardly worth discussing. Odd that I can't recall how it happened. If I didn't know better, I might believe I had been the victim of an unprovoked attack. But only a coward would do such a thing. Do you know any cowards, Hartland?"

"Only one," Caine replied, the implication clear.

The earl's hands curled into fists.

"Caine, darling," Olivia interjected in a placating tone. "What has upset you so?"

Slowly, Caine's gaze returned to hers. "You."

"Me? What did I do?"

"Don't play innocent."

"I told you, St. Giles and I—"

"I don't give a damn about the two of you. I'm speaking about the Doyle family."

The light of understanding dawned in Olivia's eyes. "What about them?" she asked defensively, her chin going up.

"You can't throw them off the property. They've lived here for twenty-two years. Will Doyle was the backbone that helped make Northcote what it is today. He and my father worked side by side cultivating the fields."

"That is truly a heartwarming story, darling. But I cannot abide tenants who do not contribute to the maintenance of the estate. What would the other tenants think, should I allow the man and his family to live freely on my property?"

"That you possess an ounce of compassion, perhaps? The man's dying, for Christ's sake."

Olivia's eyes narrowed angrily. "There's no room here for charity. The tenants work, or they leave. It's that simple."

"Sara gave you this month's rent."

"Yes, odd that she had the money. One might wonder where she got it. Her father has been ill for three months, yet she has had it each month. You wouldn't have any idea how that happened, would you?" She gave him a knowing look.

"You got your damn money," Caine said through gritted teeth. "Now leave them alone."

She sighed and studied her bejeweled fingers, as though the subject bored her. "I don't want their money.

I want them off my land." She glanced up then. "And this *is* my land, if you'll recall. My house. My tenants. I can do what I please."

"Her father is dying."

Like an imperious queen, she lifted her teacup, a silent command for one of the attending servants to refill it. "That isn't my problem, is it?"

The look that came over Caine's face was frightening, and in that moment, Bliss truly believed he wanted to do bodily injury to Olivia.

"You want something; spit it out. What will it take for you to let them stay? Name your price. You always have one."

Those cat eyes glimmered with satisfaction and a small smile played about Olivia's lips as she rose and glided seductively toward him. "You know me so well, my love." Her voluminous skirts brushed against his legs as she stepped closer to him, indecently close, her breasts almost touching his chest, her eyes on him alone, uncaring that her guests looked on. "But I wonder what you could give me that I don't already have?" Something unspoken flared between them, and Caine's body tensed. "I suspect you gave every last shilling to those filthy paupers."

She sighed and shook her head. "I always knew you harbored an unnatural fondness for the villagers, and I'm quite put out with you for going behind my back. If not for Chadwick, I might not have known." She smiled baitingly as Caine's jaw locked in anger. "I told you he was a man of many talents. Among other things, he said he spotted you visiting those people several weeks ago."

"And you've been waiting to spring your trap ever since."

She shrugged airily, her triumphant gaze briefly floating

to Bliss as she ran a slim, manicured finger over Caine's shoulder. "Well, I had to see what would happen, if you would come up with the money. Since you refuse to take what I offer you, I can only assume you put that damn horse to stud. You always manage to land on your feet, don't you, my lord? I've often appreciated your resourcefulness."

St. Giles rose from his chair. "How unfortunate, Hartland," the earl prodded jeeringly, his eyes gleaming with malice as he rubbed the bruise on his jaw. "It must be hard to see your father's people cast off."

"Shut your mouth," Caine said in a low, savage voice. "Or I'll ram your teeth down your throat."

"Caine!" Olivia gasped. "I'll not have you speaking to my guests that way. Apologize to St. Giles at once!"

Caine leaned down close to Olivia, and Bliss saw the flash of fear that blanched her face. "I wouldn't apologize to that maggot even if you covered me with flesh-eating parasites and let them feast on my body for the rest of my natural life."

"Why, you arrogant bastard," St. Giles hissed. "You should have followed your father off that cliff."

The next instant was a blur as Caine lunged toward the breakfast table and dove across it, St. Giles's eyes going wide with shock as Caine's massive hand wrapped around his throat.

A cacophony of sounds broke out with people yelling, St. Giles gasping, dishware breaking.

"Caine! Don't!" Bliss pleaded. If he killed St. Giles— Her hands tried to break his vicious hold, but his grip was too strong. The earl began turning blue.

Knowing Caine would kill St. Giles if she didn't find some way of stopping him, Bliss climbed onto the table, glasses crashing to the ground as she tried to get in front of him, to make him look at her.

"Please, Caine," she beseeched, laying her palms against his cheeks; his skin was so hot it nearly scorched her. "Don't do it. He's not worth it. Please . . . *please* let go."

His eyes, brutal and frightening and black, slashed in her direction as though she was another threat he needed to annihilate.

Her heart beat wildly, her lungs constricted with fear. Still, she held tight, forcing herself to hold his gaze. "Caine, he's not worth it. Please let him go."

A moment ticked by, then two, three. Finally, like the opening of a vise, he released the earl, who stumbled back and fell into a chair, his hands clutching his throat as he gasped for air.

"I'll see . . . you . . . charged for this . . . you bastard," the man vowed between heaving breaths, the marks of Caine's fingers a glaring reminder of what had almost happened.

"Dear God, Caine!" Olivia exclaimed, shock giving way to anger. "Look what you've done! That was my best crystal and china!"

"Bugger your damn crystal and china!" St. Giles choked out. "That lunatic almost killed me! I insist you call the magistrate. The swine needs to be locked up."

"Had you minded your own business, none of this would have happened," Olivia snapped.

"You're blaming me?" An angry flush scorched the earl's neck as he jerked to his feet.

"Get out of my sight before I'm tempted to throw something at you."

Fury radiated from the man, his gaze slicing to Caine,

a promise in his eyes that warned it wasn't over, before he stormed from the room, scattering the crowd that had gathered in the doorway, their expressions a mix of horror and fascination.

"Come with me," Bliss quietly insisted, taking Caine's hand as she got off the table, barely hearing the splintering of glasses as Caine followed her, shards crunching beneath his booted feet as he came to stand in front of her, the wild look in his eyes not entirely gone.

Bliss turned to find Olivia regarding their clasped hands, a challenge in her gaze when she lifted her head. Bliss returned the challenge, a strong need unfurling inside her to protect Caine.

He yanked his hand from hers and stalked away, his actions piercing her heart and her pride. A self-satisfied smirk curled Olivia's lips, mocking her.

"What do you want, Olivia?" he said, his voice emotionless as he stared out the window overlooking the gardens, his hands shoved into the pockets of his trousers.

"Well," she began, "there is one thing, as you know, but I believe I'll attain that wish." She cast a look at Bliss, her sly smile still in place, and Bliss knew the remark had something to do with her. Olivia's skirt rustled as she glided toward Caine, stopping next to him at the window. "It seems, my lord, that I already have everything you once possessed."

Caine turned only a fraction so that he could stare down at her. "Not everything."

"Really?" She cocked her head. "What's left?"

"Khan."

"That brute?" she scoffed. "What could I possibly want with him?"

"Khan is the best horse here. Not one of yours can compare. Breeders once traveled hundreds of miles to mate their fillies with his sire."

Olivia regarded him for a moment, then slowly nodded. "He is quite magnificent, isn't he? I could charge an exorbitant fee for his services, keeping the list exclusive enough that people will be clamoring for breeding rights. I can also mate him with my mares to beget future generations. Yes," she murmured with a growing smile. "I can see the merits."

"Then he's yours on one condition."

"I don't think you're in a position to bargain."

"Either you agree or there's no deal."

"Once I hear your request, I'll give it due consideration."

"If you want Khan, then you can't throw the Doyles or any other tenant off the land."

"What? That's ridiculous! You go too far—"

"You'll make more than enough money to compensate for any trouble. Take it, Olivia. You're getting everything."

"Well," she finally said, "I *am* getting the better part of this deal. Fine. I agree. There are other ways of keeping the villagers in line." She smiled provokingly. "Shall we toast to my good fortune?"

Caine ignored her and walked away, her soft laugh following in his wake. At the threshold, he turned and warned, "Keep St. Giles out of my sight or next time I'll kill the pompous little cock."

Then he was gone.

Thirteen

I am about to take my last voyage,
A great leap in the dark.
Thomas Hobbes

$\mathcal{B}$liss stared out her bedroom window at the endless night that blanketed the moors. A warm, sea-scented breeze billowed the curtains around her as she watched a string of glowing lights blinking and bobbing in the distance. The ghostly spectrum headed toward the westernmost point of the quay before disappearing one by one, as though falling into the gaping maw of a black hole.

The sight made her think of Caine's story about his father haunting the cliffs. Though her heart wanted to believe that deceased loved ones could somehow remain within the realm of the living, she knew what she had seen was not the glittering, demonic eyes of a pack of hounds following their disembodied master, but rather the lanterns of a group of fishermen.

She had overheard someone say that the fishing fleet often went out after midnight if the tides were low, to catch salmon. She had also seen the long rope ladders leading down to secluded inlets where coracles danced on the windswept tide. There were no ghosts, except those that existed in the imagination.

Since the incident in the morning salon, Bliss had kept to her room, claiming a headache when Court came for her at dinnertime. She knew he had heard about what had taken place. Undoubtedly he also knew her role, yet he made no comment, though his eyes conveyed she could talk to him if she wanted.

But what could she say? That he was right? That she should have stayed away from Caine? But how could she have known that the dark and brooding Earl of Hartland would become far more a risk to her heart than to her body?

She had to leave. She had decided hours ago that she would. The more time she spent with Caine, the more he drew her in. She had thought him a challenge once, but he was so much more than that. He was a journey, a winding trip that threatened to disrupt her life.

The plain truth was, she was scared. Something was happening to her, something she had never experienced before—an eclipsing of common sense, a feeling of spinning out of control, as if the very fabric of her life was shifting, and piece by piece the person she had always been was being replaced by someone else. What she feared, dreaded, was that she was coming to care for Caine.

Beneath that ruthless exterior was a man who amply matched her passion for life, who never backed down, who took what he wanted, said what he felt, and who possessed a depth of emotion she had yet to encounter in anyone.

And he belonged to another woman.

Bliss pressed her forehead against the cool window-pane, wondering when Caine had gotten under her skin and lodged there, and how long it would take before the ache in her heart dissipated.

She had thought about stealing out at first light, before the house was awake. Before Caine was standing in front of her, and the sight of him stopped her cold.

Lord, when had she become such a coward? As much as she might want to take the easy way out, if she succumbed to one fear, she would succumb to a multitude of others.

She had to tell Caine she was leaving. She owed him that much.

She knew where he was; she had spotted him entering the stables hours earlier. She could picture him down there alone, surrendering the only thing that meant anything to him. The compassion Caine could not bestow upon another human being, he conferred upon his horse. And now he had lost his final salvation.

As she quietly let herself out of her room and padded down the shadowed hallway toward the front of the house, Bliss didn't know if the course of action she now planned to take was right. But she feared that where Caine was concerned, she might never know.

He was drunk.

Drunk and numb. But not numb enough, Caine thought. Not nearly numb enough.

God, what had happened to his life? How far back had everything gone awry? When had he taken that first step down the wrong path? Perhaps he had been born this way, his arrival into the world a death sentence to whoever cared for him. First his mother. Then his father.

All this time, he had lived under a self-indulgent delusion. But pretense was so much easier to face than the truth. Yet the lie had led to one mistake after the next, until his transgressions compounded so high, he couldn't scale his way over. And it was all because he possessed the one trait he couldn't abide in anyone else.

Weakness.

He was an illusion, just like his once-perfect life; his rage directed outward because he was too bloody spineless to accept the blame himself.

He had failed everyone.

Now, Bliss.

Sweet, fatal Bliss. Fatal to be near her. Fatal to see her, to touch her, to want her.

Fatal to care for her.

Christ. For a short while he had let himself forget who she was, allowed her to slip beneath his defenses and make him think that maybe . . .

He shut out the thought, closed off any emotion other than the bitterness that kept him going. Everything he had was taken from him. Whatever he desired was lost to him. He should have let St. Giles bed her, and good riddance.

He jammed his eyes shut and ground the heel of his hands into them, trying to block out images of St. Giles doing to Bliss what Caine had done to her that afternoon. Feeling her soft skin. Drowning in her heat. Hearing those hot whimpers as she built toward her climax. Then spreading her. Filling her. Taking her in absolute possession. Finding peace.

Caine sucked in a long, drowning breath as the quicksand of his own stupidity dragged him down and closed over his head. Damn Bliss. Damn her to hell. She had created a chink, a shift in the already precarious balance of his life, and he didn't know how to change everything back.

God, why did she haunt him so?

"Your life's a bloody damn mess, old man," he mocked himself, his tongue thick, his words slurred as his equilibrium rocked from one mammoth swell to the next. He leveled the half-empty bottle of vintage Armagnac on top of Khan's stall door. His horse looked at him with a jaundiced eye, as if to say, "The bugger's in his cups again."

Suddenly Caine found the whole stinking situation enormously amusing. "Here's to the phantom of the hall!" He lifted the bottle, one of three. Now one of only two. Soon to be none. "Bottoms up."

He tipped the potent liquor to his lips and drained the remainder. Then, with a growl, he twisted around and flung it out the stable doors, glass splintering with a satisfying crack against the ground. A startled gasp jerked his gaze around, and there in the doorway, stood the very source of his torment.

Bliss. Lovely, wary. Lush. And damning the last shred of decency that remained in his soul.

She stared at him wide-eyed, as though believing he had gone mad. Too late; he had traversed the road to madness long ago.

Two years ago, in fact. Two years in which to stew, to wonder what form his revenge against Exmoor would take. Two years of waiting for this moment.

Tonight, he would no longer be denied.

*   *   *

Bliss stood rooted to the spot, Caine's piercing gaze holding her captive, her body trembling under the blast of his fury and longing.

His shirt was undone and pulled free of his trousers, the tails hanging along his lean hips, a sheen of sweat clinging to his bare chest. And yet it was another heat that assailed her, drawn from her own body, stirred by the power of seeing him there, tall, defiant, boldly assessing her, daring her to run.

Hating her, yet wanting her.

"Odd, isn't it, how we keep ending up here together?" His deep voice washed along her nerves and raised the fine hairs on the back of her neck. "I wonder if it has some special meaning? What do you think?"

"I think you're drunk." He looked reckless, wild. Dangerously compelling with that strange, inhuman beauty of his, like a glorious pagan, ready to rape and plunder.

He smiled, and the sensual, sulky curve of his mouth was self-deprecating, barely civil. "I always knew you were a clever girl. Care to tell me what I'm thinking now?" He crudely ran a hand over the front of his trousers, bringing her gaze to the rigid length pressing against the buttons. "I see you've figured it out. Good girl." He started toward her from the shadows, the wolf stirring from his lair.

Self-preservation made Bliss retreat until she'd backed up against a post, immobile as Caine approached. Moonlight glimmered through the open door, creating sinister shapes on his face. The menacing line of his mouth conveyed that nothing short of divine intervention would save her from his wrath.

"I won't allow you to hurt me," she told him in a shaky voice, thrusting out her hand to ward him off, as though a speck of sand could hold back a raging tide.

"It's not hurt I plan to inflict, my love. On the contrary. You will finally know the true meaning of your name."

Bliss shivered and maneuvered around the post as he continued to advance. "I understand how you're feeling. But I had nothing to do with what happened. You didn't have to give up Khan."

His jaw set hard. "And I told you what would happen if you came to me again with false offers of kindness." He paused, deliberately, and for effect. "You do remember what I said, don't you?"

Bliss remembered, and her trembling increased as she mentally replayed his coarse words: *I'll screw you, your ladyship . . . I'll give you all the gratitude your tight little body can take.*

Her heart began to pound until her ears were full with the sound, a faint dizziness skimming the edge of her vision, threatening to engulf her.

"I didn't come here to offer kindness. I came here to say goodbye."

That stopped him. "Goodbye?" Something flared in his eyes, something that seemed almost like despair. Then it was gone. "Well, I guess I'd better hurry then."

He shrugged out of his shirt, muscles rippling and flexing as he divested himself of the garment, tossing it heedlessly to the ground, his skin taut and smooth, but incredibly powerful . . . incredibly provocative.

And infinitely dangerous to her senses.

"Caine, listen to me. Please. I wanted to tell you more than just goodbye."

"How kind of you," he mocked in a dark drawl, slowly circling her, a ravenous predator who knew its prey was trapped and helpless.

"I don't want to see you give up Khan."

"Moot point, my lady." His tone was softly savage. "The deed is done. Let's move on to other, more pressing matters, shall we?"

"You were right," she said, her breath coming in shallow bursts as she kept just out of his reach. "I owe you a stud fee. I want to pay you."

A muscle worked in his jaw, his eyes glinting with renewed fire, the likes of which she hadn't seen since that first day he had come upon her in the stables. "You want to pay me now, do you? And which stud service would that be for? Mine, or my horse?"

"You know which."

"I'm not sure I do. But it doesn't matter. I don't want your damn money." His eyes smoldered like a wildfire. "I'm not here to assuage your sense of pity."

"It's not me who is doing the pitying. It's you!" Her anger at his foolish pride and arrogant refusal to see the truth made her want to scream. "You're father's gone, Caine, and no amount of wishing you had done things differently is going to change that."

His jaw clenched, telling her she was pushing him too far, but she didn't care. Someone had to tell him, someone had to care enough.

"Let it go," she pleaded, desperate for him to listen. "This house, this land, it's not all there is. You've got so much to offer. You're not just Olivia's lover, or any other woman's lover. You think you've failed, but you haven't." Bliss didn't realize she was crying until a salty tear touched her lips. "Please. Just take my money. Tell Olivia you made a mistake and get Khan back. It's not too late."

He stood looking at her, his eyes hard and implacable. "It is too late. For all of us."

Deep down, Bliss knew he was right. The minute she had set eyes on him her fate had been sealed, her life careening headlong down a path of certain destruction.

"Don't," she whispered, shaking her head as he moved in, leaving her only a single instinct, to run, to get as far away from the threat as she could.

With a sob breaking from her lips, she hoisted her skirts and fled into the darkness.

Fourteen

*A pleasure so exquisite
as almost to amount to pain.*
Leigh Hunt

"*Bliss!*" Caine's voice was anguished, the sound tearing at her soul. Yet she kept running, stumbling, blindly seeking some sanctuary in the blackness around her.

She could hear his footsteps pounding behind her. She knew she could never outrun him, yet she kept going, falling to her knees, scraping her palms, pushing upright, hearing the distant roar of the waves pounding against the rocks, closer, closer . . .

Then the air was forced from her lungs as an iron-hewn arm clamped around her waist, lifting her off the ground, her feet swinging wildly, her arms flailing, Caine's chest a hot, hard, unrelenting wall against her back, before she was jerked around in his embrace to face him. He looked fierce and powerful and catastrophic, his mouth swooping down to silence any protests.

May God forgive her, but she wanted him. Their

mutual panting blurred with the sound of the ocean's mounting fury as he pressed her down on top of a flat boulder, still warm from the day's sun.

"God," he growled, nudging her head back and teasing the flesh on her neck, "don't deny me, Bliss. Please . . . I need you."

Bliss shook her head wildly, fighting a battle she had lost the moment he touched her. She could not relinquish herself, give in as scores of women had before her, women who had possessed him.

As Olivia did night after night.

An aching sound rose in her throat. "Don't!" She pushed against his chest, rock solid and unmovable, and hot and hard and masculine. She wanted to feel every inch of him, absorb the full, searing length of his body, reach down and smooth her hands over the bulge rocking intimately against her. "I won't be one of your women, damn you! Stop. Please, stop."

He gripped her shoulders, shaking her lightly, their warm breath mingling as he stared down at her, his stormy eyes blazing with desire and self-loathing.

"You're the only woman I want," he growled. "Damn you for doing this to me. For making me need you so much."

"I'm leaving. I told you."

"No." He refused to listen to her.

He bore down against her, his mouth ravaging her neck, one hand undoing the buttons at her bodice while the other hand moved with frantic urgency under her dress, the contact of his hot palm against her skin erotic and maddening.

She writhed against him, opening her legs wider to

accommodate his massive size, a voluptuous pressure pinning her, heat against heat.

"Don't leave me, Bliss. Don't leave me," he repeated over and over again as his mouth made her body burn up in flames.

A gasp of pleasure burst from her lips as he sipped at her nipple and then drew the tight point into his mouth, suckling, laving, tormenting the sensitive peak while the hand between her legs tore at her pantalets, leaving her bare and vulnerable and on fire as he slipped a large, callused finger between her slick folds, finding the ripe tip of her sex.

Broken moans welled up in her throat, the sound equal to the husky groans coming from Caine as his lips moved feverishly between her breasts, tugging, nipping, teasing until her nipples were two lush points of pleasure, distended, begging for his touch as he massaged the sensitive nub between her nether lips, his fingers saturated with her wet heat.

She gripped his hair as he lifted her hips to his mouth and took her in the most carnal way a man could take a woman, suckling the tiny bud as he had her nipples, his tongue working magic she had never thought imaginable, playing wildly, exploring the entire length of her, slipping inside her like a hot flame, in and out, bringing her to the brink and holding her there, torturing her with his seductive mastery until she begged him to enter her. She wanted him inside, to be impaled, to be his, if only for tonight.

"Bliss . . ." he groaned as he slid up her body, his hardness pressing intimately against the sweet spot that throbbed for him.

She captured his gaze and held him there while her trembling fingers slid down his chest to the buttons on his trousers. She wanted to feel him, to hold all that hot, hard power in her hands, to caress him as he had caressed her.

"Bliss," he tried again, his voice ragged, pained. "I'm on the edge."

Such a confession from this man made her feel her own power, as though, at least in this moment, she held him in thrall. He was hers.

The last button came undone. Then the full, silky length of him was in her hands, burning her as she explored him—the thick ridge, the throbbing vein, down to the tight sacs she cupped in her hand. His harsh intake of breath told her she was giving him pleasure, increasing her confidence as she massaged him.

He pumped against her questing fingers, his eyes shut tight. A dark, sensual growl tumbled from his lips, the sound breaking over her like an erotic tide, making her bolder. Her finger toyed with the satiny tip, spreading the single pearl of moisture on the crest.

His eyes snapped open then, tearing the breath from her lungs at the heat and passion centered there. "Fight me," he said hoarsely, the words an ardent plea for salvation. "Don't let me do this."

Bliss arched up against him, pressing his erection against her wet valley and sliding slowly, so very slowly along his shaft, a tantalizing, brazen invitation. "I want you."

"Why?"

Because she knew in her heart this was right. No other man made her feel so much like a woman. No other man made her feel the power of every instinct inside her.

No other man was worth her virginity.

"Because it's my choice . . . and I choose you. I don't expect declarations of love or vows of fidelity. All I ask is that when you are with me, you are mine and mine alone. I don't want you thinking about any other woman, Caine. Only me."

"There is no other woman. No one exists but you." He braced his hands on either side of her head, his chest a massive slab of heat and muscle above her as his head descended, his lips brushing over hers in a heartbreaking kiss. "Help me . . . please."

"I will," she promised in a whisper.

He closed his eyes, looking anguished, torn between the devils of desire and denial. "Is it me you want? Or this?" He increased the friction against her.

"It's you." She threaded her fingers through his hair. "I want *you* inside me. *You* to be the first." He groaned and dropped his head, his soft hair like the brush of a feather across her skin. She captured his face in her hands, forcing him to look at her. "I don't know what you did to me. You rip apart everything I believe in, yet I can't stop thinking about you, aching for you."

"God . . ." He pressed his forehead against hers, still sliding against her, the tip of his shaft scoring her taut nub with each stroke, his hands gripping hungrily at her hips, igniting a searing tumult of desire, his breath rough beside her ear. "I've thought about this . . . about being inside you, how you would feel. Jesus, I want to hate you. Why can't I hate you?"

"What have I done?" The question came out a raw, broken plea, a need to understand what inner turmoil tore him apart. "Tell me, Caine. Is it Olivia?"

His head jerked up, a savage light reflected in his eyes. "Don't speak her name. Not now; it's just the two of us. No matter what happens, remember that I tried to deny you. God, I tried, but I can't." He groaned, his shoulders trembling. "I can't."

"Then don't," she breathed, pulling his head down and kissing him the way she had wanted to kiss him all night, all day. Always, it seemed.

The mating of their mouths was carnal, wet, his tongue plunging into hers as he rocked harder against her, faster, his fingers barely teasing the sensitive tips of her nipples, an erotic whisper of sensation giving nothing but pleasure, drawing her down into a hot, dark labyrinth of sexual hunger where he was her only salvation.

He wrapped an arm beneath her back, lifting her up to kiss her nipple, that simple touch pushing her over the edge. Her body convulsed, breaking into a million pieces, as though she had been thrust down upon a rocky shoal.

"Yes . . ." He laved the tight bud, giving her no reprieve from the tumult he had created inside her, slipping his longest finger deep into her, testing her readiness, a pained expression on his face as he tried to hold himself in check until she lifted up against his hand and the dam on his control burst.

Gripping her wrists in one hand, he raised them above her head. "You're mine," he growled. As the pulses still rippled hot, scalding pleasure through her veins, Caine entered her in one swift, rending stroke, the penetration so deep it burned, pain and pleasure, heat and dark fire.

Bliss cried out, her nails digging into his back as he pushed further. He was so big, too big. "Caine—"

"Ssh. I'll make better, I promise." He rocked slowly at

first, in and out, giving her a little more each time, a sweet pressure culminating where they were joined as he filled her, high and tight, lifting her with each powerful thrust.

Bliss kissed the curve of his neck, tasted the salt on his skin, savored his scent, and the heady musk of their love-making. Instinctively she lifted her legs around his flanks and tipped her pelvis up, increasing the pleasure that thrummed between their heated bodies.

Oh, God, he was hers, all of him, inside her, hot and hard and deep. And she felt insatiable. On fire. He had awakened something in her, something she desperately needed.

Something she feared no man would ever bring to life again.

And all the while, he looked into her eyes as he made love to her. He refused to let her turn away, to deny him even an ounce of what she was feeling—unbridled passion and an emotion so intense, it swamped her every sense.

He leaned forward and wet her nipple, blowing his warm breath across the puckered, aching tip and whispering, "Give me what you've given to no other man."

She did, shattering once more, all the pleasure and pressure spearing down to the core of her. Her muscles tightened, squeezing his shaft, drawing his long, hard length inside her, deep and deeper still. His hands gripped her hips as he pounded against her, a guttural groan tearing from his throat as he finally found his own release.

Bliss drifted down to earth in a haze of satiation. Cool night air skittered across her body as she lay there, boneless, replete, staring up at the indigo sky.

An overwhelming sense of happiness mingled with

bittersweet despair. What had just happened between them was explosive, incredible—yet nothing had changed. She could not be with him like this, with another woman's specter dancing between them.

She wanted more, a commitment she knew he would never be able to give, and the realization that she desired something stable and genuine from Caine shook her to the core. She had never believed any man would mean this much to her.

She sat up, wincing at the ache between her thighs. Caine was leaning back against the boulder, his gaze focused somewhere in the distance, once more lost to the roar of the ocean, a tormented Odysseus searching the world for his home.

He was so achingly beautiful, his body limned by moonlight; his entire aspect silent, still, stripped of its usual harshness. He appeared defeated, and so impenetrable it seemed as though he was no more than an extension of the stone behind him.

"Caine . . ."

"Don't say it."

"What happened—"

"Was a mistake," he injected in an emotionless tone. "I told you I was no good. I told you to tell me no. Don't blame me now because you regret what happened."

"I don't regret it. Not a minute." She should. Perhaps eventually she would, but not now.

Now she understood the true meaning of being a woman, what it was like to be free. She had been missing the most essential element: the power of her own body. All the books in the world could not have given her what Caine had given her tonight.

She slid off the rock and went to stand in front of him. He gazed over her shoulder, and when she shifted into his line of vision, he focused over her other shoulder.

She laid her hand on his arm. "Look at me. Please."

Reluctantly, he did as she asked, but Bliss couldn't see his eyes, just the stubborn jut of his jaw, the tension in his neck, the barely contained aura of a man on the verge of anarchy.

"I didn't use any protection," he said into the ensuing silence.

"I know."

"Don't you understand? You could be carrying my child." His laugh was harsh as he dragged a hand through his hair. "Christ, what have you done to me? I've never been careless. You've muddled my mind."

"I wanted it as much as you. I'm to blame, as well. But it was my first time; certainly nothing could come of it. I really don't think—"

"That's right," he cut her off brutally. "You don't think. You're like poison. And you're killing me." His voice seemed to hold a lifetime of condemnation. "God, you're killing me."

For a haunting second, he stared at her as though she was a stranger and he had lost his way, a displaced, uncertain traveler who had ended up somewhere he had not intended. She wanted to reach out to him, to ease the fierce line of his jaw, smooth away the harshness around his mouth, but the moment evaporated.

"You're so smart and yet so bloody damn naïve," he said in a rough voice. "Go home. Run as far and fast as you can—and leave me the hell alone."

He pushed away from the boulder, brushing her aside

as he walked toward the cliffs . . . almost as if he would walk right off.

"Caine!" She raced after him, grabbing him by the arm and swinging in front of him.

He stared out at the sea, the water whipped into a sudden fury by a sweeping blast of air, the tempest swirling around them, leaving them at its center.

"What do you think it's like?" he said, his voice borne on the rising wind. "To fall to your death. No way to turn back. No way to undo it. Seeing flashes of what an abysmal failure your life has been." A shudder went through his frame. "Do you think you're free?"

"No." She shook her head, the wind whipping her hair across her face. "That's not freedom."

"Don't you wonder about death? What it would be like to take your fate in your own hands, and just let go?"

"No, because I want to be here tomorrow, no matter what may happen."

"What if there's nothing to look forward to and tomorrow no longer matters?"

She stared up at him gravely, terrified that she had stumbled into something beyond her ability to handle. "There's always something left. You just have to reach for it."

"You have all the answers, don't you?"

"Not nearly enough," she said helplessly, "and none where you're concerned."

He looked down at her finally, studying her face. "Why did you give yourself to me?" he asked, an intensity in his eyes that she could not interpret.

She could lie, spare herself the hurt that honesty might bring. But something told her he needed the truth, that it might make a difference.

"You told me when I first arrived that I was denying the attraction between us, and you were right. I didn't want to spend the rest of my life wondering what being with you might have been like."

Moonlight reflected off the glittering blackness in his eyes, telling her that he had misinterpreted her words. "So did I appease your curiosity? Touch all the right places?"

"Please," she begged in a whisper. "Don't ruin it."

He turned abruptly away from her. "Go back to the house."

"Not without you."

"I won't jump, for Christ's sake," he ground out, his face stark. "Just go."

Bliss didn't want to leave him. He seemed on the edge. And she thought in that moment that he possessed more fortitude than she did. She had floated through life armored in her beliefs, shielded from most of the world's harsh realities simply because she was the daughter of a duke—and a woman.

She had always scorned the role she was destined to play. But she hadn't considered what it might be like on the other side; how a man, deprived of all he had once known, might feel.

She opened her mouth, wanting to say something, but they'd be wasted words that he wouldn't hear. And would they change anything?

She couldn't stay here. Couldn't take the chance of opening herself up for the heartbreak he could so easily inflict. *Go home,* he had said. *Or else,* were his unspoken words. If not, he would systematically destroy her.

Her tears flowed freely as she leaned up and kissed his

cheek. "Goodbye," she whispered, then turned and fled into the night.

Caine reached for her, a voiceless panic clutching at the back of his throat, closing off the words to call her back, to beg her to stay in his arms another hour, with nothing but his body and hers bound in primitive communion.

He dropped his arm and damned her for ever coming into his life and making a mockery of everything he had steadfastly believed, for causing him to yearn for things he had vowed he never would.

He had thought himself immune, believed the walls he had built stone by stone, day after unending day, were impenetrable. But one whisper of his name on Bliss's lips, a single earthy surrendering to his will, and he had been lost.

He moaned low in his throat, the sound whipped by the wind as a storm worked its way across the landscape. The far horizon vanished as black clouds billowed toward the hall, thunder rumbling and jagged forks of lightning splitting over the ocean. But the approaching maelstrom was no equal to the roiling ferment inside him.

He tried to summon up his rage with images of his father's laughing face and then the unopened casket. The scar on his cheek seemed to suddenly burn. He had been branded, and everyone knew his disgrace. He could not look in a mirror without the constant reminder, without the pain, the anger. The blame.

But he had gotten his revenge, hadn't he? Slaked his lust on the daughter of his enemy? He'd had her exactly as he had envisioned her, beneath him, writhing, panting his name, welcoming him into that tight, hot sheath, her fingernails scoring his shoulders as he drove into her.

He had won.

So why the hell did he feel no satisfaction?

And why did he long for the one thing she hadn't relinquished?

Her heart.

Bliss entered the silent house, her mind plagued with mounting doubts about leaving Caine in such a volatile state of mind. If something should happen to him . . .

"My lady?"

Bliss started, her heart in her throat as she turned to find Olivia emerging from the shadows.

"Are you all right?"

"Fine, thank you," Bliss lied.

"It's late to be out wandering the moors. You could have hurt yourself, or worse, taken a deathly fall."

Caine had saved her from that fate, and what had followed had changed her. "I couldn't sleep."

"I understand. I, too, had difficulty sleeping. It seems my lover is not in residence. Perhaps you've seen him?"

Her lover. The words seemed a purposeful taunt. What did Olivia know? Something glimmered in the woman's eyes, something that made Bliss feel she was toying with her.

"Lady Bliss?" she prompted when Bliss made no reply.

"I'm afraid I don't know where your . . . where the earl is. Now if you'll excuse me, I'm quite worn out."

"Yes. I imagine you would be."

Something in her tone stopped Bliss. "I beg your pardon?"

The woman glided across the floor to stand in front of her, her gaze slowly running over Bliss, malice showing in full measure.

"Making love to Caine can be quite an exercise in endurance," she said with an odd smile that chilled Bliss to the bone. "He can pleasure a woman for hours. Frankly, I'm surprised to see you back here so soon. I expected he would have you until dawn, his obsession to possess you was so strong. I guess his need wasn't as great as I'd thought."

Words of denial automatically sprang to Bliss's lips, even as a worm of dread uncoiled inside her. "I don't know what you're—"

"Your eyes give you away, my dear. You're not quite as worldly and sophisticated as you've allowed us to think, are you? I must confess to being surprised Caine was willing to put aside his loathing long enough to do the deed. Then again, he had substantial motivation—and I certainly know how devoted he can be to a cause when he puts his mind to it. Quite delicious."

Somewhere in the house a clock ticked, measuring each unbearable second.

"I almost envy you," Olivia went on calmly. "Caine is a prime specimen when angered, utterly superb. I only hope he hasn't used all that lovely pent-up frustration on you. I'm feeling ravenous for his brand of lovemaking at the moment. It is the reason I allow him so much leeway, after all."

"You knew . . . ?" Bliss uttered, struggling desperately for a normal voice.

"Of course. I know everything Caine does. I even watched for a while. He was quite the rutting beast, wasn't he?"

Bliss's face grew hot and her body cold. "You watched us?"

"I suspect half the house watched. We are, as you may have noticed, a rather debauched group." She ran a finger down Bliss's neck, laughing softly when Bliss jumped back. "My friends, who used to believe I exaggerated Caine's extraordinary prowess, simply had to discover the truth for themselves. None of them, to my knowledge, has ever found him lacking. I wouldn't have tolerated his black moods this long if not for the length of his . . . endurance, shall we say?"

Bliss's throat could barely form words. "I don't believe you."

"Oh, but you should. I know him far better than you. In bed and out, though the latter is a much less frequent occurrence."

Denial burned in Bliss's lungs, but she could not voice it. "Why would he want to hurt me?"

"You really don't know, do you?"

Bliss wanted to slap the woman and wipe that gloating expression off her face, then find Caine and demand an explanation. But she would not allow Olivia the pleasure of seeing her fall apart.

"No. I don't know," she replied, maintaining her composure by the barest thread. "But I can see you're aching to tell me. So what was it? Did he find me too much of a challenge to resist? Or was it simply that he must seduce any female who steps foot in this house?"

"If only it were that simple. Caine, as you know, is quite the complicated man. He spends a good deal of time plotting revenge against those who have wronged him. And you, I'm afraid, were an irresistible target."

Caine had once told her that he hated her, but Bliss had never truly believed that hate could result from the incident with their horses.

"What have I done to him?"

"Nothing, exactly. It has more to do with your father. You were just the unfortunate recipient of Caine's formidable wrath."

"What has my father done?"

"You are surprisingly uninformed, aren't you? Though I suspected as much. Had you known what you were facing, perhaps you would have been prepared to fend Caine off. Maybe I should have warned you, but, really, where was the fun in that?"

For a moment, Bliss could only stare at the woman's coldly beautiful face. "You put him up to what happened tonight?"

"No, no, my dear. I was merely a bystander to his plans. Caine thought up this scenario entirely on his own. And it's no wonder, considering your father was the cause of Caine's ruin."

Bliss shook her head. "I don't believe you. My father would never hurt anyone."

"No? Why don't you ask him what he knows about Henry Ballinger, then? Ask him about the debt Caine's father owed him, that led to the earl killing himself."

"You're lying."

"Ask Caine, if you don't believe me. I'm sure he'd be happy to confirm what I've said. The debt that sent his father to a tragic, untimely demise was owed to your beloved papa, whom Caine hates with a ferocity that is unparalleled. And defiling the daughter of the man who destroyed his father is a fitting revenge, wouldn't you say?"

In that moment, Bliss could see it all so clearly. Caine's anger, his cruelty, how easily he claimed to hate her. He had refused to open up about his father, refused to let down his guard. Every heated kiss, every searing touch had been a ruthless, calculated prelude culminating in her downfall. He had sworn he would be her ruin.

And she had gone willingly to the slaughter.

PART TWO

France

*Love is a deep well from which
you may drink often, but into
which you may fall but once.*
Ellye Howell Glover

Fifteen

To go away is to die a little,
It is to die to that which one loves:
Everywhere and always,
One leaves behind a part of oneself.
Edmond Haraucourt

La Ville Lumière.

Paris—the City of Light. But tonight, Bliss's section of the city was dark. Hardly a street lamp was lit outside the apartment she shared with her mother on the *Rue de la Chaussée d'Antin*.

She had been home for nearly a week, determined to put Caine out of her mind, but the task proved harder with each passing day. Her anger was the only thing that kept her from despair, from thinking about how she had started to believe he might actually need her.

He had told her that she should refuse him, push him away, but she hadn't had the strength to do so. Blaming him for her downfall was much easier than blaming herself, for to blame herself might mean acknowledging deeper feelings.

It had taken her a few days to summon up the courage

to write her father, to question him about what had transpired between him and Henry Ballinger. She didn't want to believe her father could have been involved in destroying another man's life, but she had to know the truth, for her own peace of mind. Just that morning, she had received his reply.

> *My darling daughter,*
>
> *I do not know what has happened to precipitate your inquiry into this matter, though I suspected you might hear of this terrible tragedy when you informed me you were traveling to Northcote.*
>
> *Perhaps I should have prepared you for this possibility, but I will confess to cowardice when the time arose. I was afraid of what you might think of me, for I knew the reason behind Henry Ballinger's death, though it was not common knowledge.*
>
> *I hope you will believe me when I say that I would have gladly given the earl more time to pay back the monies he owed me. I knew Henry for years and found him to be an honorable man. I would never have wished him any harm.*
>
> *As for his son, I am baffled by the information you have imparted. Caine never came to see me, for if he had, I most certainly would have spoken to him.*
>
> *Perhaps I should have gone to him, but I will admit that I felt at a loss for the right sentiment to console him. I worried he would think I was only assuaging my own conscience. For the first time in my life, words eluded me.*
>
> *I am still bereaved over Henry's death, and I feel a certain responsibility toward his son. Perhaps you*

might convince Caine to come to London and take his place in the House of Lords? He would have my full support should he wish to do so.

I miss you, daughter. Come home again soon. And tell your mother . . . well, tell her that I hope she is faring well.

Your loving father

By the way, your cousin Court has just informed me that he intends to ask Lady Rebecca St. Claire to be his wife. I wholly approve of the match. He sends his love.

Relief coursed through Bliss as she folded the letter and tucked it away in a drawer. Her father was innocent of Caine's charge, as she knew he would be. So why did Caine believe her father had a hand in the earl's death? Had his accusation merely been a result of grief? A need to place blame, rather than believe his father capable of killing himself? Or had something else happened? Something that could have led him to believe her father was at fault? But what?

Bliss pushed aside her questions. Caine was no longer her concern, nor had he ever been. She had to concentrate on moving forward, to think about the good news her father had imparted.

Court was to be married. She was not surprised; he had been completely taken with Lady Rebecca, and Bliss knew they would be very happy together. She was only sorry she had made him worry when she had announced her decision to leave Northcote a day early and return to Paris.

He had known she was running away, and that her

leaving had something to do with Caine. She prayed he'd never discover the full extent of her folly. She would never forgive herself if her own selfish actions caused him to lose Lady Rebecca or have him foolishly call Caine out.

Since returning home, Bliss had strived diligently to force Caine from her mind, keeping herself busy working on portraits for her patrons. Her studio was set up in the garret, a bright, cheery spot, and the only room in the house that gave her a view of the very heart of Montmartre.

There was nothing lovelier than the butte when sunlight played on its rich red-ochre soil and peppered the winding gullies and narrow footpaths. Or the evening sky, when it transformed from a soft slate-blue to a crimson-laced pink.

But no matter how full her days, there was no escaping the long and lonely nights when she had nothing to occupy her thoughts, and dreams of Caine haunted her.

Some mornings she'd awaken to find her pillow wet from tears, tears she would not allow herself to shed during her waking hours. Not for a man who had used her as a tool for revenge. Other mornings she'd stir in a fitful slumber, plagued with images of Caine's heated possession, his hands and lips branding her flesh as he bound her to him with the sensual rhythms of his body.

Sometimes she would touch the places he had touched, a tingle burgeoning in her nipples, craving the warm tug of his lips, the hot rasp of his tongue, the erotic massage of his fingertips as he teased and tormented. He had cast a spell over her body, ensnaring her in a luxuriant web from which she could not break free.

"We are mooning again, *non?*"

The male voice, so dear and familiar, stirred Bliss from her thoughts. She turned to find her friend, confidant, and often temperamental model, François Gervaux, regarding her from his position on the settee, his eyebrow raised in a concerned question mark, his angelic good looks at odds with the charming devil she knew him to be.

She had met François five years earlier when she had been sketching a group of gaunt urchins and bedraggled waifs along the *Avenue de Clichy*, her ire rising as she watched one wealthy peer after the next stroll callously past those young, starving faces without a backward glance.

François had stood over her shoulder, startling her when he spoke. He, too, had once been among the ranks of the poor, he told her. Abandoned at the age of seven, he had run away from the orphanage where he had been beaten regularly.

He had made a life for himself on the streets, selling his body, giving himself over to lascivious men who liked the lithe charms of young boys.

Then a respected artist had spotted him and was struck by his startling beauty. He took François from the streets and set him up as one of his models.

Since then, François had posed for most of the up-and-coming artists of the Salon, proudly boasting that he had been painted in the buff by such notables as Renoir, Bazille, Degas, and Maître. The man who had taken him in was an elite among the group. His name was Manet.

Paintbrush still in hand, Bliss moved back to the canvas sitting upon an easel in the middle of the room. "I'm not mooning," she replied, toweling off the blotch of yellow paint that had dribbled down her thumb. After cleaning her brush, she dabbed it lightly in a pocket of blue.

"*Chérie,* I know mooning when I see it. I am an expert on the subject, after all. I have perfected the art of drifting about in a state of melancholia, looking pale and tragic. You've painted me this way"—he waved an airy hand—"hundreds of times, *mais oui?*"

"I am not pale and tragic."

"Perhaps not pale, as you spend too much time with your face turned up to the sun, but you, *mon ange,* are most definitely tragic. I feel your pain."

"Please, François, do not get dramatic."

"This, too, is something I excel at. We French have a flair for drama. It is in our blood. Now tell your darling François, whom you treasure above all others, what has put you in such an unhappy state?"

"I am not unhappy." She almost sounded convincing, but François was too sharp to miss a thing.

"Poor François is now to be lied to?" He sighed. "You break my heart, *jolie.* You think I do not see that you have not been the same since you returned from that heathen England?"

"England is not heathen." Though some of its occupants were.

He sniffed disdainfully, staring at her with betrayed eyes that conveyed he was horrendously misunderstood and gravely wounded.

He claimed his loathing of all things English was inherited, but Bliss knew his animosity had begun when he had been smitten with an Englishman who had scorned his adoration. For a Frenchman, to be scorned in love was akin to being hacked to bits with a dull cleaver.

"Look at me," he said. "I am about to expire on the spot with curiosity. Why must you torture me so? You know how sensitive I am to unwanted agitation. Why, I feel a terrible affliction coming on as we speak!"

"Turn to the right and raise your arm a little higher," Bliss instructed, hoping he would let the matter drop.

"This is the first time you have requested my services since you arrived home. If I did not love you so, I might feel wounded beyond all hope of recovery that you did not call upon me the very moment you stepped foot back in Paris."

"Tilt your chin up, please."

"Fille méchante," he huffed, growing impatient with her. "You are so difficult to dredge information from when you are feeling testy."

"I'm not feeling testy." Melancholy, perhaps, but soon she would be back to her normal self. Her feelings for Caine would run their course and that would be that. She only wished she knew how long that would take, because the hollow feeling inside her had yet to abate. Some days it nearly overwhelmed her. "Remove the sheet now, if you please."

He did as she asked, whisking the sheet away as though he was a Roman conqueror flinging his gauntlet to the ground, revealing what his male admirers most admired about him. He was fond of saying that he need not swing from the gibbet to be well hung.

Normally the sight of that proudly erect part of him interested her not at all. It was simply another piece of the human body, like an arm or a leg, its only value aesthetic.

But today, the sight of that very elemental part reminded her of Caine—of the pleasure he had given her, of all the delicious and wonderful things he had done to her body, and she found herself warming to an uncomfortable degree.

She forced herself to blot out thoughts of Caine and concentrate on the task at hand, her brushstrokes light and fluid across the canvas. She was so absorbed that she didn't immediately notice that the image being rendered looked less like François and a great deal more like Caine.

"*Mon ange?*"

Distracted, Bliss glanced over at François. "Yes?"

"Have you, by chance, lain with a man?"

For a moment, Bliss blinked dumbly at him, then a sudden heat crept up her cheeks. She should have expected such a blunt and probing inquiry, as François possessed no compunction about discussing anything.

At her telltale flush, François sat bolt upright, staring at her as though the Virgin Mary had just materialized in front of him. "*Dieu doux dans le ciel!* You have! Oh, you have broken my heart, you wretched girl," he bemoaned. "I was to be your first. I was to initiate you into the art of lovemaking. No man does it with the skill of a Frenchman."

Bliss avoided his accusing gaze and studied her canvas. "I don't recall ever having that discussion."

François waved a dismissive hand. "Inconsequential details. You miss the point."

"Which is?"

"*Mon Dieu*, did you learn nothing in that country of the swines? You have been ruined. You will never want a real man between your thighs. It would be too much for you to handle." As though this was the most dire sentence the heavens had thought to cast down upon a mortal, he threw up his hands and sank back on the cushions in his best imitation of a beleaguered sulk.

"It wasn't that bad." Bliss waited for a crack of thunder to rend the sky at her blatant understatement. She had never imagined that making love to a man could be so wonderful.

François lifted his forearm from his brow, gazing at her with one aggrieved eye. "Not that bad? A woman's first time should be the most memorable experience of her life, not some clumsy rutting. You have dealt me a mortal blow. I think I will never recover."

"And I think you will recover as soon as the dance hall opens its doors this evening."

He glared at her. "Not only does the cur take your virginity, but now he has left you a viper-tongued shrew whose affections he has usurped from your beloved François. I think I shall kill this interloper."

"You're forgetting something," Bliss said, striving to sound indifferent as she refocused her attention on the canvas.

"Oh?" he queried, sounding offended.

"You prefer men."

"That." He shrugged in a careless fashion. "Not the same, *chérie*. In this one instance, I would have put aside my natural revulsion for female flesh. You are the exception, of course."

"Of course." Bliss laughed softly.

"I am your friend, therefore I had a certain obligation to perform this momentous favor for you. But," he said with a bereaved sigh, "the deed is *fait accompli*. So now the question remains, who is this man who has won your heart?"

"He hasn't won my heart."

François's gaze was unnervingly direct. "You, who have cast aside men as though they were so much fodder—"

"I have never cast anyone aside like fodder."

"You, who have left hearts scattered all over Paris, never giving one man more than a cursory glance, their pride in shambles—"

A knock at the door saved Bliss from whatever probing question loomed on the horizon. She would welcome the devil himself at that moment, if it distracted François.

Moving to the door, Bliss swung it open, thinking it was her mother with a supper tray.

Instead, leaning negligently against the doorframe was the very devil she had summoned, looking every inch the aristocrat in a navy superfine jacket that molded his rugged shoulders, cream brocade waistcoat that emphasized his broad chest, and dove-gray trousers that hugged his muscular thighs.

The devil known as the Earl of Hartland.

Sixteen

〰️

A bolt is shot back somewhere in our
breast,
And a lost pulse of feeling stirs again . . .
Matthew Arnold

*B*liss was unable to catch her breath, her gaze riveted to the piercing midnight eyes she had just painted.

"Surprised?" Caine murmured, his deep, resonating voice making her shiver.

She shook off the traitorous thrill caused by his unexpected appearance and stiffened her resolve. This man had used her. He had no right to suddenly appear on her doorstep as though he had done no wrong, especially looking so calm and fascinating.

"What are you doing here?" she demanded.

"I've come to pay a visit." He leaned close to her, assaulting her with that incredible heat. "I'm the very soul of sociability." His mouth was suddenly next to her ear, his breath a soft pressure against her throat as he whispered, "I've missed you."

A sharp ache rose inside Bliss, infuriating her. She

forced herself to remain rigid, glaring at him. "Your arrogance knows no bounds, my lord."

He straightened slowly. "None at all." There was a suggestive intimacy in the curve of those full lips, which had kissed her with such carnal abandon. "May I come in?"

"No."

"Still an expert at chiseling me down to size, I see. Good thing I'm not easily deterred." He pushed away from the doorjamb and took a step toward her. Impulsively, Bliss held her hand out to block his path. He quirked that infuriating eyebrow at her, challenge written plainly on his handsome face. "Are we to engage in a scuffle? I'd prefer to avoid it, if possible."

"Then leave and it won't be an issue."

He chucked her under the chin. "Remind me to take you to Gentleman Joe's for a bout in the ring. My money's on you." Then he entered her apartment, the hand she intended to use to push him out the door brushing across his chest instead, leaving a telltale heat in its wake.

"Cozy," he murmured, his gaze scanning her belongings before a dark scowl formed on his face. "Who the hell are you?" His belligerent tone told her he'd spotted François.

Naked.

"Who the hell are you?" François demanded in return, not sounding the least intimidated, though Caine had to outweigh him by at least two stone.

Swallowing back an unexpected laugh, Bliss was greatly relieved to see that François had tugged up the sheet, though the thin silk sculpted his bounty in all its glory. To the unknowing eye, it might appear she was having an afternoon tryst. And from Caine's tense profile, that was exactly the conclusion he had drawn.

His eyes, now far more black than blue, settled on her. "Have you already begun gathering your information?"

It took Bliss only a second to deduce his meaning. He had once tauntingly questioned her about the degree of pleasure he had aroused in her, and she had replied that she would need to seek out other men to make an adequate comparison of his skills.

Lifting her chin, she replied, "Yes, as a matter of fact, I have. Now, if you wouldn't mind leaving so that I can continue my lessons? I'm a very studious pupil, if you recall. But some things require a good deal of time and devotion to master."

The possessive light that suddenly blazed in his eyes warned that pushing him was not advisable. "You mastered that particular lesson quite aptly, if memory serves."

The carnal undertone of his words evoked images Bliss had yet to forget. "How did you get in here?"

"A plump, rosy-cheeked maid welcomed me with open arms. She didn't seem to find it remotely unusual that you were entertaining men in your bedroom."

"This isn't my bedroom." His gaze slid to the cot she kept in the corner, and for some unfathomable reason, Bliss heard herself say, "Sometimes I work late into the night."

He slanted her a disarming smile. "A captivating image."

Her heart missed a beat. "If your insatiable curiosity has been appeased—"

"Far from it."

"That was your hint to depart, *monsieur*," François

interjected, knotting the sheet around his lean hips and
standing, his own impressive height of six-two a fairly even
match to Caine's. "Unless you need help finding the door."

"I presume you think to assist me?" Caine's gaze
flicked over his potential opponent, unconcerned.

"*Mademoiselle* has expressed her desire for you to
leave. If you do not feel so inclined, then most assuredly, I
will show you the way out." François took a step toward
Caine, which Caine matched.

Bliss hastened between them, her back to François.
"Stop this."

Caine raised an eyebrow, a glint of anger in his tumultuous gaze. "Saving your lover, sweetheart? How charming." He caught her chin between his fingers. "Then
again, you always were quite passionate when riled."

"I want you to leave," she told him furiously, hating the
fact that part of her still responded to him and didn't
want him to go.

Faint lamplight caught the saturnine curve of his
cheek. "I have something to say to you."

"Then say it and go."

"It's a private matter." His gaze cut over her shoulder
to François. "Why don't you scuttle off, old boy? Later, if
you feel so inclined, I'll take you up on your offer to step
outside. For now, however, get out."

Bliss had to block François as he lunged forward. He
may prefer men to women, but that didn't make him any
less male when it came to his honor.

"This is foolishness!" he said in an impatient tone. "Let
me dispatch this boor so we can return to what we were
doing."

"And what was that, again?" Caine asked, now making

a lazy circuit of the room as though he had every right to snoop.

"Perhaps we were making love," François taunted.

Caine glanced over his shoulder. "And perhaps I'll wring your bloody Frog neck."

"Jealous, English?" François draped his arm over Bliss's shoulder, the gesture intended to provoke.

"Of you?" Caine said with a scoffing laugh. "I've seen what you have to offer, and I highly doubt the lady was impressed."

Bliss's temper soared. "Why you pompous, pig-headed . . . Out! Both of you!"

"But, *chérie* . . ." François cajoled, only to be silenced by her glare.

"You, of all people. How could you?"

"I only meant—"

"I know what you meant, and I suspect I'll eventually forgive you. But not at this moment."

He sighed dejectedly and retrieved his clothes, once more the old François. "What of that one?" he muttered, his gaze flinging daggers at Caine's back.

Bliss glanced toward Caine. His tousled, sable hair was painted with streaks of golden candlelight. He was an enigma to her, yet she could not seem to shake her fascination for him.

Turning back to François, she said, "He'll be following on your heels."

"Are you sure you would not like me to put a few lumps on his thick skull? Nothing would give me greater pleasure."

"I've retained that right for myself. But thank you anyway." She took hold of his hands and tried to smile reassuringly. "I know you were only trying to protect me."

"He's the one, isn't he?"

Bliss's first thought was to utter a denial, but she knew François would see through her. "Yes," she answered softly. "He's the one."

A flicker of reluctant interest revealed itself now that a conflict had been avoided. "I do not know what you see in him. Those muscles are ostentatious. And that face! All harsh planes and rough, brooding angles. Utterly gauche. The spawn of a long line of bare-knuckled brawlers and bourgeoisie, I suspect."

As though sensing he was the topic of their conversation, Caine glanced over at them, raising that provoking eyebrow, his grin clearly challenging.

"Barbarian," François huffed with a disdainful sniff. "I shall remain within shouting distance, should you require my help." Clothes in hand, he sailed regally out the door, the sheet trailing behind him like the robes of an emperor.

"Close the door," Caine softly commanded.

Bliss wet her lips, exhaling slowly. "No."

He leaned a shoulder against the wall, arms folded across his chest, showcasing those ostentatious muscles as though a person could possibly miss them.

She had felt them for herself not so long ago, running her hands up and down their supple strength, reveling in their barely restrained power, the way they molded her against his body, her hands clinging to them as he drove into her. She shivered.

In four long strides Caine stood face to face with her, something unreadable in his eyes. "Has he made love to you?" When Bliss remained mute, he took hold of her arms, his grip bordering on painful. "Has he?"

"No!" She wouldn't give him the satisfaction of knowing it would be a long time before she allowed another man into her bed. "Now please, just leave."

With surprising gentleness he brushed back a stray lock of her hair, the light sweep of his fingertips along her neck as intimate as a kiss.

Bliss stepped back. "I won't let you come in and out of my life, wreaking havoc with impunity. I know all about your ploy; Lady Buxton delighted in rubbing your dirty secret in my face."

He reached out and traced her cheek with his finger, the tender gesture at odds with the strange severity in his eyes. "She shouldn't have done that," he murmured, sounding almost sorry.

"Of course not." Bliss backed out of his reach. "It took the pleasure away from you."

His hand remained suspended for a moment, then dropped away. "Are you so sure I would have enjoyed it?"

"Why not? You did before. But you did warn me, didn't you? What a laugh you must have had, bringing me down a notch. Another idiotic chit throwing herself at you."

"If I recall, I threw myself at you."

He was trying to charm her. Bliss stiffened her resolve. "If you've come all this way hoping to find me steeped in regret and self-pity, you'll be sorely disappointed. Self-pity is your territory."

"Perhaps you're right."

She didn't want his agreement. She wanted him to feel as angry and hurt and betrayed as she felt. "I made love to you and I enjoyed it. You thawed the duke's frigid daughter, so count yourself a success. But having made the wrong choice with you, I'll know better than to repeat the mistake. You may have been the first, my lord, but you won't be the last."

He continued to observe her in that resigned fashion. "I didn't come here to gloat, regardless of what you think."

"Why *did* you come? Something must have motivated you, and I don't delude myself that it's concern for my feelings. That would undoubtedly be a first."

"I understand you're angry."

"I'm not angry, my lord. I'm furious."

He regarded her for a long moment, then asked quietly, "Have you given any thought to the possibility that you may be carrying my child?"

"Pray don't concern yourself. I wouldn't demand that you give me the honor of your name. I'd rather bed down with a nest of asps."

A muscle worked in his jaw, telling her how hard he was working to rein in his temper. "If you're pregnant, I'll take care of you and the babe."

"How magnanimous of you." The image of his baby at her breast while he looked on nearly broke her heart. "But in case you haven't noticed, I don't need you. What possible reason would compel me to subject myself to your ill humor?"

"Perhaps because you have some small feeling for the man who could be the father of your child."

Bliss wished it wasn't so, but she did care. She'd glimpsed sweet, vulnerable things beneath Caine's hardened exterior. But he didn't care about her. She had been a means to an end, nothing more.

"If I were pregnant, what then? Would you be performing nightly in Lady Buxton's bed to support us? For you certainly wouldn't be anywhere near mine."

The inferno that suddenly flared in his eyes was the only warning she got before his control snapped. He stepped in front of her until her spine was pressed up against the wall, his hands braced on either side of her head.

"Don't tempt me to prove how easily I could change your mind. If you didn't feel something for me, you wouldn't be acting like such a shrew. You care for me, damn you. And I . . . I feel something for you."

Bliss trembled. God, how she had missed him, the loathsome, beautiful wretch. She realized that she had been trying to incite his temper, wanting him to explode. She was too proud to tell him she wanted him to kiss her and whisper roughly in her ear that he would never let her go, as he had once before.

"The only feeling you have for me, my lord," she said with contempt, "is between your legs." She boldly laid her hand against the front of his trousers, the heaviness surging hotly against her palm telling her that she still affected him.

He hissed sharply through his teeth, the fire in his eyes blazing nearly out of control as he moved against her, leaving her no escape as he molded her body between his hot, hard form and the wall.

Her breath was suspended in her throat as she gazed up at him in challenge. She nearly sobbed with relief when his mouth came down on hers, the contact sending sparks everywhere.

Seventeen

When there is no peril in the fight,
there is no glory in the triumph.
Pierre Corneille

*H*e kissed her fiercely, his mouth opening over hers, his hips grinding against her, letting her feel the hard press of his arousal that she had so brazenly caressed.

His hands seemed to be everywhere, not allowing her a moment to catch her breath, forcing every hungry, eager thing from her soul.

Bliss tried to retain a shred of defiance, tried not to give Caine what he wanted. But he took hold of her arms and settled them at his shoulders, leaving her hands in reach of temptation—the firm contours of his shoulders; the warm, pliant length of his neck; and that hair, that soft, untamed hair that begged someone to caress the smooth strands, to run it through her fingers and then tighten it in her grasp, bringing his head down even closer, his groans mingling with her soft cries until the world around them was no more substantial than a wisp of smoke.

She was drowning in him, consumed by his heat, the taut line of his body flush against hers, powerful muscles shifting as his mouth took hers in flagrant, willful possession.

His fingers dug into her hair, loosening the heavy mass from its topknot and letting it spill down her shoulders. He grabbed a fistful and imprisoned her with it, tugging her head back so that he could taste the curve of her neck, the sensitive spot behind her ear. An aching pant built at the back of her throat. He captured the sound with his mouth.

Her heart beat a wild tattoo, excitement coursing through her veins as Caine tilted her mouth up to his; a piercing ecstasy arrowed from her nipples to her belly and blossomed between her thighs.

But behind her closed eyes, images began to invade: flashes of Caine with other women, disarming their inhibitions as he was so masterfully doing with her, all of them succumbing to his seduction, all of them feeling the sinuous strength of his body, writhing beneath his expert touch, their faces blurring and then sharpening into one.

Olivia Hamilton.

The woman's cold, mocking countenance appeared before Bliss's eyes, her cruel words ringing like a piercing knell that tore at her heart.

He spends a good deal of time plotting revenge against those who have wronged him. And you, I'm afraid, were an irresistible target.

Bliss tore her mouth away. "Leave me alone." She shoved at him, and then again, until her fists were pounding against his chest.

He grabbed hold of her wrists, manacling them at her

side, his breathing labored and his eyes heavy-lidded with passion as he stared down at her. "Stop it."

"Let go of me."

He hesitated, and then with a wordless sound of frustration, he released her. Bliss escaped to the other side of the room before facing him again.

"Wasn't once enough for you?" she said, despising the slight catch in her voice. "You've vindicated yourself. You've taken my virginity as your prize. Your father's memory has been avenged. What else do you want?"

Silence filled the room as Caine regarded her, his gaze embracing and damning all at once. "Perhaps," he finally said, his voice slicing through the quiet void to pierce her heart, "it's you I want."

The confession stunned Bliss, a pang of joy flickering to life inside her. But she couldn't believe him. She wouldn't. He was toying with her again.

"Why?" she asked angrily. "Is there some other family member you believe my father has wronged?"

He walked to the window and looked out. Clouds laced the night sky, their shadows briefly filtering across his face before moving on. Slowly, he turned to her, the moonlight exaggerating the chiseled lines of his jaw. His mouth was firm, his eyes a tumult of emotion she could only guess at.

"This is no longer about my father or yours," he said.

"Isn't it? You made it about our fathers the moment you set out to seduce me."

"I tried to stop."

"Does passion come so easily to you, my lord, that you can simply turn it on and off at a whim? Did you desire me even a little? Or are you so adept at seducing women that you can make them believe they mean something to you?"

His jaw tensed. "You know I wanted you, damn it."

"A lust for revenge and too much alcohol has the power to motivate even the most reluctant individual."

"Revenge had nothing to do with what happened between us."

"You'll forgive me if I disagree." Bliss realized her hands were gripping her skirt. She dropped the material and forced her feet to move. "So tell me, what truly prompted your visit today? Have you discovered you only have a week to live and must now make amends before God? Or did a sudden bout of conscience miraculously overwhelm you?"

"According to you, I have no conscience."

At the dark note in his voice, Bliss glanced at him, uneasy at the way he seemed to track her movements.

"Whatever your reasons for coming here, you've at least given me the opportunity to tell you what I think." She faced him, her voice trembling with anger. "I don't believe your claims about my father. He would never intentionally set out to hurt anyone. He is not that kind of person." She could have told him about the letter, perhaps offered to let him read it, but she wouldn't give him the satisfaction of knowing she had doubted her father for even a moment. "I'm sorry about what happened to your father. I truly am. But I won't take the blame."

The shadows enshrouded all but his eyes, intensely blue and determined. "I took my anger out on you. I had convinced myself I hated you. But somewhere along the way . . ." He paused, his voice sounding weary as he said, "Somewhere along the way, things changed. Once you were gone . . ."

"You realized you had lost your whipping post," she finished bitterly.

He gritted his teeth, his expression stony. "No, I realized I had made a mistake."

The admission stopped her short. Then she remembered she was dealing with a master manipulator and seducer. "Forgive me if I'm not flattered, but I never want to see you again."

She whirled on her heels, her skirt making a furious snap as she started for the door. In a flash, Caine reached her and spun her around to face him.

"I think the kiss we shared a few moments ago says you feel otherwise."

"Think what you will. If you'll excuse me, you've interrupted my work and chased off my model."

"So that's what that buffoon was doing here? Modeling for you?"

"Yes."

"Then I think it only fair to make it up to you by offering myself as a replacement." One corner of his lips lifted, sinful intent in his expression as he shrugged out of his jacket, the expensive material falling in a dark pool at his booted feet.

"W-what are you doing?"

"Disrobing." He divested himself of his waistcoat next, that unprincipled grin daring her to stand her ground.

"Well, stop it."

He ignored her, his gaze holding her immobile as he undid his cuff links, each one making a small ping as it hit the floor. Then his hand rose to pull away the cravat around his neck, the snowy white material drifting to the floor in slow motion. He unbuttoned his shirt in the same unhurried fashion, revealing his heavily muscled chest inch by tantalizing inch.

As much as Bliss tried to look away, she couldn't. And when his shirt whispered to the floor to join his other belongings, leaving him standing in a golden glow of lamplight, her palms began to sweat.

The moment he reached for the top button on his trousers, she found her voice. "Don't!"

"Why not?" Caine asked in a silky tone, noting the heightened color on her cheeks, and the way her tongue darted out to lick her dry lips, the quick rise and fall of her chest. "Scared?"

He closed in on her, taking perverse delight in the way her eyes devoured him, making him disintegrate in little pieces. That look had been what had haunted his dreams the most. Those hot eyes skimming over him, missing nothing, incapable of telling lies.

She had awakened something inside him that he couldn't face, and he had done whatever he could do to get away from it, allowing himself to believe what he felt for her was still hate.

But once she was gone, and one empty day melted into the next, he realized hate had stopped being a factor. He had missed her—her smile, the way she smelled, how she walked, how she stood up to him. Hell, he had even missed the way she could whip him into shape with that sharp tongue of hers.

But what he had missed the most was the way she felt in his arms, how she fit, and how she held nothing back when he kissed her.

He wanted that again. She couldn't hide her true self from him when he touched her. She wasn't experienced enough in playing the game to know how to disguise her emotions.

He reached into his pocket to retrieve the item he had brought with him. "Remember this?" he asked.

Her eyes widened, slow heat flushing her cheeks. "That's my garter." Her gaze lifted to his, those pretty eyes mortified. "Where did you get it?"

"Off your thigh." The telling blush on her face rose to new heights and Caine smiled to himself, knowing she was thinking he had taken it the night they had made love. He would enjoy enlightening her. "You don't hold your alcohol at all well, love. Any number of unscrupulous scoundrels might take advantage of that fact."

It took only a moment for understanding to blossom. "Are you saying . . ."

"That I undressed you when you were too intoxicated to do so yourself?" He smiled as an answer. "You do make a fetching drunk, sweetheart. Quite hard to resist." As she was at that moment, with embarrassment and rising anger sparking in her eyes. "All and all, I consider myself a rather noble fellow."

"Noble!" she exclaimed in a furious tone.

"Had you seen how tempting you looked with the moonlight bathing your skin, and your breasts so luscious . . . Besides, it was either myself or St. Giles, and I'd like to think you would have preferred me."

"I would have preferred neither of you!" she fumed, and in the same breath, "He was in my room, too?"

"It was a busy evening."

"He wouldn't have . . ."

"Let's just say sleep wasn't on his mind."

She shivered, comprehension dawning on her. "The bruise on the earl's jaw . . . You hit him, didn't you?"

"Would it dilute my chivalry if I said I enjoyed it immensely?"

"I don't understand you."

"A common lament, I'm afraid. But what is uppermost in my mind at this moment is exactly what form your gratitude might take. I was thinking that you could put your mouth against mine, maybe run your fingers through my hair and whimper a little bit. You know the whimper I mean, that soft—"

"I want it back," she demanded, holding out her hand. "Please give it to me."

" 'It,' as in the garter?"

"Yes," she snapped.

"I don't know," he said tauntingly, working his way around her desk, trying not to startle her into bolting as he closed the distance between them. "I've developed a fondness for it." He stroked the silk across his lips; taking pleasure in the way Bliss's gaze followed his action, her breathing shallow. "But I might be willing to part with it—on one condition."

"Which is?"

He grinned wolfishly. "If I can put it back where I found it."

Her cheeks flamed with color. "Absolutely not," she retorted hotly, lifting that stubborn chin and staring down her pert nose at him, a rather impressive feat, considering her lack of height.

"Guess I'll have to keep it, then." Caine continued to casually stalk her until the backs of her legs came up against the edge of the bed.

Her gaze shot to the door, that lovely closed door, all the way across the room. He could see she was calculating the distance, wondering if she could make it to freedom before he was upon her.

"Don't try it, sweetheart." His fingers slid around her wrist and he stared down into her furious, beautiful face, committing to memory the exotic tilt of her brows, the blunt perfection of her nose, the siren's lashes that framed eyes whose glare was lethal.

He realized that somewhere along the way, the neat lesson he had once planned for her had turned on him. He was at her mercy.

"Did you miss me?" he murmured, gently shaping the soft flesh beneath his hand.

"Not in the least." Her breath fanned his skin in warm, soft pants that roused his desire.

"Your eyes tell me a different story." He tipped her chin up with his forefinger and saw the pulse leap at the base of her throat.

Bliss jerked her head away, praying only fury showed in her eyes. "Really? And what are they telling you now?"

He smiled, a chastened half grin that did strange things to her heart. "They're telling me that you hope I suddenly burst into a ball of flame and wither into a pile of ashes at your feet."

"Nothing so mild as that, I'm afraid."

He laughed softly. "That may be true, but it still doesn't change the fact that you want to kiss me."

"Have you always been given to such delusional thinking?"

His warm breath caressed her cheek as he leaned down to say, "I find myself nearly insane where you're concerned."

For the space of a heartbeat, he almost had her believing in him again. Then she blinked and rational thought was restored. "You want another tumble," she charged.

A spark of anger flared in his eyes, belying the casualness of his words. "Of course. I traveled all this way just for the privilege of climbing between your sweet thighs and easing into your slick, tight heat, to feel your nails scoring my back as you arch up against me, your pretty nipples teasing my chest, your legs squeezing my flanks, your hips tipped up to sweetly receive every last primed inch of me—"

"That's enough!"

"—when there are hundreds, perhaps even thousands of women between here and Devon whom I could have plowed, who would have willingly tossed up their skirts instead of clawing and hissing at me."

"You've made your point," she said breathlessly, betrayed by the images his words aroused. "You'll forgive me if I'm not properly appreciative of your devotion, considering it is so fleeting and unpredictable. I suggest you use your powers of persuasion on one of your other women. Someone without a brain in her little head. Now, step aside."

The regal demand only incited Caine's hunger for her. And he knew then that he wanted to hear her say that she loved him. Perhaps the reasons no longer had anything to do with Olivia and her damn wager.

He didn't even know himself anymore. Every day, it seemed he understood less and less what motivated him. After Bliss was gone he'd convinced himself he was better off, that even though he hadn't succeeded in getting his home back, he had still reaped his revenge. But it hadn't brought any peace to his soul.

He had been forced to recognize that the absolution he was searching for had to come from within. All this time, he had been looking outside himself to mitigate the weight of the guilt pressing in on him, to find someone else to take the fall. But even though he had reached a milestone in the slow, painful progress toward redemption, he was still not ready to let go of the blame. He could not yet forgive himself.

"Are you sure you don't want to give me another go, since I'm here?" he asked provocatively, blowing a loose tendril away from her cheek, smiling inwardly at the slight shiver that chased over her skin.

"The only thing I want is to see your back as you leave."

"Fine," he consented, his sigh sounding sufficiently martyred. "I'll go. But I require one thing before I leave." He closed the small distance between her lips and his, and tasted her sweetness.

Her hands fluttered like the wings of a dove before settling into the crook of his neck. Every muscle in his body trembled in response. God, how he had missed the simple pleasure of her touch. No matter what he did, he had not been able to put the feel of her from his mind.

He had not touched Olivia since Bliss left. Olivia thought he was angry that she'd ruined his chance to get back Northcote, but it had stopped being about the damn house the moment Bliss had surrendered to him, as she did now, her soft whimper spiking his temperature.

He nudged her back until she sank down onto the bed, her head tipped up for his kiss. His hands fisted into the coverlet to keep hold of his sanity, when what he really wanted was to drive his body against hers and bring out the passion she only revealed when they were like this.

It took his fuzzy brain a moment to realize Bliss had stiffened and pulled away from him. It took another moment to realize that the startled sound he heard had not come from her.

Slowly, Caine turned his head and discovered a petite, auburn-haired woman staring wide-eyed at him, the doorknob in her hand, as though the sight she witnessed had frozen her in place.

The woman appeared to be an older version of Bliss, who now sat stock-still on the bed . . . while he hovered over her, half-dressed and looking anything but saintly in his intentions.

"*Pardon*," the woman said, her soft voice tinged with a French accent. "I am interrupting."

Caine didn't expect her nonchalant attitude. He had envisioned a different scenario entirely, one that entailed his body parts littering the floor, the most rigid member of his anatomy the first to go.

Bliss, plague take her, didn't do a single thing to ease his discomposure. Instead she sat there, her lips bruised from his kiss, appearing to all the world like a virgin about to be sacrificed on the altar of lust.

"Should I go?" the woman inquired, an amused smile playing about her lips as her gaze moved between the two of them.

"No, Mama," Bliss said, confirming Caine's suspicions, a groan strangling in his throat. "His lordship was just leaving." She looked up at him, daring him to say otherwise. "Weren't you, my lord?"

"Yes . . . I was just leaving." He retrieved his clothes

much quicker than he'd divested himself of them, and Bliss had to stifle a laugh. Never had she thought to see the day when the mighty Earl of Hartland looked like a shame-faced lad caught red-handed with his fingers in the pie.

He fumbled, dropping first his cravat and then his waistcoat on his way to the door, which he practically dove through. Had Bliss known that all she needed to do to make him leave was call in her mother, she might have done so before he had kissed her—though in truth, that was doubtful.

She should be ashamed of herself, but she had missed him desperately. Missed the way he kissed her, with rough tenderness, and the way his large hands never remained still when he touched her, and how the slight stubble on his jaw gently rasped her cheeks when he hadn't shaved, and how the deep cadence of his voice never failed to make her skin tingle. She had even missed his gruff barbs and brooding looks.

Yet the man she had met today was a far greater danger to her heart. An angry, mocking Caine she could defend herself against. But not a Caine whose eyes held a differ-ent light, whose words bespoke a newfound tenderness, who could easily charm if he so desired.

"So that is the man you have been mooning over?"

Her mother's voice roused Bliss from her reverie, and she heard herself repeating what she'd told François. "I'm not mooning." She smoothed an imaginary wrinkle in her skirt. "Between you and François, I don't know who's worse."

Her mother tipped her face up, regarding her with knowing green eyes. "François and I are French, my love. We know all about—"

"Mooning. Yes, I know. But you are both wrong. The

day I moon over that irritating, sapheaded, arrogant . . ." Bliss searched for words.

"Handsome?" her mother supplied.

"Highhanded boor," Bliss countered, "is the day I will become a model of feminine behavior."

"If you say so, daughter," she replied, with an airy shrug. "But you are hopelessly infatuated, nonetheless."

"I am not!" Bliss protested far too vehemently.

Her mother spoke over her denial. "I have found infuriating men to be the most passionate, and quite often the most devoted of lovers. It comes from an excess of pride and an overwhelming virility. And from what I saw, that lovely specimen possesses those traits in abundance. You really should have painted him nude. I imagine he is stunningly built."

"Mama!"

Her mother glanced at her, all innocence. "This bothers you, *ma douce?* Such conversations never disturbed you in the past."

Bliss shrugged helplessly. "This is different."

"Ah." Her mother nodded. "You have feelings for this man. I knew something had transpired during your trip to England. You returned with the look of the lovelorn." She sat down on the bed and took hold of Bliss's hand. "Tell me what happened."

When Bliss was a child, her mother had the uncanny ability to get her to confess every wrongdoing simply by giving her that look that said she could confide anything—which she usually did.

Bliss capitulated with a resigned sigh. "I might have felt something for him. Something small and hardly worth mentioning, as I don't feel it anymore."

"*Non?* Your eyes, my love, they give you away. They always have." Her words mirrored Caine's, and Bliss decided she would have to start wearing a blindfold. "You still feel strongly about this man. I wish I'd had the opportunity to speak with him. He must be quite spectacular to have ensnared you so thoroughly."

"He has not ensnared me. And he is not spectacular! He's a liar, and a cheat, and a bully."

"All that?" A note of amusement laced her mother's voice.

Bliss sprang up from the bed and whirled around to face her mother. "Just once, I wish you'd be like other mothers and swoon or cry, or take something heavy and smash him over the head."

Her mother folded her hands in her lap and regarded her. "You have never needed me to smash anyone over the head, most especially a man."

Bliss held onto her indignation for another moment, then sighed and flopped back down on the bed. "Well, maybe this time I do."

"This sounds very bad."

"It's horrible. I shouldn't feel a thing for him."

"But you do, *oui?*"

"It makes no sense whatsoever. He used me and then made a fool out of me, and still, every time he's near, I . . ."

"Feel lightheaded?"

"Yes. It's utterly preposterous."

"My love, take what I am about to impart in the kindest of terms, from mother to daughter." She patted Bliss's hand gently, her smile warm as she said, "You are being a ninny."

Bliss's mouth opened on a protest, which her

mother forestalled with a raise of her hand. "Stop pushing everyone away, or someday you'll be all alone. Like me."

"I'm not pushing anyone away!"

"Whenever a man has shown the slightest interest in you, you have found a way to punish him in some form."

"I have not!"

"What about Jacques? He adored you, would have thrown rose petals at your feet for the rest of your life had you but given him an encouraging word, yet you barely acknowledged his existence."

"He was only two inches taller than me!"

"So now your affections are based on a man's height?" Her mother shook her head. "I did not think this was how I had raised you."

"It was more than that. He was . . . boring."

"Perhaps, but he cherished you."

"He could speak of nothing beyond banking."

"But when you spoke, he hung on your every syllable."

"He slurped his tea."

"He thought the sun rose and set at your feet."

"He had hair in his ears!"

"He existed just to see you smile."

"He—"

Her mother's soft laugh cut her off. "So many excuses," she said with a knowing smile. "You must face the truth this time. You have met your match in this Englishman, and you were looking for a reason to break free. He may have used you, as you say, but I imagine you had a hand in your own downfall. I know you too well, *ma petite*. No man could ever take advantage of you if you were not willing. If he forced you, of course, we will take action. He shall be imprisoned in the *Conciergerie* this very evening. Are you telling me that you were not willing?"

Bliss shivered at the thought of anyone being sent to the *Conciergerie*. It was a bleak, dismal place, and had a bloody history. Nearly three thousand men and women had been imprisoned there during the Revolution before they were beheaded.

Hugging herself, she glanced away from her mother. "No, he didn't force me."

"Tell me what happened." Her mother waited patiently for her to begin. Bliss poured out the whole story, including the revelation Olivia had made. Her mother digested the tale before saying, "Your young man sounds greatly troubled. Quite a bit like your father at the same age."

Bliss stared. "Father? Why, he's the soul of morality! He's nothing like Caine."

"There is much you don't know about your father. He was quite the man about town once."

Bliss couldn't picture her sweet but stuffy father being anything close to a rake. "Perhaps you're exaggerating just a bit? I suppose all men have their reckless moments," she said dubiously.

"Oh, your father was indeed reckless." A wistful smile flickered across her lips. "A true hellion. Big and bold and arrogant and ready to fight anything or anyone."

"*My* father?"

Her mother nodded, her eyes alight with remembrance. "He came into my life like a whirlwind, and though I was quite able to stand up to him, when other women simply flapped their fans coyly and swooned ridiculously whenever he smiled, I knew I could not resist him forever. In truth, my heart belonged to him from the first moment I saw him, though I denied it until he forced me to realize what I felt. He took my virginity beneath that ancient Scots pine by the stream on the edge of Exmoor's borders."

Bliss could do no more than gape at her mother, who chuckled at her stunned expression. "I never thought to see the day when I left my headstrong daughter speechless."

"Well, you can hardly blame me. You've never told me any of this."

"I never felt the need to do so, until now. There are so few times these days when I have the opportunity to impart any wisdom. You do not need me as much as you did when you were a little girl."

Bliss gently squeezed her hand. "I'll always need you."

Her mother smiled lovingly at her. "And I, you. But perhaps I should have stepped in earlier, when I saw how you closed yourself off from men who became too interested in you. I fear that perhaps you did not want to end up like me, separated from the man you love."

Bliss felt as though she was finally getting a glimpse inside her mother's heart. "Do you really still love Papa?"

"Yes, *ma douce,*" she said softly. "I still love him. And I suspect I always will."

The question that had haunted Bliss since she was ten years old and standing motionless in the hallway listening to the horrible fight between her parents, believing she was the cause of it, lodged in her throat. She had run away from the truth then, and she was still running from it now. To speak the words would make it real.

Warmth glowed in her mother's eyes. "When a woman falls in love, she follows her heart, even if it might not be the most sensible thing to do—as you already know. Men are fickle creatures. Ask for marriage, and they will run faster than the wind to elude the bond. Show the same disinterest they do, and they cannot get you to the altar fast enough."

Bliss shook her head. "This is all quite a bit to take."

Her mother's arms encircled her shoulders. "Would you prefer me to swoon like a proper mother, so you may revive me accordingly?"

Bliss laughed. "Thank you for the offer, but I believe I can muddle on."

Her mother gave her arm a reassuring pat. "I always knew you could. You are very much like me, my love: you like your angels fallen. Have faith that the answer will come to you when you are ready to hear it."

Eighteen

I presume you're mortal, and may err.
James Shirley

The *Cimetière du Père Lachaise* was Paris's largest and most impressive cemetery, with its grand gothic architecture and ornate tombs, their extraordinary statues rising up from beds of granite as though they had heard a noise or had turned to stone without warning in the midst of a dance.

The mournful image of Jacob Robles peered at Bliss as she strolled down the *Rue du Repos*, his face and gesture of finger to lips invoking a reverent silence.

The residents' most faithful companions, the hundreds of cats that made *Lachaise* their home, rested peacefully in the shade of trees or on the tops of headstones.

Bliss breathed the cool, crisp air deeply as she walked, the serenity a balm to her soul. The French did not consider cemeteries depressing, or fascination for them morbid or unnatural, but rather an extension of life itself.

And *Lachaise* was one of the lovelier burial places, especially now as dusk fell, painting the sky with vivid streaks of light plum and dark sapphire, ribbons of crimson-gold sparking hints of fire amid the silvery gray headstones, and fingers of mist rising from the dew-laden grass, the remnants of a light afternoon shower.

Today she needed to feel her grandparents' presence, to hear in the stillness and silence the words of advice they would impart, perhaps hoping they would lessen the guilt she felt about her role in the dissolution of her parents' marriage, and to help her sort out the confusion she felt over Caine.

When he had left the night before, she had thought he would return, materialize in that startling way of his, and tell her again that he had missed her. She had remained home all day under the pretext of working, but he had never appeared.

Perhaps he had returned to Devon, whatever reason that had prompted him to come to Paris dissolving upon seeing her. And wasn't that what she wanted? For him to leave? If only he hadn't come in the first place and reopened the wound, forcing her to think about him, to want him.

All night Bliss had told herself that she would not have succumbed to his kisses, yet he had managed to position her on the bed with devastating speed.

Had her mother not arrived when she did, Bliss could not say what might have happened—which frightened her desperately. She feared her mother might be right, and Caine was the one man she would not be able to put from her mind.

Have faith, she had said. Perhaps that was what Bliss truly hoped to find here.

Her thoughts heavy, she turned down the final tree-lined path, her steps echoing faintly on the flagstone. She came to a stop in front of two tombs nestled side by side, the figure of a man carved on top of the first and a woman on the other, captured at the height of their youth and vitality, their bodies turned toward each other for all eternity.

Bliss pressed a hand to the hard stone, a sudden aching wrench of emotion tugging at her heart. "*Bonsoir, Grandmama et Grandpapa,*" she murmured, removing the wilted flowers from her last visit and replacing them with fresh sweet williams and larkspur.

She sat down on the small marble bench at the foot of their graves. The last time she had seen them alive she had been ten years old, and France had been in the middle of a building revolution that would usher in the Second Republic.

Her grandfather had been gravely ill, and her mother had decided to visit, fearing that once the borders were closed, she would not see him before he died. Bliss had been determined to go with her to France. Her father protested that it was too dangerous, but her mother had defied his edict and they had gone, traveling clandestinely to keep out of the arms of rebelling factions.

What happened that December changed her life forever. She had lost both her grandparents within a week, and afterwards, her parents' abiding love for one another had irrevocably begun to crumble.

If only she had heeded her father and stayed home where she belonged. If only she hadn't been so headstrong, perhaps her father would not have blamed her mother for nearly getting herself and his only child killed.

A tear slid down Bliss's cheek, falling on to her sketch-pad, the wet spot blossoming as other tears mingled with it. She could not seem to stop them. She didn't want to end up like her parents—alone, unhappy, full of pride that would not allow either of them to heal old wounds. But she feared she was heading down the same path.

The sensation of being watched brought her head up, a pang of awareness propelling her to her feet. She whirled around to face the intruder, her heart lurching in her chest.

And there, only a few feet away, was Caine, his body cast in moving shadows of dark and light, an elegant silhouette against the backdrop of the descending sun, standing as still as one of the statues and regarding her with unfathomable eyes.

"Y-you frightened me," she told him, tears stinging the back of her eyes, emotions threatening to bubble forth.

"I'm sorry," he said quietly. "I didn't mean to startle you. I thought you heard me walk up."

She didn't want him to see her like this, yet she ached to lean her head against his shoulders and allow her tears to fall.

She averted her gaze for a moment and blinked them away. "What are you doing here?"

"I saw you leaving your house as I was arriving, and I followed you."

"Why?"

"I want to apologize to you." Shadows hugged the sleek curves and hollows of his face, the fading light creating dancing patterns on the ground between them. "It isn't my strongest suit," he admitted with an uneasy smile. "I haven't had a great deal of practice. I know I bungled things yesterday. It's just that when I saw you and the Frog—"

"His name's François."

His disgruntled look almost made Bliss smile. He stuffed his hands into his pockets. "I got a little crazy. I'm sorry." He looked at her through those indecently long lashes, his eyes penitent as he softly added, "For everything."

In that moment, it might have been easy for her to forgive him. Part of her wanted to believe that what had begun as a means of striking out at her father had turned into something else along the way.

It truly frightened her, how much she wanted him. Nothing in her life had prepared her for Caine, and nothing had ever made her so afraid.

She turned from him, the words to send him away not coming as they should. A moment ticked by, then he came up behind her, his body a solid wall of heat against her back. She could feel his chest rising and falling, his scent, so masculine and evocative, enveloping her.

"Tell me why you were crying when I arrived," he murmured in a tone that was hard to resist.

Bliss shook her head, pain resurfacing at the reminder.

"Whose graves are these?"

She closed her eyes briefly and tried to breathe past the tight knot in her chest. "My grandparents."

"You miss them."

"Very much," she said, despair creeping into her voice. "I only got to see them a few times the year before they . . ." She bit her lip to keep it from trembling. "The year before they died," she finished.

Caine's fingers lightly traced her temple. "But you still have fond memories of them, don't you?"

"Yes."

"Tell me what you remember most."

Bliss hesitated, glancing down at her hands. "My grandmother liked to sing," she heard herself say. "She had a wonderful voice, a pure soprano. She was always smiling. Always happy."

An image of her grandparents unfolded in her mind's eye and brought with it a tide of emotions. How she wanted them back. She would do things differently this time. Not make so many mistakes.

"My grandfather had a way of captivating people with his stories. He would recount the legends and struggles of the First Republic with such passion and fire. He gave me an appreciation for the plight of the underdog."

"They sound like wonderful people."

"They were. They cared deeply about many issues and hated injustice of any sort. It was through their eyes that I started seeing the world differently, though I expressed my feelings through my art."

"I saw some of your work last night. You're very talented." He paused for a moment. "May I?" He gestured to her sketchpad that sat on the marble bench.

Bliss hesitated. Rarely had she shared her personal work with anyone. "Yes," she finally murmured.

He stepped away and took hold of the book, her private diary of the life that existed outside the sanctuary of the cemetery walls. Opening the first page, he studied the drawing, and then looked at her, an expression in his eyes Bliss had never seen before. Sorrow and compassion.

"Her name was Fantine," she said to his unspoken

question. "She was a shoe-stitcher. I came across her begging for credit at the butcher's shop. The owner turned her away."

"What happened to her face?"

"Her husband beat her," Bliss replied, her voice flat with the sickening taste of the words. "He would spend what little money they had drinking at the tavern, and then stumble in the door expecting his supper to be on the table. When it wasn't, he blamed her, as though she had any control over his squandering. It didn't seem to matter to him that his children had little or nothing to eat."

Caine cursed beneath his breath. "The son of a bitch should be hung from his testicles," he said fiercely. Bliss only wished the solution could have been that simple. "So where is this woman now?" he asked.

Bliss closed her eyes. "She's dead. She had to find a way to feed her family, and began selling her body down along the Faubourgs. One of the men got too rough and strangled her."

"Jesus."

"Her children are at a workhouse now." She opened her eyes and met Caine's concerned regard. "Do you know anything about the workhouses?"

"Not enough."

"They're horrible. Most people would rather eke out whatever existence they can find on the streets, than submit to the near starvation and indignities such places foster." Bliss would never forget the overwhelming sense of sorrow that had pervaded the dank walls and dirty faces when she had gone with the vicar to visit the children. "They're like prisons, with the workers allowed few visitors and often subjected to strict discipline, many of them separated from their families."

"Can't the government do anything about it?"

"The government sanctions it. And even if there are complaints, they turn a deaf ear." Bliss flipped to the next page in her sketchbook, showing him a picture of a little girl, her once cherubic face frozen in a mask of pain. "She has phossy jaw. It's a form of necrosis caused by the phosphorous the match-tippers handle. They allow children as young as seven and eight years old to work alongside adults, twelve to fourteen hours a day for ludicrous wages, shut up in unhealthy workrooms, beyond the reach of either air or light or sunshine."

Caine rubbed a hand over his eyes, as though the sight was too much even for him. The remaining sketches were all similar, faces of hungry women and children, many of them working by the light of a single candle, their hands raw and chapped.

"Isn't there anything anyone can do about this?"

"Care," Bliss replied. "Our society punishes the poor, as if poverty is the result of laziness alone, not of misfortune caused by hard times or other circumstances beyond the person's control."

"It's clear you care a great deal about their plight."

"I paint them, but what have I really done for them?"

"You've also spoken up on their behalf."

"But my voice is not enough. I'm a woman; I can't change the laws. And I don't possess the same strength my grandparents had. If they believed in something, they fought for it staunchly."

"You're a lot like them."

She shook her head and glanced up at the night sky,

stars beginning to shine through the velvet canopy. "I try to be as steadfast as they were in their beliefs, but I'm on the outside looking in, capturing emotions and feelings on canvas, but never expressing them from the heart."

Caine's finger whispered down her neck, his nearness almost an embrace. "I've never known a woman who is more passionate about something she believes in. You took me on, didn't you? If you can do that, you can do anything. You should show your art. Let the world see this cruelty for itself."

Bliss lowered her gaze and wrapped her arms around her waist. "I don't know."

Caine held his hand out to her, palm up, a tender offering of support. The unexpectedness of it nearly made her cry. She put her hand in his. The pads of his fingers slipped along hers, sending a frisson of awareness through her before his hand closed over hers, brown and firm and strong, his warmth taking away the coldness that seemed to go bone deep.

"What does that inscription say?" he quietly asked, gesturing to the epitaph on her grandmother's headstone.

Bliss gazed at the words that had been etched in the marble. *ILS FURENT ÉMERVEILLÉS DU BEAU VOYAGE QUI LES MENA JUSQU'AU BOUT DE LA VIE.* "They marveled at the beauty of the voyage that brought them to the end of life," she softly recited.

"It's a wonderful sentiment."

"Yes. They loved each other quite a bit." Her voice shook and Caine gave her fingers a reassuring squeeze, resting his cheek against her hair. "They died within a week of each other. My grandfather was already ill, but I believe my grandmother's unexpected death made him give up the battle and let go. He had lost the most important reason he had to stay alive."

"It must have been devastating for you to lose two people you loved so suddenly."

"It was."

"How did your grandmother die?"

"She was killed."

"I'm sorry," he murmured, pressing a light kiss to her temple.

The tears Bliss had been trying to hold back began to trickle down her cheeks. "It was so peaceful that day," she said. "But looking back, I realize that it was more of an unsettling silence."

"Can you tell me what happened?"

She hesitated, but the memories poured out of her. "The tension that had been building between the government and the people had escalated. The district around the *Rue Montmartre* and the *Rue du Temple* stirred with growing anger. Dozens of barricades suddenly sprang up; some occupied by more than a hundred guardsmen with rifles. I could see the soldiers from the window of my grandparents' home." She shivered in remembrance.

Caine's arm came around her waist, holding her close. "You must have been terrified."

"I don't think I understood what was happening. I remember feeling strangely detached, as though I was watching the scene from outside myself. My mother forbade me to come along when she and my grandmother went out into the street, but I followed them anyway, keeping far enough back so that they wouldn't see me.

"A woman stood on the summit of the hill. She was

reading a proclamation written by Victor Hugo. Several hundred people gathered to listen. Nearly a thousand of the king's men stood guard."

"What happened then?" Caine gently coaxed.

"I heard the cathedral bells of *Notre Dame* chime the hour. It was three o'clock. A moment later, someone shouted, "Long live the Republic!" and then a shot rang out, no one knew from where. While the crowd stampeded, the soldiers fired on them.

"The entire incident lasted no more than five minutes, but in the end, a dozen people lay dead in the streets. I can still see the unblinking stare of an elderly man stretched out against the curb, still holding his umbrella, and a young boy whose body had been riddled with gunshot . . . and my grandmother."

Her tears began to fall in earnest. "It didn't seem possible. I thought that it was a nightmare and I would wake up any minute. I stood there, unable to move, my mother kneeling by her side, a terrible keening sound coming from her. I was frozen to the spot, staring down into my grandmother's eyes as the light faded from them. I remember thinking that she would get up and the nightmare would be over. There was only a small bloodstain on her chest, surely not enough to fell a woman who had survived so much.

"She reached for my hand then, but I couldn't take it. I knew she was saying goodbye and I didn't want her to go." A sob broke from her lips. "It was my last chance and I . . . I let it slip away."

Caine turned her around and enfolded her tightly in his arms, letting her cry. His fingers twined in her loose hair, holding her there, his other hand gently caressing the nape of her neck.

They stayed that way for long minutes. When her tears began to subside, he moved to the marble bench and sat down, pulling her onto his lap.

"Feeling better?" he murmured.

She nodded, dabbing at her eyes with the handkerchief he had slipped into her hand.

"You were only a child," he told her in a comforting tone. "You can't blame yourself for being afraid of something you didn't understand."

"I should have begged them not to go."

"How were you going to stop them?"

"I don't know," she said with a half sob. "But I should have tried. I should have told my mother to stay home when my father forbade her to come here. He knew it was too dangerous. Perhaps if I had pleaded with her she would have stayed, and then she and my grandmother would never have gone out into that street, and my mother and father would still love each other."

Caine cradled her head against his chest, his hands stroking rhythmically through her hair. When her last sniffle dwindled away, he cupped her chin and tilted her face up to his, kissing her lightly on the lips.

Love blossomed in Bliss's heart, fragile and frightening. Somewhere along the way, she had fallen for the disreputable Earl of Hartland. Who would have believed it? England's staunchest defender of women had fallen for England's staunchest defiler of women.

"If you could paint anywhere in the world," Caine said softly, twilight aglow around them, "where would it be?"

Bliss's gaze drifted to the beautiful winged angel perched atop the tomb behind them, the seraphim's stone eyes seeming to light on her in soft inquiry. "I don't know," she replied. "I suppose here. All aspiring artists seem to find their way to Paris eventually."

"You suppose? Or you're sure?" His eyes, as he stared down at her, were as dark and deep as the sky overhead. "Where else would you like to go?"

The answer came to her in an instant. "Back home. To Exmoor."

"Why?"

"Because I was happy there."

"And you're not happy now?"

"Happy enough," she murmured, touching a finger to his neckcloth, so perfectly tied, so neatly presented, as though he had eradicated the beast he had been in Devon, who took what he wanted and the devil with the consequences. And yet beneath that veneer of decadent glory, Bliss suspected both men existed, and the possibility made her weak.

"What do you miss the most?" he asked.

"A real family," she answered from her heart. "It seems a lifetime ago that I was part of one." Hearing her foolish yearning, she glanced away from him. "This must sound silly to you. I'm a grown woman now, not a child."

"Family is family, no matter what your age." He stroked the line of her jaw, coaxing her to look at him. "It was only my father and I for as long as I can remember." He glanced briefly toward the twinkling lights of the boulevard, where the dance halls were just opening their doors. "I never really knew my mother. She died when I was four."

"I'm sorry."

There was certain despair in his eyes when his gaze returned to hers. "Nothing to be sorry about. You can't miss what you never had."

"I think you can."

The expression on his face became intent. "Tell me what you see when you look at me."

It was the easiest question he had ever asked her. "I see a man who has been devastated," she said in a soft voice. "Who's haunted. Pained. Who makes me weak, but also makes me strong. Who's compassionate when no one's looking. Cruel when he's hurting. Gentle when he wants to be tough."

He stared at her for a long moment, as if she had succeeded in rendering him speechless. Then he touched his finger to the corner of her mouth. "You accused me once of never asking for something I wanted."

Bliss's pulse quickened, her voice breathless as she said, "And what is it that you want?"

"A kiss to begin with," he murmured, his hand sliding under her hair to take hold of her nape and lifting her mouth up to his. "Then I want your heart."

Nineteen

It is not enough to conquer;
One must know how to seduce.

Voltaire

Caine's mouth covered her soft gasp of surprise, his words making hope flare in her heart as she wrapped her arms around his neck. One large hand gripped her waist, gently kneading the flesh beneath her dress, making a bonfire begin to burn brightly inside her.

He kissed her cheeks, her jaw, her throat; her body arched up against his mouth as he pressed his lips to the flesh above her bodice. He skimmed his hand along her side and up to her breast, outlining the full swell, then boldly cupping her. Bliss whimpered into his mouth at the first touch of his fingers across her nipples.

"God," he groaned. "You're so damn sweet and responsive." He nuzzled her throat, his warm lips a heady caress. Bliss whispered his name, encouraging him. He pressed his cheek against hers, his voice hoarse with restraint. "I have to stop, or else I'm going to take you right here, love."

It took Bliss a moment to realize that they were outside, where anyone might see them.

She nearly leapt off Caine's lap. His low chuckle teased her as she scrambled upright, glancing around to see if anyone was nearby. Luckily, the growing lateness of the hour had left the cemetery virtually empty.

She glanced over at Caine and noted the amused glimmer in his eyes, along with simmering passion. "You're wicked," she chided, a reluctant smile tugging at her lips at his lecherous expression, the scar on his cheek barely noticeable in the darkness.

Her gaze moved over the thin line. She hesitated, then reached out to touch it. He didn't stop her. The skin was silky beneath her fingertips, a marked contrast to the rough texture of his jaw.

"I wrote to my father," she said, feeling the tension that moved through Caine's body at her admission. "He told me that he never knew you came to see him. That if he had, he would have spoken to you." She ran her finger down the length of the scar, and felt a slight shudder wrack his frame. Then she leaned over and pressed a kiss to it.

"Bliss," he groaned, the word a plea.

"He's sorry for what happened to you, Caine . . . just as he's terribly sorry about what happened to your father. He never wished the earl harm." She paused, hoping he would say something, but he remained still and silent. "He told me to tell you that should you wish to take up your position in the House of Lords, you would have his support."

He looked at her for a long moment and Bliss braced herself, thinking he would explode, but instead he just nodded. He had listened, and he had heard her. She could ask for no more.

She shivered as a gust of cool air rippled across her skin, reminding her she had not brought her shawl. Caine shrugged out of his coat and put it around her shoulders. The warmth from his body infused the lining, the scent of sandalwood and smoke comforting as he helped her to her feet.

Bliss pressed her fingers to her lips and then placed her palm on each of her grandparent's graves. *"Je t'aime,"* she whispered, and let Caine guide her away.

They walked for a few moments in companionable silence, the wind caressing her cheeks, the hoot of an owl and the distant chorus of cats sweet music to her ears.

At the end of the footpath, Caine came to a stop. "What's that?" He nodded to the crypt in the corner, with a mournful Victorian maiden adorning the front.

"That's Chopin's grave."

"What are all the little pieces of paper there for?"

"Lovers tuck notes in the cracks. It's become a bit of a legend that the maiden is really a guardian angel."

Caine gazed speculatively at the statue and then glanced at her sketchpad. "Do you mind?"

Bliss shook her head, watching as he flipped to the back of the book, where he tore out a small square of an unused page. Using the fine edge of her charcoal drawing pencil, he scribbled something. She tried to peek over his shoulder, but he blocked her view. Then he walked over and inserted the scrap of paper into a sliver of space beneath the maiden's heel.

"What did you write?"

He smiled down at her. "That's for me and Chopin to

know." He laced his fingers through hers, refusing to satisfy her curiosity as they headed out of the cemetery and on to the boulevard, where he hailed a jarvey, giving the driver her address.

He helped her in. Bliss arranged her skirts and then glanced up to find him still standing outside, his hands shoved in his pockets, appearing uncertain.

"Are you coming?" she asked.

"Do you want me to?"

The answer came easily. "Yes." She wasn't ready to see this night end. She wanted to get to know this new and solicitous Caine Ballinger, to learn what she could about him.

The side of the conveyance dipped slightly as he climbed in and closed the door behind him, encasing them in a cocoon of darkness but for the dim glow of a single lantern mounted beside the box.

The gentle clip-clop of the horse's hooves on the cobblestones and the light swaying of the carriage lulled Bliss. Caine's long legs were stretched out on either side of hers, their eyes locked on each other, the yearning they had managed to contain still simmering beneath the surface.

"If you could be anywhere right now," she murmured, repeating a form of the question he had posed to her, "where would you be?"

The squabs beneath him creaked slightly as he leaned forward and took her hands in his, skimming his thumbs over her knuckles before slipping underneath to caress her palms in slow, rhythmic strokes.

"I'd be right where I am now," he said. He kissed her then, softly, reverently, but with a hunger that burned her.

"Caine . . ." His name whispered longingly from her lips as she brushed the back of her fingers across his cheek. He tilted his head into her palm and placed a warm kiss in the center.

"Come here." He took hold of her wrist and gently coaxed her across the small distance separating them, settling her on his lap again. "That's much better."

Lifting her hand, he kissed each of her fingers, then the inside of her wrist, working his way up her forearm and finding the sensitive flesh at the juncture of her elbow with a diligent sensuality that was maddening.

Bliss closed her eyes and sighed in grateful surrender, knowing how much she had wanted this intimacy with him. His chin skimmed over the upper swells of her breasts to the place where no material hindered his seeking lips. Then he kissed her again, hot and possessive.

He raised his head slightly, his eyes heavy-lidded as he stared down at her. His hand trembled slightly as he lifted it to her neck and splayed his fingers, nearly spanning her collarbone.

"So fragile. So sweet." His palm slid down until it was between her breasts, and Bliss bit her lip, waiting, wanting.

He began to work the small mother-of-pearl buttons free, easing her bodice down until her breasts were exposed, her nipples already erect.

"Lovely," he said, his voice hoarse with desire as he kissed each aching tip. The whispered caress made her throb with anticipation and excitement. "They're so tight and pink." He tasted her again, a long suckling that had her writhing. "They feel like silk against my tongue. And when I suck hard, they conform to my mouth, so that one flick of my tongue"—he teased the tips, creating a vortex of pleasure inside her—"and you moan my name. Yes, like that. A kittenish sound in the back of your throat. God, it makes me crazy." He lapped at the jutting points.

Bliss felt a slave to her body, craving how delicious Caine could make her feel. "The driver," she murmured hazily as the carriage began to slow.

His body shielding hers, Caine slid back the panel behind the box and called up to the coachman, "Keep going until I tell you to stop." Then he drove the panel home with a crisp thud.

"What will he think?"

"I don't give a damn. Now where were we? Ah, yes. Your beautiful nipples and how they feel in my mouth." He leaned down and drew one aching peak between his lips, his teeth lightly grazing it, heightening the sensitivity.

Bliss felt his hand at her ankle, pushing up her skirt, his warm palm skimming her calf, teasing a sensitive spot behind her knee before moving between her thighs, gently bidding her to open for him. She did.

He cupped her, sliding his middle finger through her curls to find the hot pearl within. "You feel so good," he said with a heavy groan in his throat. "But you taste even better, like rich cream. And this"—he massaged the nub in slow circles—"is like a sweet berry."

His words made a cascade of heat pour through Bliss, with visions of his mouth down there, suckling with the same delicious rhythm he used on her nipples.

He lowered his head to the curve of her neck. "Are you thinking of my mouth on you?"

"Yes," she breathed.

She could feel his smile against her skin. Then he sat her up, so that her back was to his chest.

"Put your legs over the tops of mine."

Willingly, Bliss did as he asked. He pushed her skirt up to her waist, leaving her perched on his lap like a wanton, her thighs open, her softness exposed. He shifted his legs wider, spreading her until she was taut and quivering.

He kissed her shoulder and the nape of her neck, his hands pressing against the outsides of her breasts and then molding them, pushing the peaks high and massaging them with his thumbs.

"Like how that feels?" he murmured against her ear.

"Yes," she said with a low, husky moan. "Oh, yes."

He slid one hand slowly down her stomach, her muscles trembling in anticipation as his fingers glided into her slick valley and found her throbbing nub once more.

Bliss arched back with a broken whimper, the feel of Caine's large finger against her swollen flesh so very exquisite, every nerve ending on fire. Her breasts pulled high and tight made the soft scrape of his fingers across the tips of her nipples that much more divine.

"Caine," she said in an aching voice, as her body climbed to that heavenly pinnacle.

"Yes, love. Let me feel it."

She panted as he massaged her nipples, the spread of his hand so wide he could rub both hot points at the same time, the finger stroking between her wet nether lips slipping inside her, moving back and forth while his thumb tantalized her slick sex.

"Think of me inside you," he said in a low, hoarse voice, his breath warm against her neck. "Deep inside you, as deep as I can get. Pumping like this." He slipped another finger into her and pushed hard, lifting her.

Bliss felt mindless, drugged, nothing existed besides Caine and what he was doing to her.

He watched his hands playing with her nipples, his jaw clamped tight as he rolled the tight buds, plucking and squeezing and flicking until her womb throbbed and her muscles tightened around his fingers.

"Yes, that's it," he urged, drawing her down over his arm.

With a groan, he tugged one distended peak into the hot inferno of his mouth, and with the first lash of his tongue over the aching tip, Bliss climaxed, the throbbing tremors dragged from deep inside her, one after the next, until she spiraled down to earth in the molten aftermath.

"Beautiful," he whispered against her ear, making her blush as she thought about how she had writhed against him, demanding more. "You're so incredibly lovely when you're being pleasured. I can't get enough of watching you, how passionately you respond to me, or how my hands feel against your body."

Bliss tucked her head beneath his chin, feeling uncharacteristically shy. "I want to make you feel good, too."

"You did." He tipped her head up. "Just touching you makes me hot as hell. When you came, and my fingers were inside you, that hot, wet release squeezing against me . . . Christ, I almost came right along with you. That's never happened to me before. I'm so primed for you, I'm about to explode." He nudged his groin up against her bottom to prove his claim. "But not here. Not like this. I want you in a bed with soft sheets and candles."

He kissed her nipples one last time, groaning as he

straightened. With gentle hands he fixed her bodice and tugged down her skirt, before cradling her against his chest as he had done earlier.

He eased back the panel and spoke to the driver again as Bliss lay languid and sated in his arms. She had forgiven him. He had come to Paris for her. He had missed her. Certainly that had to mean he cared for her.

A few minutes later, they came to a halt in front of Number Twelve *Rue de la Chaussée d'Antin*, her home. Caine kissed her passionately and then reluctantly returned her to the seat across from him, his hot blue eyes promising delights she could only imagine.

He took hold of her hand and placed a light kiss on the back as the driver alighted to put down the steps. Then the door swung open.

But it was not the driver who stood on the other side, staring up at them with a taunting lift of brows and that cruel smile.

But Olivia.

"Darling!" she crooned. "How devilishly naughty of you to keep me waiting. You did say to meet you here at nine sharp, didn't you? Pleasuring the little chit must have taken longer than you expected." Her gaze shifted to Bliss, the implication clear as she raked an assessing glance over her, not missing Bliss's disheveled hair and mussed clothing, or the flush on her cheeks and upper chest. "Clearly you succeeded, from the looks of things."

Bliss stood frozen on the bottom step, Caine's hand burning where it pressed against her back, his body rigid with tension. The happiness she had so recently felt began to deteriorate before her eyes.

"What the hell are you doing here, Olivia?" Caine

demanded in a furious tone, helping Bliss down the final step when her limbs refused to work.

Somewhere in her mind, Bliss realized he held on tightly to her arm as though he thought she would bolt, but she could not summon the strength to wrench away, to run up the stairs and block out both of them. To save herself from what she feared was coming.

"As I said, I was waiting for you."

"You know what I'm talking about. What are you doing here, in Paris? I left you back in Devon to rot in hell."

Olivia laughed, tapping her fan coquettishly on his forearm, as though they stood in the middle of a ball-room rather than on a dusty street. "Don't be ridiculous, darling. We arrived together."

"Get out of here, Olivia," Caine warned. "And don't come back. If I see you again, you won't like the out-come." His grip unrelenting, he dragged Bliss toward the front steps of her house.

"Oh, dear. I've arrived too soon, haven't I? She hasn't said the words yet, has she?"

Time seemed to exist outside of that moment as Bliss drew to a halt and turned her gaze up to Caine's, praying in the depths of her heart that he had not made a fool out of her again.

"Damn it, Bliss, don't listen to her. I didn't come here with her. I swear it. She's lying."

"What is it I was supposed to say?"

"Nothing. Jesus . . . It all changed, don't you see? I couldn't do it. I . . ." His face was a mask of regret and despair. "I couldn't do it."

"What couldn't you do?"

"It doesn't matter anymore. I didn't do it. I wouldn't. I told her so."

"My dear Lady Bliss . . ." Olivia reached out to console her, placing her hand lightly on Bliss's arm.

Bliss jerked back. "Don't you dare touch me," she commanded, a rising tide of fury replacing the numbness that had settled over her.

"I understand what you must be feeling," Olivia said with false sympathy, "but please don't blame Caine entirely. I fear I'm as much at fault as he is. It was only a game, you see, devised by two jaded lovers who were simply looking for some sport to relieve their ennui."

"Shut up, Olivia," Caine growled through clenched teeth.

"We've been found out, my lord. There is no need to pretend any longer. We owe it to the lady to confess our wrongdoings." She looked back at Bliss. "I really didn't think it would go this far."

"Bliss," Caine said roughly, coming to stand in front of her, blocking out Olivia. "Don't listen to her. I love you. I should have said it before now, but . . . Jesus, I was afraid. You were too damn good for me. I thought I could let you go, forget about you. But I couldn't."

"Tell her the truth, Caine. Tell her how you used her to win back your home."

"I didn't use you, Bliss. I wanted you. I'll always want you."

"Tell her how we made a wager," Olivia taunted.

He stared at Bliss pleadingly. "I couldn't follow through."

"You see, my lady," Olivia went on, "what I didn't tell you back in Devon was that your defilement was not solely about revenge. Yes, Caine wanted to get back at your father—"

"Shut up, damn you," Caine threatened, whipping around to face her.

"But he also wanted his home back," Olivia continued, undaunted. "I, too, wanted something. Caine's child. And he was more than willing to provide me with one, if he didn't succeed in fulfilling his part of the bargain."

Caine advanced on her. She backed away from him, but the words kept coming. "What better way to avenge his father's death by not only taking your virginity, but making you fall hopelessly in love with him? He didn't want your heart, my dear. He wanted your soul."

"*Shut up!*" Caine roared.

"You lovestruck bastard." She laughed viciously. "You stupid, bloody fool. Do you think she could ever care for someone like you? You and I are two of a kind, my lord. Sinners to the end, caring for nothing but our own personal gratification. How do you think you fell so far? Because you're a vice-ridden swine. The only thing you cared about was sticking your rod into the next willing female, letting your poor father suffer because your cock needed appeasing."

"That's enough." The command came from Bliss.

"No," Olivia said forcefully. "That's not nearly enough. You've been duped by a master, my girl. Since I had quite a bit at stake here, I had to protect my investment. Caine is so very skilled at seduction, you see, I knew he would bed you and have you professing your undying love for him before you knew what had happened. Do you think he would be here now if he had managed to get you to tell him you loved him back in Devon?

"Think, my dear: Caine was willing to give me anything I wanted, do anything I say, perform any sexual act I desired, to remain in that house. Do you think he would let all that hard work go to waste on a silly virgin like yourself? I've done you a momentous favor, my dear. Caine is an exercise in poor judgment. Ask him yourself if you don't believe me."

Bliss's entire body ached with despair; her movements slowed as she faced him. "Is it true what she's saying? Was everything . . . all of it because you wanted to get your home back?"

He leaned against the wall, his head tipped back, his gaze focused on the night sky. "I thought it was going to be so simple," he said, his voice hollow. "I thought I knew how each part was going to play out. I wouldn't care about you; wouldn't want you. And by Christ, I sure as hell wouldn't need you.

"But you challenged me at every turn. You changed me." His head shifted against the hard stone, his eyes empty as he looked at her, as though he was no longer there. "For a short while, you made me forget who I was."

"How very maudlin," Olivia drawled in a disgusted tone. "He's so wracked with guilt, it's pathetic. Well, darling, since you've gone this far, you might as well tell your beloved the rest. It is such an interesting tale, after all."

"Don't," he begged. "If you care for me at all, Olivia, don't do it."

"Yes, I care for you—as much as you care for me, and we both know how much that is. I warned you not to treat me so callously. There was only so much I would take from you, even with your lovely cock that could do such sublime things to my body. But St. Giles has taken your place in my bed, and though neither his performance nor his manhood measures up to yours, he does what I say. So you see, I don't need you anymore. Your usefulness is at an end. You're worthless anyway. What do you have? Nothing. You're an outcast, a homeless earl. You can rot in the street, my love. That's how much I care."

"Why are you doing this to him?" Bliss asked, hurting for Caine, knowing that no matter how he had broken her heart, she could not simply stop loving him. She had to defend him, because he had been brought too low to defend himself.

"Why?" Olivia countered with a bark of laughter. "Because I can. But really, what would a simpleton like you know about it? You wage wars with words, when any war against a man is best won with sex. Their brains are in their pants, my dear. I'd advise you to keep that in mind."

"I don't want any advice from you. You're a cruel, calculating witch."

"La, you're finally figuring it out. But before you start labeling me and feeling sorry for this weak excuse for a man, consider this. He plotted against you. You were a pawn." She turned her malicious regard on Caine, who was slumped against the wall, his head in his hands. "Now tell her, Caine. Tell her why she should lay all the blame on your shoulders. Tell her the one thing that makes everything you've done to her that much worse."

"Please, Olivia," he groaned, shaking his head. "Don't."

She scoffed, "For all your hard talk, you're utterly

spineless. Fine. I'll tell her." Her gaze leveled on Bliss while she calmly adjusted her gloves as though she was not verbally annihilating a man in the street. "His father didn't jump from that cliff, my lady. He was killed by his own son."

Twenty

*The iniquity of oblivion blindly scattereth
her poppy, and deals with the memory of
men
without distinction to merit of perpetuity.*
Sir Thomas Browne

*B*liss stared at the woman in stunned silence for the
space of five heartbeats. Then she forced herself to think.
"No." She shook her head. "Caine wouldn't have done
something like that."

"It's not common knowledge, of course. For the sake
of my sexual gratification, I felt it behooved me to keep
silent about the earl's untimely demise." Olivia dusted off
a speck of dirt on the sleeve of her dress. "Now there's no
more need to do so."

A hundred thoughts tumbled through Bliss's mind,
but one thing was sure. Olivia's claim could not be true.
Caine had loved his father.

"You weren't there when the earl died," Bliss countered. "You can't possibly know anything."

"Oh, but you're wrong. I know quite a bit. Though
Northcote offered little in the way of amusements, one of

my maids was privy to the entire incident. She worked for Henry Ballinger during that time, and saw the earl and his son arguing at the edge of the cliff. Then she saw Caine push the earl to his death."

A terrible, grief-stricken sound pierced the air, frightening Bliss. Caine had slid down the wall, his eyes anguished, his face blanched of color.

"I tried to save him . . . I couldn't . . . He was out of reach. I tried. God, please believe me, I tried."

"Yes, darling," Olivia mocked in a condescending tone, as though talking to a child. "I'm sure you tried to save him. The man who had ruined your future by piddling away every sou he'd ever made, along with the money your lover's father gave to him." She cast a sidelong glance at Bliss. "While it's true the earl was in debt, the real reason he was at the cliffs that night was because he could no longer contain the fact that his son was—"

"*No!*" Caine shot to his feet, reaching for Olivia. "Don't . . ." He fell to his knees before her.

She laughed down at him. "This is priceless. The mighty Earl of Hartland has finally found his proper place." She leaned forward, cruelly whispering in his ear, "Remember who brought you to your knees, my love."

Bliss had never seen Caine looking as he did at that moment, as though he was waiting for someone to ram a knife through his heart and finish him off. She wanted to scream at him, shake him, make him fight.

"It was so hard for you to find out you weren't who you thought you were," Olivia murmured in an almost loving tone as she stared down at him. "Not a beloved son. Not a true heir. But the by-blow of a whoring mother."

A low groan of abject misery came from Caine as though from his very soul, a violent shudder wracking his body.

"Leave him alone," Bliss commanded. She would *not* let this vindictive witch hurt him. No matter what else he had done, he didn't deserve this.

Sardonic amusement glittered in Olivia's eyes as she looked at Bliss. "But there's so much more to tell you, my dear." She glanced down at Caine. "Isn't there, my love?"

"Please . . ." he whispered in a hoarse, broken voice, and Bliss died inside, aching for him. No man had ever been brought so low. She understood now why he had looked at the cliffs and the sea with such longing, as though he wanted to step off into oblivion and make all his guilt and pain go away.

"I remember those first few months after you had come to stay with me," Olivia said. "How blistering drunk you would get and how deliciously rough you were with me in bed. But alcohol and guilt are terrible bedfellows, aren't they, darling? Piece by piece, you revealed the sordid tale. And once the little maid had confessed what she had seen, I discovered that most of your father's old retainers knew the truth—though only the threat of making their already miserable lives even more wretched forced them to fill in the gaps."

Olivia looked up at Bliss then. "I'm not sure what he told you, but his mother killed herself rather than live with her own shame. Her husband never knew why until many years later. The week before his death, the earl sent a messenger to fetch his son home from whatever brothel or married woman's bed he happened to be in at the time.

"When Caine arrived that fateful night, he found his father at the Point, empty liquor bottles strewn around him. After harboring his ugly secret for years, faithfully deluding himself, just as his son now deludes himself that it was all a terrible, unfortunate accident, the earl could no longer bear the burden. He felt his son deserved to know the truth about his lineage, which would certainly explain Caine's prurient behavior, son of a whore that he is. Well, I'm sure you can envision what transpired next, having been treated to a dose of Caine's temper yourself."

When Bliss remained silent, Olivia went on. "He didn't believe he could be a common bastard. Our boy has always been so full of himself, so arrogant and self-assured of his place in this world. He was the crown prince of Devon. But that night, he realized he was a fraud. Doubtless it set off his explosive temper and he lashed out at his father—"

"No," Caine bellowed, his voice raw, kneeling there on the hard ground like a postulant seeking forgiveness before the Lord. "I didn't push him. God help me . . . he wanted to die. He wanted to be with her. He only stayed all those years for me, he said." The words tumbled from his lips, prayer and confession. "And I wasn't even his real son. But he had been willing to give me everything, and I threw it all back in his face, cursing him, cursing my mother. That's when he hit me. He'd never hit me before, and I burned with rage and grief. I told him that he should have followed my mother to the grave. That he was better off dead."

His body trembled uncontrollably, memories returning him to that terrible time. "I left him there, knowing he was drunk and unstable. Halfway up the hill, I stopped and turned around. I saw him standing at the edge of the cliff, staring down, the wind buffeting him toward the yawning depths below.

"I knew then. And I ran . . . *God, don't do it! Don't!* I yelled his name over and over, pleading, but he just looked over his shoulder, as though he had already gone away. And then I was reaching for him, but he had leaned forward . . . and . . . oh God." He squeezed his eyes shut.

Tears streamed down Bliss's cheeks, her heart aching for the torment Caine had lived through for the last two years, believing himself responsible for his father's death, when it was clear that his father had gone to the cliff to die.

She hated his father in that moment. He had dragged Caine home so he could make his grand revelation and then kill himself before Caine's eyes, leaving his son to blame himself for something that wasn't his fault.

"Caine . . ." She moved toward him, her hand outstretched, but he scrambled to his feet and backed away from her.

Olivia laughed. "The wild stallion has been broken to the bit at last," she jeered. "It's a shame, in a way. Tame horses have no spunk or spark to them." She shrugged. "Well, I shall at least have the enjoyment of bringing Khan to heel. Unlike his once-proud owner, that beast will fight me all the way, but he *will* be made to do my bidding, have no doubt." She inhaled with satisfaction. "It seems I've won all the way around. How lovely for me. Well, I will bid you a fond fare-thee-well or *adieu,* as the French say." With a flourishing twirl, she turned to go.

Bliss's words stopped her cold. "Don't leave yet, my lady. You'll miss the best part."

Olivia glanced over her shoulder at Bliss, a hint of wariness in her expression. "And what is that, dear child? Are you going to make the scoundrel lick your boots? For that, I would gladly stay."

"No. I'm going to do something much simpler," she replied, walking over to stand in front of the woman.

"Please don't bore me with one of your sanctimonious speeches," she said with a sigh. "They are so dull."

"No speeches. Just a few words."

"And what could you possibly say that I might be remotely interested in hearing?"

"Just this: I love Caine."

Olivia stared at her in disbelief. "Certainly you're joking."

Bliss met her stunned look unblinkingly. "No, I'm not. I love him. With all my heart. And since you made such an effort to travel all this way, I couldn't possibly deny you the pleasure of hearing me tell you so."

Olivia's lips melded together in rising fury. "You don't mean it. You couldn't. He made a fool out of you. Used you and ruined you for other men."

"Oh, but I do mean it. Though you were right about one thing: Caine did ruin me. I won't ever want another man. Only him."

"My God, you're as mad as he is!"

"Perhaps. But that's none of your concern. Now," she said, "since Caine has met with the terms of your agreement, I expect his home to be signed over to him immediately."

Olivia gaped at her. "Absolutely not!"

Bliss took another step toward her, nose to chin. Olivia outweighed her by at least two stone, but Bliss didn't care.

"Either you sign over Northcote to Caine by tomorrow morning, or I will hunt you down, and I promise you won't like what I'll do to you when I find you."

"You wouldn't dare!"

"I most definitely would."

The woman sputtered unbecomingly, her glare promising retribution. "Fine," she snapped in a furious undertone. "He can have his damnable house back. The place is like a morgue anyway. Let him live in it and wander its drafty halls until the floorboards rot beneath his feet. It won't change the fact that he is and always will be a social pariah. And by tomorrow morning, all of England will be privy to the news of his tainted blood and murderous tendencies."

Bliss had never felt such blistering anger in all her life. "It would be unwise of you to threaten exposure. Your actions will only make you look like a spurned lover."

"Spurned?" Olivia's laugh was short and brittle. "No man has ever spurned me. *I'm* the one who walks away." She then turned to Caine, who stood with his back to them. "You were not the only one with revenge in mind, my lord. Each and every time you pleasured me, always holding a piece of yourself back, I plotted the final stroke of your downfall. You thought you were playing me for a fool, but I was playing *you* for a fool. Now you will go down in flames."

Without a second thought, Bliss slapped Olivia across the face, sending her reeling to the ground, the force dislodging her hairpiece.

Her hand pressed to her reddened cheek, she stared up at Bliss, shock etched on her face. "You hit me!"

Bliss glared down at the woman cowering at her feet,

fury coursing through her veins. "And I will do so again if I find out that you have spoken one word about what has transpired here. I will use all my father's substantial influence to ruin you if you try to harm Caine. Do you understand me?"

Her palm still fused to her cheek, Olivia nodded. As she rose to her feet, she hissed, "Have joy of him. You two deserve one other."

She stormed into the darkness, the sound of her angry voice snapping at her driver followed by the slamming of a coach door, and wheels thundering along the cobblestones.

Bliss stood there for a minute, still trying to grasp all the startling revelations that had been made. She had been hurt at first, and yes, angry. But then a strange calm had descended over her and she knew exactly what she had to do.

Her mother's words seemed so prophetic now. The answers *had* come to her when she was ready to hear them, and when she had looked at Caine down on his knees, everything was clear. For better or worse, she would not forsake him.

"She won't forgive the slight, you know."

Bliss turned to look at Caine, who had not moved. His posture was rigid, tense, and she longed to wrap her arms around his neck and hold him tight.

"I don't care," she said. "The spiteful witch had it coming. I hope her cheek stings for a week."

Caine shook his head. "Lady Bliss Ashton, a bully. Who would have known."

"Perhaps, but it felt good."

"Retribution always does."

There was something in his tone that suddenly unnerved her, as though he was mocking her. "Are you upset with me?"

"Upset?" he said. "Why should I be upset? That would be rather misguided of me, don't you think?"

"I don't know."

"Really?" He stepped out of the shadows that partially cloaked him, allowing her to see the contempt in his expression. "And here I thought you knew everything. You certainly act as though you do. Defender of women's rights, and savior of reckless, cold-hearted earls."

"Caine—"

He held up his hand. "What's done is done."

Bliss walked toward him, her skirts making only a whisper of sound as she came to a stop in front of him, laying a hand gently on his arm.

He looked at her, a long hard look, as though passing judgment and finding her wanting. His eyes were so cold, so unlike the man she had glimpsed only a few short hours ago.

Then he walked away from her, leaving her standing there, confused and alone. He was shutting her out again. Didn't he realize that she understood the reasons for his cynical and unforgiving outlook on the world?

She hastened after him, stopping him in the middle of the street. "Where are you going?"

His gaze flicked briefly to her, killing in its lack of emotion. "Away from you."

"Caine, please. I understand that you're hurting—"

"Hurting?" His short bark of laughter cut through her like a knife. "Christ, open your eyes! You've been used. Didn't you hear Olivia?"

"I heard her," Bliss quietly replied. "But I don't believe what she said."

Her valiant belief in him nearly broke Caine. He wanted her to hate him, needed her to. Damn her beautiful, faithful soul. "Well, believe it. I screwed you with only one purpose in mind, and that was to get back my home. I've succeeded, so your services are no longer required. Consider this your congé, my dear."

"Why are you acting this way?"

Because he had nothing to offer her. He was penniless. Northcote's tenants could barely support themselves, let alone fill his coffers. How would he support her? By living off her father's largesse? He'd kill himself first.

His sole commodity lay between his legs, but he could never touch another woman in that way again. Bliss had ruined him for anyone else. He had caused and suffered so much pain in his quest to get his home back, and the victory was hollow. It meant nothing without her.

"I told you there were lessons I could teach you," he said with calculated brutality. "Consider yourself a more valuable commodity now. Men will kill to bed a passionate woman, and you, my dear, are rich in that particular blessing." Leaning down, his cheek brushed hers as he whispered in her ear, "You should have gone with your first instincts and not trusted me. Ironic, isn't it, that you were right about my reasons for coming after you? I did just want to toss up your skirts."

"But you didn't," she said, torturing him with the tenderness of her response, belief still shining in her eyes.

"An oversight," he bit out. "I figured you would invite me to your bedroom when we returned, and you'd be so hot for it, you'd give me the best ride I've had in a long while."

He framed her face between thumb and forefinger, feeling her tremble as he forced himself to look coldly into those trusting eyes. "Chin up, sweetheart. There'll be other men. Perhaps some poor fool might even fall in love with you."

She stood there looking at him with her heart in her eyes. He couldn't leave her like this, but he had to leave her. Olivia had exposed him for what he was: the son of a whore. Even if he had the wealth to go with his title, he still would not be good enough for Bliss. Too much sin and depravity marked his past.

"I love you, Caine," she said softly, but with conviction, the tears glimmering in her eyes ripping into his gut.

No woman had ever said those words to him. No woman had ever seen him as more than a means of pleasure. He hated her in that moment, hated her for giving him a glimpse of something he could never have, never be. He wanted to punish her for loving him, for not walking away before she had destroyed him.

He grasped her upper arms, his fingers biting into her flesh as he dragged her forward. "I warned you time and again that I would ruin you. I gave you ample reason to run, but you and your idiotic ideas of salvation kept you from saving yourself. Do not blame me for your stupidity." He gritted his teeth, forcing the words out. "Find yourself a husband. Breed him a half-dozen brats and forget about me. For I will surely forget about you." He released her with a shake and she stumbled back, a single tear coursing down her cheek.

"You won't forget me," she whispered in a heartbroken voice.

"I already have," he lied, and forced himself to walk away.

Twenty-one

Behold, I have played the fool,
and have erred exceedingly.
1 Samuel 26:21

*B*liss stared out the garret window, watching the sun fade from the sky, leaving behind a vibrant ribbon of color, a sight that would have inspired her only a week ago. Now it simply meant the passing of another day.

After Caine's cruel dismissal, she had believed he was simply angry with her for interfering on his behalf with Olivia and that he would come back. He possessed a great deal of pride, and she had fought his battle for him.

But as the third day moved into the fourth, then the fifth and sixth, she realized she had to stop deluding herself. Caine had used her and forgotten about her, just as he said he would.

That should have been enough to make her hate him, but her emotions wouldn't allow her the benefit of catching up to her common sense. She found herself shedding tears without provocation, which nearly threw poor François into a panic, as he had never seen her cry.

She had never believed she would become the kind of woman who loved a man so much she was willing to overlook his sins, or allow herself to believe that he cared when he had told her he didn't. But that was exactly the woman she had turned into. Only time would make a difference. Only distance. And Caine was surely long gone from Paris by now.

A scratch sounded at her door, but Bliss felt too listless to answer the summons. The door swung open a moment later, the clatter of dishes telling Bliss someone had come with her supper tray, the heavy tread and even heavier sigh telling her it was François.

"I've brought your food," he said, sounding put out with her.

"Thank you," she murmured, watching the windmill on the *Moulin de la Galette* slowly turn.

François muttered an expletive and thunked the tray down, making his displeasure known. "There are two full plates still sitting here. *Mon Dieu,* you must eat! You are wasting away to nothing."

"I'm not hungry."

"This I have heard before, and I am most tired of it. You will eat if I have to force every bite down your throat."

Bliss was so lost in her thoughts that she didn't hear him come up behind her. She jerked when he laid his hands on her shoulders.

"Relax, *ma belle.* You are too tense." He began to gently knead her shoulders, and Bliss waited for his reproach, but only a companionable silence stretched out around them.

"I'm sorry," she finally said. "I know I've not been myself lately."

"I understand, and I do not like to see you hurting."

"I know."

He paused, then said, "The Englishman, you still care for him?"

Though it was foolish and transparent to lie, Bliss did so anyway. "No, he's long been forgotten. I'm just . . . tired." It seemed her whole world had become an ache of weariness. But she would get over this. She had no choice.

"That is because you do not eat and have not gotten any fresh air. You have locked yourself away in this tower room like a melancholy princess. This is not like you. You are a woman of spirit and fire."

Bliss turned to face him, a dreaded tear coursing down her cheek. "What's happened to me?" she whispered, her voice trembling.

François cupped her cheek, brushing away the tear. "Love, my girl. Love is what has happened to you. I know, as I have felt it many times, and each time I'm sure the pain will not be as great, but it is. It does not get any easier. But it will subside."

"When?"

"Much of that depends on you. You must take yourself in hand and force yourself to go forward. Before you know it, things will be as they were before. And there is no time like the present to start. We will go to the *moulin* this very evening."

"No." Bliss shook her head. "No, I couldn't. Not tonight. Not yet."

"*Oui*, tonight."

"It's too soon."

"Nonsense. It will do you good."

"But—"

"I was going to keep this a secret, but now you have forced my hand. Manet will be painting there tonight, and he has specifically asked that you come."

Bliss momentarily forgot her troubles. "Manet asked for me?" To be extended an invitation by the artist was not only rare, but coveted. He was an intensely private man who associated with only a select few.

François nodded. "He has seen some of your work and thinks you show a great deal of promise. Now, do you want to miss the opportunity to watch him paint?"

She had been an admirer of Manet's for many years, and one of the thousands to crowd into the Salon to view a showing of his work.

Somewhere deep inside her, the old fire flickered back to life. Perhaps François was right. Maybe she needed to force herself to get out, to forget. Caine had most likely forgotten all about her. In fact, he was probably toasting his good fortune by bedding some pert-breasted, doe-eyed trull, who would offer him no trouble, no lectures, nothing but pleasure. Endless hours of pleasure.

"Oh, sweet God, not the tears again!" François said with a mixture of exasperation and concern as he gathered her into his arms.

"I hate him," Bliss whispered in an emotion-clogged voice, angrily swiping at her tears.

"As you should. He's a scoundrel of the lowest order."

"But I love him."

"Of course," he sighed, waving a handkerchief in front of her tear-blurred vision.

Bliss glanced up at him through wet-clumped eyelashes and murmured a weak, "Thank you." Then she straightened, determined that would be the last time she would shed a single tear for a self-proclaimed hedonist. With a final sniff, she lifted her chin and said, "Give me a few minutes to get ready."

Caine had lost track of the days, having been fairly hammered with drink for most of them. But he greatly preferred his new role as Montmartre's town lush to his old role as England's biggest bastard and prime jackass.

At least when he was drunk, the images of Bliss were not so piercingly clear, those blue eyes not so hurt and confused, that chin not so stubborn and proud, those lips not trembling from the pain he'd caused.

He had been so immersed in liquor and despondency that he hadn't been able to lift a single damn finger to pummel that stupid Frog into the floor when the man had boldly sat down at the tavern table Caine had occupied nearly continuously since leaving Bliss standing in the street.

The Frog had had the balls to stare Caine in the face and tell him what a profound fool he was and that he didn't deserve Bliss, and that half the men in Paris were in love with her. Caine had managed to summon up a belligerent glare, but the blighter was right. Yet if even one of those bloody fops laid a hand on her, he would cut it off.

He stared down at his drink and then lifted it to his lips, wondering, as he had for the past week, if at the bottom of this glass he would finally find the oblivion he sought.

*   *   *

Bliss looked out the hackney window as it rumbled down the rutted street. The weather was thickening, gray showers scudding across the horizon that would leave the city with muddied lanes and glistening treetops by morning.

She had brought along her pad and charcoals, thinking to do a few sketches of her own. The nightlife of Montmartre was replete with the most unusual characters, many of whom meandered right outside her window as the hired conveyance trudged up the hill.

She watched a rag picker searching through discarded items in the gutter. The woman raised her head as a light mist began to fall, her face revealed in the yellow glow of her lantern. Isabelle Boudreaux, a well-known figure about the boulevard.

Beneath her tattered scarf, her skin was pale, crepe-thin and seamed, a toothless hole for her mouth and inflamed bruises for eyes. A gust of wind whipped at hair that used to be like spun silk.

Isabelle had been a beautiful woman once, an elite among the demimonde, and all of Paris had been taken with her. But her admirers were long gone. Disease and an addiction to absinthe had stolen everything from her.

Bliss called out to her, wanting to take the woman out of the drizzling rain. But when Isabelle looked up, a hunted expression clouded her face. It was the look of someone who had seen too much hardship and abuse. She scurried off into the darkness of the surrounding alleys.

With a defeated sigh, Bliss sat back against the squabs. Women like Isabelle were the reason she painted. Her face, like so many, was a canvas of the harsh life she lived, the daily struggle for survival.

Perhaps it was for Isabelle and her kind that Bliss traveled to such a licentious nightspot to meet with Manet. Caine has been right: she needed to take the next step, to show her art. If she could gain Manet's interest, she might be able to get her paintings viewed at the next Grand Exhibit.

The hackney came to a rattling halt in front of the *Moulin de la Galette,* whose windmill Bliss often watched from her window. The establishment sat atop an incline, its façade beaten down around the edges. Yet its haphazard appearance took nothing away from its welcoming allure.

Amid the din of voices spilling out the open doors arose a throatily sung *musette* about a fallen girl who comes to a tragic and untimely end. The tune was an all-too-accurate portrayal, Bliss thought as she spied a homeless *pierreuse* offering herself to a passerby.

A thin veil of smoke wreathed Bliss as she and François entered the pump room. On the stage, dancers in multilayered petticoats flared out their skirts, showing glimpses of ankles and calves.

Bliss found a spot in the corner where she could watch everything, her eager gaze searching the room for a glimpse of Manet. "I don't see him," she said, glancing up at François, who appeared ill at ease. He had been acting odd since they had left her apartment.

"He should be here any moment. Would you care for some refreshment?" Before Bliss could respond, he blended into the crowd, a path opening up behind his fleeing form.

Her gaze suddenly collided with fierce blue eyes and her world shuddered on its axis. Caine sat directly across the room from her, slouched in a sprawl, brooding and savagely handsome, an empty glass clutched in his hand. He had stayed in Paris. In Montmartre. Why?

The joy she felt at seeing him was eclipsed a moment later when a scantily clad barmaid sashayed toward him and boldly sat down on his lap, wrapping her arms brazenly around his neck, her ample bosom pressed against his chest. A group of onlookers hooted loudly at the spectacle.

Bliss prayed he would push the woman away, but instead, he put his hands on her waist, and holding Bliss's gaze, he pulled the barmaid close for a deep kiss that sent the revelers into gales of whooping.

The blow was the worst he could have ever inflicted, and though she wanted to run from the sight, her feet would not move.

A hand suddenly grasped her arm. Her gaze jerked up, thinking to find François—never expecting to see the Earl of St. Giles staring down at her.

Twenty-two

❦

Thou tyrant, tyrant Jealousy . . .
John Dryden

"I'm sorry," he said, smiling apologetically, his aristo-cratic features pronounced in the gilded light, silvery eyes intently regarding her. "I didn't mean to frighten you."

Bliss took a steadying breath, remembering the story Caine had told her about the earl, how he had come into her room when she was asleep, intending to take advantage of her. Had that been true? Or simply one of his tales to make her believe he had come to her rescue?

"What are you doing here, my lord?"

The black and blue mark on his jaw was completely gone, and he was once more the charming rake with the angelic face that turned every female head in the room.

"I'm sure you must be surprised, my lady, as was I. I never expected to come across you in such a place."

"I'm with a friend." Where was François?

Her gaze nervously shifted back to Caine. He had not

moved, and neither had the barmaid, who was now boldly kissing his neck. The only thing that told Bliss he had even noticed the earl's arrival was the violent glare he sent her way, the look a clear warning, which galvanized her anger.

How dare he look at her as if *she* were the one in the wrong! He had told her in no uncertain terms that he no longer wanted her.

The need to return the pain he had so willingly inflicted on her pushed in on Bliss, and she returned the earl's smile with a warm one of her own.

"You are a beautiful woman, my lady," he said in an appreciative tone.

"Thank you, my lord," she murmured, lowering her lashes.

He crooked his finger beneath her chin, tipping her face up. She saw the desire simmering in his eyes and knew she should be concerned, but she could not get the image of Caine and the serving girl out of her mind.

"I will confess that coming upon you like this makes going out in this weather well worth the effort. I hope you'll allow me to take this opportunity to further our acquaintance. There were things that impeded my ability to do so back in Devon."

Bliss didn't need him to elaborate on what "things" he referred to. The biggest one was sitting across the room, the heat of his gaze like a weight on her back.

Even as a voice told her not to allow the earl to think she harbored any interest, she said, "I'd like that." A harmless flirtation would not amount to anything, and Caine was enjoying his dalliances. Why should she not do the same thing?

Bliss spotted François striding across the room, a deep frown dragging his brows together, his displeasure obvious as he drew up beside her.

"Come with me," he said without preamble, clamping his fingers around her arm and dragging her toward a corner of the room.

Bliss wrenched away and glared up at him. "What has come over you?" she demanded.

"That man is a viper."

"You know nothing about him."

"I know enough to see that he only wants to get between your thighs."

"That seems to be a common flaw among you men," she returned hotly. "Heaven forbid you should get to know a woman."

"Your anger is misplaced."

"Perhaps, but I'm getting heartily tired of men thinking they can dictate to me."

"I am advising, not dictating. Though it is obvious you are not thinking clearly, or you would see this for yourself."

"*You* are the one who told me I must forget and move on."

"*Oui*, but you are going about it the wrong way. I must protect you when you are too pigheaded to protect yourself."

"I don't need protecting. I'm perfectly capable of taking care of myself."

"Pigheaded, as I said. You refuse to believe you are as fallible as the next person."

"The next female, you mean."

"You will not draw me into that trap, *chérie*. I am

going to be your friend whether you like it or not, and I will not allow you to make a mistake you will regret."

"You have no say."

"You are playing with fire, *mon coeur*. You are hurt over seeing the man you love with another woman. It is clouding your judgment."

A tiny screw of pain pricked her heart. "He is not the man I love."

François made a rude noise, but before he could retort, a voice interjected, "Is everything all right, my lady?"

Bliss glanced up to find the earl standing at her shoulder, his gray eyes alight with concern.

"Fine," she lied, plucking the glass from François's hand and saying in a voice only loud enough for him to hear, "Do not treat me like a child. And do not follow me." Refusing to meet his warning gaze, she walked away.

"Would you care to go someplace quieter to talk?" the earl asked gently, the look in his eyes sympathetic.

Bliss stole a glance at Caine and found him disappearing through a door at the back of the taproom, impatiently tugging the barmaid behind him, who went more than willingly, grinning at her friends as she passed. They fanned themselves as though they were about to faint dead away at her good fortune.

The last piece of Bliss's battered heart broke irrevocably, but she willed back the tears as she looked up at the earl and nodded agreement.

He smiled and took hold of her hand, leading her in the same direction Caine had just taken the buxom serving wench, then guiding her through an adjacent door.

They moved along a narrow hallway, the muted sounds of revelry reaching them, dim sconces shrouding them in shadows. Bliss shut her eyes tight, trying to will away images of Caine and the pretty barmaid.

A sudden heat washed over her and she jerked open her eyes. The earl held aside a red velvet drape leading to an anteroom. Flickering candlelight cast writhing shadows on the wall as Bliss's shocked gaze took in the scene before her. Moans rose from the men and women shamelessly entwined upon garish damask sofas and satin cushions on the floor, proclaiming this part of the tavern for what it was. A bordello.

A crash of thunder shook the floor, the power of it wrenching groans from the joined couples, as if the dynamics of the storm had infused their desires with the electricity of the lightning bolts stabbing at the earth.

Before she had a moment to return to her senses, the earl led her to one of the adjoining rooms, his grip rough as he yanked her in front of him and notched back another curtain, forcing her to look in—to see Caine sprawled in a chair, his head resting on the back, his eyes closed . . . and the serving girl kneeling submissively before him, running her hands up his thighs.

"See what a whoremonger he is," the earl hissed in her ear. "This is his life, and you can't change it."

The barmaid's hands skimmed across Caine's groin and a sound of despair spilled from Bliss's lips. The small noise brought Caine's head up, his eyes jerking open, a look of pain and regret passing fleetingly over his face before fury overtook him.

With a strangled cry, Bliss turned and fled, Caine's bellowing roar echoing after her, St. Giles dogging her heels. He hauled her to a stop and whirled her around to face him.

"What did you think, my lady?" he jeered. "Quite a show, wasn't it? Much better than that tripe on stage."

Bliss numbly stared up at him, and she could see her own foolishness in the gleam of his eyes. "I want to leave," she said in a raw voice. "Take me out of here."

"Leave? But we just got here."

"I made a mistake."

"Yes," he said with a snarl, "you made a mistake, and it started back in Devon when you allowed that swine to shove his cock into you, and you laid there panting for it like a bitch in heat." He backed her up against the wall, his arousal grinding against her stomach, sickening her.

"Stop it!" She tried to wrench away from him, but his fingers bit into her arm, her sketchpad sliding to the floor, scattering papers at her feet. "My work!" she cried, reaching out to retrieve her papers, a gasp of pain bursting from her lips as St. Giles yanked her up by her hair. His hand clamped over her breast, squeezing painfully, and her scream was muffled by his mouth as it brutally slammed down over hers.

The next moment, he was gone; his body pulled away so violently a breeze fanned her skin. He crashed to the floor with Caine standing over him like a god of war, the muscles straining in his forearm as he took the earl by the collar, his other fist plowing into the man's jaw with a force that cracked the bone.

The earl whimpered at his feet as Caine raised his fist again. Bliss grabbed his arm to stop him before he killed the man, and his half-crazed eyes whipped to hers.

He swallowed convulsively, both of them trapped in some strange vortex of time before his gaze cut back to the earl. "Touch her again," he snarled, "and I'll cut off your balls and stuff them down your throat." The earl's head dropped hard against the floor when Caine released him.

Bliss caught sight of François's frantic face as he shouldered his way through the crowd that had gathered to watch the spectacle. She shook her head, silently pleading with him to stay back.

Caine manacled one of her wrists with his hand and dragged her away, the mob parting as he led her through a heavy set of double doors to an unoccupied room, the bolt slamming home behind him.

With a vicious yank, he spun her away from him, sending her tumbling back against a gaudy purple velvet settee. He stood there staring at her, his gaze full of the storm's tumult, his face damp with sweat. His presence was all-consuming, and Bliss couldn't breathe.

When he began to advance on her, she leapt to her feet, backing further into the room. The anger in his gaze transformed into lust, intensifying the heat in the room.

Bliss's body vibrated with fear and longing as Caine continued his steady progression toward her, his every movement embodying hedonism and simmering rage. Then he stood before her, his shadow enveloping her, his big frame a solid force impeding escape, his hand wrapping around her nape, pulling her forward and hard against his chest.

A burst of rain-moistened air blew in from the open window and the water drummed heavily against the eaves, a syncopated rhythm to the tumult inside Bliss at having Caine so near again, her love for him a crippling entity she could not shake.

"I should have killed St. Giles for touching you," he growled, his eyes wild as he stared down at her. "I'll kill any man who touches you."

Bliss struggled against him. "Go back to your whore!"

His grip tightened. "This thing between us . . . I can't fight it anymore." His lips grazed her cheek. "You're mine, Bliss. Mine."

"I'm *not* yours." She tried to break free from his hold. "You walked away. You let another woman touch you. I'll never forgive you!"

His jaw clenched, and in the next instant he swung her up into his arms and carried her to the settee, laying her down. "I'm going to make love to you, Bliss. Then we'll both know the truth."

His mouth was against hers before she could protest, his arms imprisoning her as his lips slanted over hers, taking away her breath, her reason; her hands reached up to cling to his shoulders, to pull him down to her.

"God, I've missed you," he whispered harshly against her ear, feathering his lips across her jaw, down her throat. "Every day, every night. You haunted me, drove me from my bed. Made me crazy."

"You hurt me," Bliss half cried as he kissed the corners of her mouth, her eyes. "I thought I would die when I saw you with another woman."

"I know, love. I know." He soothed her with his mouth, heat building everywhere he touched, his fingertips lightly scoring her nipples through the material of her dress. "When you smiled at St. Giles . . . Christ, I couldn't stand it." He wedged his head against the crook of her neck, his hungry mouth trailing warmth. "I need you. I want to be inside you. I can't let you go. You're a fever in my blood."

His hands were trembling as Bliss took hold of them and pressed her lips against his palms, feeling his shudder, her own need as great as his.

Her heart beat a wild rhythm as he undid the buttons at her bodice, her gaze holding Caine's until the last pearl popped free, revealing the swells of her breasts beneath her chemise.

He made short work of her corset laces and pushed aside the material, baring her breasts, his fingers whispering over her nipples. She gasped with pleasure.

His hands were so large, so brown against her skin as he weighed the soft globes in his palms, massaging, then rolling the aching peaks between thumb and forefinger, making heat burgeon deep inside her.

He stood her up then, peeling her clothing away, his sensual appraisal stirring her blood until she stood before him completely naked.

"Straddle my lap," he urged in a husky rasp.

Bliss did as he asked, craving the pleasure he could give her as his fingers settled between her mound, delving into the slick crease to stroke her. Her body was on fire for him, and a desperate moan rose from her throat as he slipped a finger inside her.

"Lean forward," he ordered in a low, urgent voice, taking her nipple into his mouth and nipping it lightly between his teeth, grazing her, watching her.

She wanted to touch him, to give him a taste of how he made her feel, and her hands drifted to his groin. She unbuttoned his trousers, then took his erection and sheathed it in her hands, his silky shaft thickening against her palms as her fingertips smoothed over the head and around the crest. When a drop of moisture pearled on the tip, she swiped it with her finger and lifted it to her lips, sucking it into her mouth. Salt and heat.

"Jesus God, Bliss," he groaned, bucking up against her.

She shimmied off him and settled between his thighs, wanting to pleasure him. "Show me what to do," she whispered against his rigid flesh, her hand shaping his erection, the skin so smooth as she circled the head with her tongue. "Does this feel good?" She wrapped her lips around his shaft and took a little more of him into her mouth.

"Yes . . . sweet Christ, yes . . ."

Just touching him in such an intimate way spurred her excitement, her tongue trailing along a vein, down to the tight sacs at the base, where she tentatively licked. In reaction his every muscle contracted and tensed; his eyes were nearly black as he looked down at her, his hips lifting up to ride her tongue.

Cupping him with one hand while the other gloved the base of his shaft, her mouth slipped over him and closed tightly, pulling him in as deep as she could, again and again.

"Jesus . . . Jesus . . ."

He tasted so good, so hot and male.

He pulled her away, and positioned his turgid length between the pillows of her breasts, holding them tight against him. He began to pump, slowly, slowly, until his body was on the very edge. Then he lifted her across his lap. Her moans of passion filled the room as he suckled her, his mouth moving back and forth between her nipples, turning them into burning points of pleasure as his finger stroked her faster, lighter, focusing on the very tip of her sex.

On the verge of an earth-shattering climax, he gripped her hips and turned her over onto her hands and knees, rising up behind her, his rock hard shaft cradled against her buttocks, lightly rocking back and forth. Then he positioned his erection between her thighs.

"Hold me there against you."

Bliss was frenzied with need, pressing his shaft against her wet heat as he began to slide back and forth, a silky pressure along the engorged tip, teasing so exquisitely, his hands cupping her breasts, her nipples more sensitive in this position as he tugged and lightly pinched, the core of her tightening, her moans escalating as he worked her body toward that bright pinnacle, moving faster and faster . . .

He entered her swiftly as the first molten spasm took hold of her, driving himself in deep, his hand against her shoulders, pushing her down and bringing her hot core up tighter against him as he plunged into her, his thrusts powerful, taking all of her.

He showed her his endurance, promising to pleasure her for as long as she could take him, bringing her to another shattering release before pulling out of her, turning her around and bringing her down onto his straining erection, pumping into her as the last ripples still moved through her body.

Then he stood up, his shaft still deep inside of her as he pressed her body against the wall. Bliss wrapped her arms around his shoulders, clinging to him as he rocked inside of her, filling her.

"Caine . . . please, *please*."

She was so mindless, Caine knew she didn't realize that he was purposely holding back. Only in this, when their bodies were merging, could he give her the only thing he had ever been able to give a woman: pleasure. And he would give Bliss as much as was in his power to give.

He drove into her, the wall vibrating with his thrusts. He loved the way she responded to him, how she quickened and held him tight inside.

"Come on, love," he whispered against her neck. "Shatter for me." He pressed his chest against her nipples, those beautiful hard points that drove him crazy, and buried himself as far inside her as he could go. "Feel how deep I am inside you. Feel how much I want you." He made his thrusts long and hard, and felt her tighten. "That's it," he groaned as her slow, sweet pulses squeezed him.

Finally, she sagged against him. Caine smiled and kissed the top of her head, carefully carrying her back to the settee, where he cradled her against his chest until her eyes blinked open a few seconds later.

He kissed her then, a fierce, consuming mating that said what he couldn't. He knew this could never happen again, that he had to walk away and leave her alone. He had to give her the chance to find someone else, even if it killed him to do so.

"Let's get you home," he murmured, refusing to meet her eyes.

They dressed in silence, but Caine could feel her gaze

on him, wanting to hear something from him, to tell her that he hadn't just used her again. But he would let her think the worst; it was better that way.

He led her out into the deserted hallway and down the back steps to the darkened alley, the mewling of an unseen cat echoing along the crumbling stone. Caine barely noticed the rain plastering his clothes to his body as he held his jacket over Bliss's head.

A hackney barreled down the street, kicking up plumes of water in its wake, clearly not intending to stop. Caine stepped in front of it, the horses rearing as the driver pulled back frantically on the reins.

"Whoa, laddies! Whoa!" The team skittered to a jarring halt, nearly pitching the driver from his seat, his battered hat soaked with rain and drooping over one eye as he glared down at Caine. "Are ye a bloomin' madman? I could 'ave kilt ye."

Caine ignored him and threw open the coach door, handing Bliss up. He could see she was waiting for him to follow, but he wouldn't, no matter what his heart wanted. Her eyes were luminous as she stared down at him.

It took every ounce of self-possession he could muster to close the door and step back from the curb, the pale oval of Bliss's face staring out at him. He knew the sight would be forever emblazoned in his mind.

He forced himself to turn away but discovered his path blocked by two burly men, their distinctive garb clearly recognizable in the surrounding gloom. A hazy blur of bodies huddled around the tavern door behind them, watching avidly.

The taller of the two men stepped forward and took hold of Caine's arm. "If you will come with us, *monsieur*."

Caine glanced at the hand gripping him and then at the constable's solemn face. "What for?"

"We are placing you under arrest."

Caine heard the sound of the coach door opening, then his name on Bliss's lips, questioning and frightened.

"What am I being arrested for?"

The second constable moved into position on the opposite side of him and manacled his wrist, replying, "For the murder of the Earl of St. Giles."

Twenty-three

A man had given all other bliss
And all his worldly worth for this,
To waste his whole heart in one kiss
Upon her perfect lips.
Alfred, Lord Tennyson

*B*liss heard only the frantic beat of her heart as Constable Barnaby ushered her into a windowless room at the *Conciergerie*. The prison's bleak aspect and unsavory history could strike fear into even the most stalwart soul.

Kindly, the man draped a rough woolen blanket over her shoulders, assuming that her trembling was caused by the wet clothes that clung to her body. It wasn't.

St. Giles was dead, and they thought Caine was his murderer.

They had taken Caine away at the tavern, not allowing her to see him or speak to him. Only François's arms wrapped around her waist kept Bliss from going after him. Why didn't he proclaim his innocence? He had nothing to do with the earl's death.

"Better, my lady?" Barnaby asked, a flicker of concern

in his brown eyes as he regarded her from beneath wiry brows, his ruddy face solemn.

Bliss nodded, hugging herself, trying to stop her shivering. "Caine did not kill the earl," she said with all the conviction in her heart. "St. Giles attacked me. Caine was only protecting me from him."

Barnaby canted a skeptical brow. "By slitting his throat, *mademoiselle?* I would say that is a bit extreme, wouldn't you?"

"Slitting his . . ." A terrifying chill settled over her body and Bliss shook her head. "Caine punched him. That's all."

"The earl was found in the alleyway quite dead, and there was not another person with whom the man had an altercation beside Lord Hartland. We also have witnesses who say Lord Hartland had threatened to kill St. Giles."

"Who said this?"

"His ex-mistress . . ." The constable scanned his notes. "Ah, here it is." He looked up at her, studying her reaction as he answered, "Lady Buxton." He tapped the edge of his timepiece on the table. "It seems Lord Hartland had ample motivation to kill Lord St. Giles. Not only did the earl steal the lady's affections away from him, but apparently he was intent on usurping your affections, as well."

"That's not true," Bliss protested. "Caine . . . I mean, Lord Hartland broke off his relationship with Lady Buxton. She was furious and vowed to make him sorry."

"That is when he took up with you, *oui?*"

"Yes, but . . ."

"And you have reasons not to want to see him hang for his crime, of course."

"Hang . . . ?" Bliss closed her eyes to shut out the image.

"That is the punishment for such a heinous act."

"But he didn't do anything!" she hotly contested. "He was with me the whole time."

The man's brow furrowed. "He was? He did not say this to me. In fact, his lordship told me he was *not* with you. He claims he was alone. And that, I'm afraid, leaves no one to verify his alibi."

Bliss stared uncomprehendingly at the man. "No, that's not true." In a rush of understanding, she realized what Caine was doing. "Oh, God. He thinks that if people know we were together, my reputation will be ruined."

"Will it not?"

Bliss's fury mounted anew. "Do you think I care about something so meaningless when a man's life is in the balance?"

"*Non,*" he replied equably. "I think you love him, which is why I believe you'd be willing to lie for him."

"I'm not lying!"

"Calm yourself, my lady."

"I want to see him. I *must* see him!"

"I'm afraid that is impossible at this time."

Abruptly Bliss stood up, her chair tipping back. Without thought, she ran past the constable, who yelled at her to stop.

She had to find Caine, had to get him to tell the truth. But where was he? The prison was a maze of long, shadowed corridors that spread out around her like spider's legs.

Huffing from exertion, the constable caught up to her and grabbed her shoulder. "Do not fight me."

Bliss spun around to face him. "You have to let me see him! I have to get him to tell the truth."

"Forgive me if I fail to comprehend your devotion to him. From what I've heard, he willfully seduced you to win back his home. Did he not?"

"You don't understand."

"Such a man is not worth pining over, *mademoiselle*. I pray you heed me in this. You are young and beautiful. Forget about this one. He is not worth the heartbreak he will surely cause."

Bliss stared at him furiously. "This is my life and I'll thank you to stay out of it. You know nothing about Lord Hartland. You've labeled him unfairly."

His lips thinned. "As you say, *mademoiselle*. Perhaps the magistrate will show him some leniency, as it does not appear that Lord Hartland set out to murder the earl, but was overcome by jealousy and killed his rival in a fit of rage."

"He didn't kill anyone! Why won't you listen to me?"

He eyed her with ebbing benevolence, as though she was a recalcitrant child being brought to heel. "Perhaps this will make the situation easier for you to accept." He dipped a hand into his jacket pocket and handed her a small mahogany box. "We took it from Lord Hartland when we brought him into custody. He bade me to give it to you."

With shaking hands, Bliss cradled the box, staring at it for long moments, afraid to look inside. She couldn't seem to catch hold of her breath as she lifted the lid.

A sob broke from her lips. Inside were her garter, a single silk stocking, a jade and pearl comb she had believed lost, several hairpins . . . and a dried bluebell.

"No . . . I won't take this." She glanced up at the constable, tears spilling from her eyes. "Take it back. Tell him he has to keep it."

The man stared down at her with pity. "I'm sorry, my lady. I know it must be hard for you."

No words would come, only the aching need for Caine. She had to find him.

Pushing away from the constable, she ran down the corridor. "Caine!" she cried, his name echoing back along the hard, cold stone.

The constable shouted after her, then bellowed for his fellow officers to stop her. Bliss could feel them closing in on her, but she would not stop.

Suddenly, from the shadows, a hand reached out through the iron bars of one of the cells and grabbed hold of her skirt, the material rending from the force as she whirled around, a scream dying on her lips as she realized who had her.

"Caine." His haggard face stared out at her from the dark cell, the space barely large enough to contain him.

She longed to hold him, but the iron bars impeded her. Reaching between the metal rods, she pressed her palm to his face, her fearful gaze darting to the men running down the corridor toward her.

"What are you doing here?" he demanded.

"I had to see you."

"You've seen me. Now go."

"But—"

He gripped her wrist. "Listen to me, Bliss. You have to go. You're not a part of this. It doesn't concern you. Do you understand? Go back home. Do your paintings. Show them to the world and forget about me."

"No," she whispered, anguish constricting her lungs. "Never." She twined her fingers through his hair. "Tell the truth, Caine. Please," she pleaded as the men descended on her. "Tell them the truth." She was seized and yanked away from the bars.

"Leave her alone, damn you!" Caine snarled, swiping out at the men, the force rattling the door.

"Caine! Tell them the truth." The constables tried to pull her away. "Please, tell them!"

"Go home, Bliss."

"I love you! I won't leave you."

"Don't love me."

"I do. I love you."

"You're a fool, then," he said viciously. "Do you want to know what I did after I left you in front of your house that night?" His hands gripped the bars in a death hold. "I went back to Olivia. I told you that I didn't have a noble, trustworthy bone in my body. While you were crying over me, I was making love to another woman. I was willing to give Olivia the child she wanted."

"You're lying," she said firmly. "I don't believe you."

"For the love of God, take her out of here!" Constable Barnaby ordered, his men pulling her away, her blue eyes holding Caine's until he had to look away or go crazy.

He pressed his forehead against the bars, telling himself he had done the right thing for once in his life, even as he knew Bliss would haunt him until the day he died.

Bliss sought out anyone who would to listen to her, and worked long hours to rally support for Caine. But Olivia had been thorough in her quest for revenge, making sure the constable did not miss speaking with a single witness, like Lynford and Clarendon, who maliciously elaborated on Caine's threat to kill St. Giles.

It didn't seem to matter that a few people had glimpsed a finely dressed man with salt-and-pepper hair assisting the earl up from the floor after Caine punched him. But no one could describe the man's face, as the hallways were dimly lit. In the eyes of the law, Caine was guilty. He was a man capable of selling his body and soul to hold on to what belonged to him, and people were more than ready to convict him.

On the tenth day, Bliss fainted on the stairway outside her bedroom after returning from the king's residence on the *Place de la Concorde,* where she had been refused an audience with his majesty. She had held high hopes of his seeing her, since he had commissioned her to paint a portrait of his baby daughter, Marie Amelie. But he had far more important matters to attend to than the plight of a disgraced peer.

That same day, her father arrived in Paris, his drawn appearance telling Bliss he had gone to great lengths to get there as quickly as possible after her mother had summoned him.

A light tap sounded on her bedroom door. "Come in," Bliss called out.

Her father's face peered around the edge of the door, smiling warmly when his gaze lit on her. Bliss returned his smile as best she could.

"How are you feeling, my girl?" he asked, his concern evident.

"Fine," she lied, reaching out for his hand. He took it and sat down beside her on the bed. His thick gray hair, still peppered with black, stuck up as though he had been repeatedly driving his fingers through it, which Bliss suspected he had. "You needn't worry so."

"I'm your father. It's what I do best."

Bliss had never doubted her father's love, even in the worst of times. She could only image how Caine felt, to wake up one day and realize he was not who he believed himself to be.

"You're looking better today," he said as the silence stretched out around them.

"I feel better." She did not want to give him any more reason to worry. Yet she glimpsed a new tautness around his eyes, unfurling a tendril of disquiet in the pit of her belly. "Is something the matter?"

He hesitated, then replied, "I went to see Caine today."

Bliss's heart lurched. She sat up straighter against her pillows. "What did he have to say?"

"Not much." Her father stood up, his profile bleak as he stuffed his hands in his pockets. "He's a stubborn man."

"I know."

"He told me something, though." He turned to face her, distress clear in his eyes. "He said that he compromised you. Is this true?"

"No, he didn't compromise me. What happened between us was mutual." Tears unexpectedly pooled in her eyes. "I love him, Papa. I love him more than I thought it was in me to love."

He took hold of her hand and patted it soothingly. "Yes, I can see that you do. And though I suspect Caine will deny it, I believe he loves you just as much. I think he was trying to anger me with his admission in the hopes that I wouldn't want to help him."

"But you're not going to stop helping him, are you?"

He cupped her cheek. "Of course not," he said gently. "Caine's very hurt and embittered, but he's lost without you. I cannot fault a man for seeing in you what I've always seen."

"Will he accept your help?"

Her father sighed. "No. I don't think he wants me involved, for fear it will involve you. He's determined to do this on his own."

Bliss closed her eyes, her hands making fists in the coverlet. Never had she felt more helpless.

"Bliss!" a familiar voice called out, a moment before her bedroom door opened. François stood framed in the threshold, breathing heavily.

Bliss threw back her bedcovers, dread climbing in her throat and panic tightening her limbs. She clutched the bedpost for support, fearing the worst. "What's happened?"

"I have news."

"About Caine?"

"*Oui.*"

Bliss's legs weakened beneath her.

François hastened to her side. "He is fine, forgive me for worrying you. I just came from the *Conciergerie.*" He gripped her hand and smiled. "He's free, *mon ange.* They've released him."

Bliss stared at him. "Free?" she whispered in hope and disbelief.

"*Oui.* The culprit who killed St. Giles has been apprehended."

"Who—?"

"The Comte du Lac," he answered, the name sounding

familiar. "His beloved comtesse turned him in. Apparently, she discovered the comte had been having an affair with her dearest friend. Worse, the fool had chased off all *her* lovers, including Lord St. Giles, whom he—"

"—vowed to kill if the earl ever stepped foot into Paris again." Now Bliss remembered. She had heard the comte's name mentioned during that uncomfortable dinner party at Northcote. She reached out for François's hand. "Is it really over?" She was almost too afraid to believe it.

"*Oui, chérie.* It is really over."

Bliss moved to her window, her gaze drawn in the direction of the prison, where the sun dipped behind the horizon in a brilliant, fiery ball.

She stood at the window well after François and her father had left, watching each passing conveyance, hoping one would stop and Caine would alight, finally able to trust their love.

At midnight, she turned away.

Twenty-four

◆◆◆

My life is a burden without you. . . .
I want you—I want you to let me
say I love you again and again!
Thomas Hardy

*I*t was a week before Bliss found out that Caine had left France and gone back to the wilds of Devon.

Her father had stayed in Paris for a month, trying to shield her from life's miseries, much as he had when she was a child. But his concern only reminded her of her pain.

She found a certain measure of happiness in the fact that her parents were speaking again. The light touches they exchanged bespoke friendship, perhaps one day to transform into something more. They talked more frequently now, took the time to listen to each other. There was hope where once there had been none. That was something.

And during the four months that followed, her father visited Paris whenever he could break away from parliament. Bliss consoled herself with the idea that at least one good thing had come from her heartbreak.

Or rather two things, she thought with a faint smile, laying a hand on her gently rounded stomach. Beneath her fingertips, her unborn child softly stirred. She had almost lost the babe when she had taken ill after Caine's incarceration, not realizing that her lack of appetite and dizziness were symptoms of her body readying itself for motherhood.

Her heart swelled. The Lord had blessed her, and she spent her days in a sort of bittersweet euphoria, blanking her mind to the pain of living without Caine.

Her parents had tried to make her see reason, to get her to tell Caine of the baby. But she had once told him that she wouldn't seek the protection of his name should she find herself with child, and that still held true, though for a different reason than pride now.

If she told Caine about the babe and he returned, she would know that it had not been love that had brought him back to her. And she could never accept anything less than Caine's whole heart.

A knock on her door stirred Bliss and she turned to see her father entering, his gaze drifting to her belly. "How's my grandson doing today?"

"Don't you mean granddaughter?" came her mother's chiding laugh, peering around her husband's broad shoulders to wink at Bliss. "Really, Your Grace, what makes you so sure our daughter is carrying a son?"

He frowned endearingly at his wife. "Because all Ashton women bear a male child first."

Her mother snorted at that male-minded logic. "I didn't."

"That's because you refuse to do as you ought, my dear."

"Perhaps it was *you* who did not do as he ought," she teasingly returned.

Bliss smiled at her parents' playful banter, even as a pang of envy washed over her. She turned away, her fingers lovingly brushing over the quilt she had made for the babe, a patchwork of colors soft as kitten's fur. Soon the day would arrive when she would swaddle her child in it and hold him close to her heart.

A gentle hand at her shoulder made her look up into her father's concerned face. "You've done wonders with this room," he said.

Bliss had turned her studio into a nursery, painting the walls with murals of woodland creatures and fairies. For once, her art depicted something pure and wholesome.

"Bliss," her father began in a tentative tone. "I want to talk to you about Caine."

Bliss moved to the table that held her paintbrushes, her fingers absently drifting over them. "I don't wish to speak of him, Papa."

"He's your baby's father."

"We've been over this before," she said wearily.

"Yes, and you refuse to listen to me when I try to tell you how he's changed—"

Bliss pivoted around to face him. "If he's not willing to come to me himself, he's not the man I know he could be—and I won't settle for less."

"Darling." Her mother came forward, the sympathy in her eyes nearly Bliss's undoing. "Your father and I only want what is best for you and the babe."

"Then understand that I won't accept anything less than love." Grabbing her shawl, she hastened past them, needing to be alone.

*   *   *

Bliss fled to the one place she knew her aching heart would find solace. The place she had not been able to come to for four long months, for fear it would bring back too many memories of Caine.

Now she sought its refuge, sinking down on the marble bench at the base of her grandparents' graves, the babe restless beneath her wildly beating heart.

"Hush," she crooned, squeezing away the tears in her eyes. "Everything will be all right. I promise."

The silence of dusk closed around her, a soothing balm to her spirit. Yet her thoughts remained in turmoil, centered on Caine.

Her father had told her that he had changed, hinting several times that he missed her. But Bliss refused to hope. To care. She would not take the first step in allowing Caine back into her life or her heart; if he could not commit to her voluntarily, it would be pointlesss and self-destructive.

"Bliss."

Her name was a lamenting whisper on the wind, almost unreal, bringing her head up, leaving her trembling and unable to move, knowing Caine was there. She did not question how it was so.

"Look at me, Bliss," he softly commanded.

She dropped her head into her hands. "Go away. Please, just go away."

"I can't. It's taken me too long to work up the nerve to face you."

"What are you doing here?"

"I came with your father. I had to see you."

"Why? You made your feelings perfectly clear when you left."

"Please, Bliss, look at me."

She couldn't. She knew what he would see when she did, the naked desire she still felt for him, that she would probably always feel. Her long shawl hid the truth of her condition.

"How did you know where to find me?"

"I took a chance," he murmured in that soft voice that still had the power to melt her.

"And is my father the reason you're here? Did he . . . say anything to you?" she asked, praying her father had not broken her confidence.

"Like what? That you were pining away for me? I knew you were too strong for that. In fact, I was sure you had put me out of your mind." He paused, then asked quietly, "Did you, Bliss?"

"Do you truly care?" Though her heart sped up, she refused to hope.

"Yes," he said, sounding as if he had moved closer. "You kept giving me chances, but I was too damn blind to take them. I forced myself to believe that you were better off without me during those long nights when I walked the cold, empty corridors of a house that no longer meant anything to me. Not without you."

"Don't," she softly begged, wanting to put her hands over her ears.

"For the first month, I don't think I was sober for more than an hour at a clip. In my lucid moments I walked the cliffs, searching for something I'd lost, something I desperately needed to find again. I could never quite grab hold of it, but I ended up discovering something else instead. Do you want to know what it was?"

"No," she lied.

"My heart, Bliss. I found my heart. I thought it was lost forever. But loving you made it beat again, made me alive in a way I've never been before. I knew then that I had to show you I could be a man deserving of your love. I just didn't know how. But even in that, you helped me.

"You told me once that your father thought I should take up my position in the House of Lords. And I did. I made my voice heard. I spoke out about the poor, about unfair labor conditions, and workhouses. I even spoke of women's rights."

Bliss forgot her vow not to look at him and glanced up, drinking in the very sight of him. He appeared thinner, leaner in a way that made him even more handsome, the hollows beneath his cheeks pronounced, dark circles rimming those bluer-than-blue eyes, as though he truly had suffered. But to believe that was to believe he cared. Could she trust that he truly did?

"Why?" she asked quietly.

"For you. All and only for you, Bliss. I wanted to be a better man, so that you would find something worthy in me. Something worth loving, because I need you to love me, Bliss. I'm not complete without you."

"Caine—"

"Just hear me out. I spent a lot of time with your father. I apologized for blaming him for my father's death. Once the fog had cleared from my brain, I realized I had been living under an illusion. I had reinvented the story in my mind to suit the hatred seething inside of me. Hatred I wanted to direct at someone other than myself."

He walked toward her, his stride uncertain, as were his eyes as they delved into hers. "I don't want to live with the pain anymore, Bliss. I want my life back. I want *you* back."

He came to stand within a few feet of her, reaching out to brush her cheek, only to curl his fingers into his palms. "I found an untapped seam of coal on my property," he said in a reserved tone. "I have money now. Not much, but enough to buy some sheep and crop seed, and to get a good start on raising purebred Arabians." He shook his head, a slight smile lifting the corner of his lips. "I never thought I'd see the day when I'd want to be a glorified farmer. But I'm ready to settle down."

"Your father would have liked that."

"I'd like to think that maybe he would have been proud of me, too."

"I'm sure he is."

He knelt beside her, taking her cold hand into his warm one, regarding her in a way he had never done before. "I didn't mean to stay away so long, but I had to make sure that I had something solid to offer you. I know I've hurt you, Bliss. And I know I don't deserve you, but I pray you'll forgive me. I promise I'll spend every day making it up to you."

"Don't." The tight rein she had barely managed to keep on her emotions fell apart, tears streaming unchecked down her cheeks. "Don't say what you don't mean."

He took her face between his hands, his thumbs brushing across the wet path. "I do mean it. I love you. I can't live without you. Don't make me, Bliss. Please, don't make me live without you."

A gust of wind blew back the edge of her shawl and she caught it, but not in time to keep Caine from learning her secret. His gaze slid down to her stomach and his long fingers pushed back the shawl as her hand unconsciously shifted to her belly.

For endless moments he stared, a mixture of awe and shock on his face before his bewildered, questioning eyes lifted to hers. The naked emotion reflected there was so real, it hurt to look at him.

"Why didn't you tell me?" he asked in a raw voice.

A broken sob welled up from the depths of her. "I couldn't."

His gaze returned to her belly, his breathing shallow, until finally, shaking, he reached out and put his hand on top of hers. The babe shifted restlessly beneath their fingers, as though knowing its father was there.

"Our baby." The words were filled with reverence as he squeezed her hand and looked up at her. "Don't take this away from me, Bliss. I need you. Both of you. Come back to Devon with me. I'll build you an art studio overlooking the cliffs. You're all I have."

Bliss closed her eyes. "Caine . . ."

"I know. I hurt you, and I'm sorry. And if I have to spend the rest of my days making it up to you, I will."

She stared down at their joined hands. "Are you asking me because—"

"Of the baby?"

She nodded.

He captured her chin between his fingers and lifted it to face him. "No. God, no. I came here for you. Finding out I'm going to be a father only means I'm twice blessed." His smile was filled with tenderness. "It seems the maiden is real, after all. She answered my prayer."

"The maiden?"

"Over Chopin's grave." He gestured toward the winged angel perched in flight above the musician's tomb.

"But that's just a lovers' tale."

"Not to me. Go read what I wrote."

Bliss hesitated and then rose from the bench, her legs not quite steady as she came to a stop in front of the maiden, who seemed to look down at her with approval. Taking a deep breath, she unfolded the small scrap of paper tucked beneath her heel. The words were slightly faded, but the message was still clear.

All I ask is for the privilege of loving Bliss for the rest of my life.

Tears streaming down her face, Bliss looked up and met Caine's gaze.

"Do you forgive me, Bliss?" he quietly asked, walking toward her, everything he felt for her there in his eyes.

Bliss knew then that her own prayers had been answered.

As she brought his head down for her kiss, showing him how she felt, his hands gently cradled her belly, their child, nestled beneath her heart, warm and safe and loved.

The same way she felt, being held in his arms.

Epilogue

What love is, if thou wouldst be taught,
Thy heart must teach alone—
Two souls with but a single thought,
Two hearts that beat as one.
Friedrich Halm

"Is our patient all right, doctor?" Bliss asked anxiously as she watched the bald veterinarian probe Ciara's belly.

He glanced at her through thick spectacles that magnified his eyes ten times, making him look like a hoot owl. "Just fine, my lady. Coming along quite nicely. No fears."

Bliss breathed a sigh of relief. This birth was an important one. The entire future of Northcote depended on the outcome.

"And how is our girl today?" came a voice from behind her.

Bliss turned to see her husband leaning against the stable door, smiling that heart-wrenching smile that always warmed her from head to toe.

Ten glorious days they had been married, hieing off to one of the quaint chapels in Paris and speaking their vows in front of the people who meant the most to them.

François had been Caine's best man and Lisette, the girl Bliss had once taken off the streets, her maid of honor; Lisette's three children had sprinkled rose petals down the aisle.

They had made it through adversity and come out the other side better for it. And together, they could face anything.

Bliss watched Caine walk toward her now. She loved the way he moved, in bed and out. And the look in his eyes, as he came to a stop in front of her, told her they would not be waiting until the evening hours to make love. In that, his appetites were as legendary as gossip had claimed. He had taken her in nearly every room of the house, at almost any hour of the day. He seemed to find her unwieldy state a further stimulant to his ardor; he said she glowed. And Bliss suspected she did. She was that happy.

Sighing contentedly, she leaned her head against her husband's shoulder. His arm encircled her, his thumb drawing little circles on her neck while his other hand brazenly teased the outer swell of her breast, making her shiver with anticipation.

The doctor seemed oblivious to her husband's antics as he packed his instruments away and then straightened. "I can't wait to see the jewel of your new Arabian line, my lord. The little dickens should be quite spectacular." He plunked his hat onto his head. "Well, good day to you both. My felicitation on the upcoming birth of your child."

Bliss's gaze followed the doctor's retreating form until he vanished in a haze of morning sunshine. "He's a nice man."

"He's a dawdling old bugger," Caine groused. Bliss chuckled, knowing what troubled him. "Took him bloody long enough to finish. I've been itching to tumble you in this hay since the first day I saw you in here, causing trouble."

Bliss frowned up at him. "You, sir, have mistaken me for someone else." He laughed and tucked her head back against his shoulder. She sighed. "You're still a terrible wretch, you know."

He smiled broadly. "And you love me, don't you?"

"With all my heart," she answered, reaching up on tiptoe to kiss him, their breathing unsteady by the time the kiss ended.

He gathered her close, his hand absently stroking her hair. "Everything's pretty damn perfect, isn't it?"

"Well . . . not entirely perfect."

He pulled back to look down at her, his gaze serious. "What's the matter, love? Unhappy with me already?"

"Never," she vowed.

Beyond the stable doors, a hue and cry went up, signaling a new arrival. Smiling, Bliss laced her fingers through Caine's, and together they stepped out into the bright sunshine of a crisp fall morning.

"There's Hap, coming over the rise."

Through a golden prism, the stable master appeared.

The cliffs were a stunning backdrop, dappled with every hue, from the intense dark of the tideline, through the warm green and brown shadows, out of which the cracks of the strata loomed black.

Breeding gulls fluttered like snowflakes up to the middle cliff, where delicate gray faded into pink, pink into red, and red into shimmering purple. Beyond that, a knot of clambering sheep hung like white daisies upon the steep slope. Her home.

The sight stirred Bliss's senses, making her wish she

had her paints and canvas so that she could capture this moment for all time. Most especially the look on her husband's handsome face.

"Is he riding . . . ?"

"Yes," she murmured, wrapping her arms around his waist. "It's Khan."

Caine looked down at her, confusion in his blue eyes. "I don't understand. How—?"

"Well, we had to have the best Arabian stud if we are to make a go at breeding."

"But Olivia—"

"Lady Buxton was more than happy to part with him—after she and I had a little talk, that is."

A scowl began to darken her husband's adoring face. "Tell me you didn't seek her out. Tell me you didn't get anywhere near that witch."

"Mama was there," Bliss said calmly. "I was in no danger. I simply summoned the marchioness for a little *tête-à-tête* between two reasonable, mature women."

Before her darling husband could further reprimand her, Hap stopped before them. Khan whinnied and tossed his proud head, happy to be back where he belonged, with the man who treasured him.

"Go on, my love," Bliss softly urged. "Welcome Khan home."

Myriad emotions crossed her husband's face as Khan pressed his nose into Caine's outstretched hand, two proud males reacquainting themselves. The sight left Bliss choked with tears. And when Caine turned to look at her, she saw the love reflected in his eyes.

"How did you do it?" he asked. "I never thought Olivia would consent to return him."

Bliss laid her cheek against Khan's soft muzzle and stroked his sleek neck. "Let's just say that women handle things differently than men. Once I explained the situation to her, she saw the error of her ways."

"Perhaps this will help y' understand the situation better, m'lord." Hap dug something out of his satchel. "Her ladyship's father asked me to bring it to you." He handed over a five-day-old copy of the *London Post*.

Bliss's eyes widened as she caught a glimpse of the boldly lettered article. She plucked the paper from her husband's hand and tucked it behind her back. "You certainly don't want to bother with meaningless gossip, my lord."

He slanted a knowing brow at her. "Meaningless gossip, hmm?" He started toward her. "Hand it over, love."

"But—" Before Bliss could finish her sentence, Caine had backed her up against a tree, her belly the only thing keeping him at a distance. She shamelessly cradled it, staring up at him with eyes she hoped looked guileless. She had been working on those feminine tricks since becoming a married woman, needing ways to defuse her husband's ire when she did something he didn't approve of—which was often.

But he wasn't fooled by her ploy, the dratted man. She was utterly and completely at his mercy. A single sweep of his fingers along her jaw and a gentle brush of his lips across hers, and Bliss melted quite ignobly.

"Don't be angry," she prefaced before handing over her pilfered booty.

He gave her a wary look before snapping open the paper and reading the brief, but certainly inflammatory, article. "Bliss . . ." he said in a warning tone as she endeavored to creep away.

Swallowing, she turned around. "Yes, my lord?" she answered, all meekness, which he saw right through.

"Please tell me you didn't hit Olivia—again."

Bliss nibbled her bottom lip. "I didn't exactly hit her. She merely tripped over my foot when she was leaving. She wasn't too happy that she had lost our wager and I won Khan back—"

"*Wager!*"

Bliss flinched. "Well, she wouldn't take the money I offered. I thought that since she had a fondness for placing wagers, we could settle the matter with a single turn of the cards. Alas, she drew a two of spades. I drew a queen of hearts." Which had seemed rather romantically apropos, though her husband probably didn't appreciate the irony at that moment.

"And what would she have gotten if she won?" he asked far too calmly.

Bliss shrugged. "I don't recall exactly."

Hap, the louse, was in a talkative mood. "It was her ladyship's hair, m'lord."

Bliss glared at the traitor.

Far too slowly, her husband turned back to look at her. She attempted another escape, but barely took a step before Caine stopped her.

She laid placating hands on his shoulders. "Now, husband, don't be angry. I had to do it. She hurt you."

With a begrudging curve of his lips, he said, "You are the damnedest woman, do you know that? I'm supposed to protect you, not the other way around."

"Can I help it that I cherish the people I love, and won't allow anyone to hurt them?"

Caine's expression grew somber as he cradled her head

in his hand. "Would you really have cut off your hair if you lost?"

"Yes, but I wasn't going to lose."

"How do you know?"

Bliss twined her arms around his neck, feeling deliriously happy as she pressed her head against his chest and listened to the steady beat of his heart. Her heart, now.

"Because, my love, as long as I have you, I will always win."

POCKET BOOKS
PROUDLY PRESENTS

Lucien Kendall's story,
the next book in the

"Pleasure Seekers"
series

Available in paperback Fall 2004
from Pocket Books

Turn the page for a preview. . . .

From a connoisseur's standpoint, the backside so sweetly hoisted heavenward not twenty feet in front of Lucien was the most damnably provocative one he had ever had the good fortune to admire: lushly rounded, firm, high, leading to a pair of well-shaped legs and dainty feet. The entire effect was so enticing that even the god-awful breeches of indiscriminate gray were little deterrent to the overall presentation.

The sight made up for all the misery he had suffered thus far, including the everlasting drizzle that had not let up for the three days since his coach had rumbled into the rutted, gorse-infested countryside that had made this trip into the Cornish wilderness an abysmal purgatory.

Now, if only he could see the rest of the package that went along with that sweet bottom, Lucien thought, leaning against the stable door, feeling lustful as the night closed in around him. The sky was ashen black, heralding more rain to come, and a rumble of thunder growled along the distant shoreline.

But the little thief was oblivious to Lucien's presence as she continued to rifle through the drunk's pockets. The man was out cold, his head half obscured in a bale of hay, his snores resonating louder than a logging mill, which might account for why the girl had not heard Lucien arrive, horse in tow.

Content to watch, he adjusted his position to a more comfortable one, too much the cad to alert her to his presence just yet. He deserved some compensation for the rare good deed he would soon be undertaking. Might as well enjoy himself now that an opportunity had arisen—and it had most definitely arisen.

He felt a certain degree of curiosity about what the lass was intent on stealing, as she didn't seem to be taking anything, but the thought was relegated to a minor blip in the back of his mind as the floppy hat she wore tumbled from her head, unraveling a banner of silky blue-black hair, pin-straight and fine, which puddled on the floor in a pool of glossy ink.

Lucien's characteristic poise deserted him. His hands fisted at his sides as his arousal swelled, reminding him quite forcefully of how long it had been since he'd had carnal knowledge of a woman.

Five months, six days, and twelve hours, give or take thirty minutes.

He had begun keeping track, wondering when this anomaly would pass. Perhaps he should be glad business had called him away from London; otherwise his reputation as a first-rate libertine would be completely shot to hell. The oath of a Pleasure Seeker was at stake. He had been searching for a diversion, and it seemed he had found it in the form of a lush pickpocket.

The girl muttered a rather amusing curse and quickly rolled her silky mass of hair on top of her head and jammed the hat back into place.

Straightening, she stared down at the unconscious man,

hands on hips, the slump of her shoulders conveying she had not found what she was looking for. Lucien decided the least he could do was offer some assistance, preferably of a more compelling variety. God willing.

"Need any help, sweetheart?" he inquired.

The girl whirled around so fast she very nearly dislodged her hat again. Only a hand to her head kept it in place. She had no such luck with the grimy scarf meant to obscure her face. It slid down to her throat, leaving Lucien momentarily dumbstruck.

He had long ago reconciled himself to the fact that the Lord generally didn't align all a female's features perfectly; that for the most part the Almighty enjoyed the jest by giving a woman a lush body but a sparrow's face, or the face of a goddess but a body like a Buddha.

But this . . . Good sweet Christ, the petty larcenist was a fetching piece, from her dark winged eyebrows to the wide set, exotically tipped eyes that were a piercing shade of green, a pert nose, high cheekbones, and a mouth so full and wide he was already contemplating its wonders.

For a moment she treated him to the same perusal he had given her, starting at the tips of his mud-splattered boots, running up his less than pristine clothing, and over his hair and great coat, which were both damp. Overall, not his best appearance.

Rallying herself, she took a step back and said, "Don't come any closer." Then she endeavored to cover her face again, without success.

"And what might happen if I should dare come closer?" He took a step forward, amused at having this slip of a girl toss out warnings to him. He could tuck her under his arm with little effort; restrain her with one hand. Span her waist with those same hands and settle her on top of him, poised like a goddess on his erection, impaled fully, fragile and delicate, nipples taut, skin flushed with pleasure.

In a surprisingly calm voice she said "Then I guess I'd have to shoot you." A gun appeared from behind her back.

His delicate wildflower had turned out to be a determined wildcat. "That is dire, isn't it?" His gaze flicked to the hand holding the gun; it trembled like a leaf. Clearly she was not cut out for a life of crime.

"I mean it."

"I'm sure you do. But might I suggest that in the future you pick a less frequented spot to rob your victims?"

"I wasn't robbing him. I was . . ." She stopped and frowned at Lucien.

"Was?" he prompted.

She lifted her chin. "That's none of your concern."

"But you've made it my concern, now that you're holding me at gun point. What do you plan to do with me, by the by? I promise to be the most willing of captives." Provocative new images replaced the old: his hands tied to a bedpost while she did her worst to him.

As though reading his lascivious thoughts, she leveled the pistol at his heart. "You'll move out of the way, please."

Her hand was steadier, but Lucien had looked down the barrel of a gun too many times to think death might decide to take him in a dimly lit stable, by the hand of a beautiful, dirt-smudged pickpocket.

"As you wish," he said, lowering his arm from the jamb and waving her by. He had to rein in his amusement as she hesitated, wariness in her eyes. Smart girl, not to trust him.

She edged along the perimeter of the stalls until she reached the doorway, barely five feet separating them. In one lunge he could pin her to the wall, an idea that held a great deal of temptation as she stepped into a wash of moonlight, a pearlescent beam haloing her slim figure.

Had it not been for the womanly beauty of the mossy green eyes focused so intently on him and that impressive backside of hers, he might have thought her a child, she was so petite. Though—his gaze skimmed over her—the front side was equally impressive. The baggy linen shirt did little to camouflage her soft curves.

Uncomfortably aroused, Lucien leaned back against the doorframe.

She waved the gun at him. "Stay where you are."

He extracted a cheroot from his pocket. "I'd much rather stay where you are."

She scowled at him. "Turn around and count to one hundred."

Lucien decided not to remind her that he had seen her face, and that if she intended any sort of escape she should put a bullet in him, or at the very least check him for weapons—a prospect he would no doubt enjoy. But all that seemed counterproductive.

He turned to face the inside of the barn and lit his cheroot, blowing out a stream of smoke before saying, "Next time you might want to cock the hammer. Your threat would have been much more impressive."

"Start counting," she snapped.

"One . . . two . . . three . . ." She had until five; then the chase was on.

On the count of four, however, something bashed him in the back of the head. As black spots wavered before his eyes and his knees buckled beneath him, Lucien's last coherent thought was that the lads were going to have a bloody good laugh if they ever found he'd been felled by a girl.

Then he hit the dirt.

What rotten luck, Fancy thought as she stared down at the prone form of quite the most handsome man she had ever set eyes on. Black hair, thick and straight, hung well below the collar of his great coat. His chiseled profile was limned by shadows and moonlight, and the leaves overhead cast patterns on the ground beside him, framing the glorious Goliath.

She winced when she saw the dab of blood on the back of his head. She hadn't planned on hitting him with the rock. Frankly, she hadn't thought she had enough strength to actually incapacitate him, just daze him a bit so she could make her escape. The wicked glint in his eyes had been the deciding factor. He hadn't looked the least concerned about her shooting him, as though he had known the gun wasn't loaded. But she couldn't take the chance that he would follow her, or report her to the authorities too soon. She only hoped he hadn't gotten a good enough look at her face to give an accurate description.

Kneeling beside him, Fancy pressed two fingers to his neck. Relief coursed through her as she felt his strong, steady heartbeat.

He had the most sinfully long lashes, and they framed the most memorable eyes, a pale aquamarine that was startling against his swarthy skin. It had taken her a good minute to catch her breath when she'd spotted him leaning in the doorway.

Where had he come from? And was he staying at the inn? She should have hoped the answer was no, but the thought was oddly depressing. So few exciting things happened in her part of the world.

Itching to touch him, knowing she'd never get another chance, she lightly feathered his hair through her fingers, smoothing the buttery soft strands back as she whispered in his ear, "I'm sorry."

Reluctantly, she pushed to her feet and stared down at him, shamelessly admiring the way his trousers molded his backside. He was so well-built, so broad and tall. Not even Heath, her neighbor and long-time friend, whose stature and breadth was impressive, could match this stranger.

But this was no time to be acting like a bird-witted female. She had to find the drunk's partner and pray he would give her as little trouble as his friend, who had conveniently passed out in the stables. She needed to obtain proof that Rosalyn's stepbrother, Calder, whose father had married Rosalyn's mother when she was fifteen, was behind Rosalyn's attempted kidnapping that morning.

Without proof, it would be Rosalyn's word against Calder's. And now that his father was dead and he had appointed himself the district's magistrate—ousting the fair and honorable man who had held the post for nearly twenty years—finding allies who would bear witness that Calder was low enough to force his stepsister into marriage would be next to impossible.

Just the thought of what could have happened to her best friend made Fancy shiver. Calder had been furious when he learned that his father had left a considerable fortune to Rosalyn, most of it rightfully due her from her deceased father's trust, enough money so that Rosalyn would be independent of Calder—of any man, should she so choose.

Everyone knew that Calder's uncontrollable gambling and expensive tastes would lead him to bankruptcy within a few years, even though he had inherited several profitable estates, including Westcott Manor, where Rosalyn had lived until she fled two days ago.

At present she was at Fancy's house, Moor's End, protected only by Jaines, her grandmother's beloved but ancient butler, and his wife, Olinda, the housekeeper. Both of them had worked at Moor's End since their youth, and though Fancy could barely pay them, they stayed on.

Had it not been for her maternal grandmother, she and her brother, George, would have found themselves in an orphanage when their parents died. Her father's family would never have lifted a finger to help them. When Lord

Colonel Samuel Fitz Hugh, Earl of Porthaven, had met and married a common Cornish woman, his family had dissolved any relationship with him.

Fancy was all alone now. Her grandmother had died a year earlier; George, two months later. Only a few weeks prior to his demise, he had written to say he was coming home, and she had been devastated when she received the news of his death.

While she had yearned for his return, she knew he was coming home for all the wrong reasons. He still thought of her as the fourteen-year-old sister he'd had to leave behind while he fulfilled his duties to his country, rather than the mature twenty-year-old woman she had become. But she would welcome his overprotecting ways if it would bring him back.

And now her best friend's life was in danger. She had underestimated Calder's determination, but she would not be so naïve again.

Fancy took a final look at the stranger, a pang of regret stirring inside her at the thought of never seeing him again. With a heartfelt sigh, she blended into the night to seek out her quarry.

Lucien awoke with a dull pounding at the back of his skull. Memory returned quickly of a pistol-wielding spitfire whose intent he had obviously misjudged. He never would have believed she had it in her to harm a fly, let alone brain a man who outweighed her by at least five stone.

Wincing, Lucien rose from the ground. He figured he'd only been unconscious for a few minutes. Not long enough to be completely humiliated, but long enough for the little thief to escape. He'd been outfoxed, damn it, and he didn't like the feeling one bit.

Lucien listened, hearing nothing but the wind through

the trees and the drunken revelry coming from the tavern a short distance away, where he intended to enjoy one more night of blessed freedom before reluctantly taking charge of his ward, Lady Francine Fitz Hugh. George's sister.

Lucien dragged a hand through his hair, coming away with blood on his fingertips. This was his reward for his foolhardy agreement to come to this benighted dirt hole. George should be here; not Lucien. He should have protected the boy better. He had been his commanding officer, after all. From the first day, George had been overzealous, eager for action, eager to please—and he should have stayed the hell back in England, with his family.

Instead he had landed in Lucien's regiment, all battle-hardened soldiers who understood their leader was fallible and weren't foolish enough to worship him. Most knew how he had earned the nickname Renegade.

He should have gotten out sooner. Before his demons took control of him. Before he had caused the death of a twenty-four-year-old boy.

A familiar anguish twisted in his gut as he grabbed his horse's reins and led him into a stall, removing the bridle and saddle and brushing him down, then stocking his hay and water.

As Lucien was leaving, the stable boy ambled in, a disheveled ragamuffin with sandy brown hair and a pale, freckled face. He was rubbing the sleep from his eyes, which widened upon spotting Lucien.

"Cor, mister . . . y' scared me." His gaze traveled up Lucien's tall form and he blinked. "Y' is a big 'un, ain't ye?"

The boy's reaction was not uncommon. At six-four, Lucien generally received a second look. He had to duck to enter most taverns, as the entranceways were constructed for men of lesser height. A damnable nuisance when one was inebriated.

"Where've you been, boy?"

A flush spotted the lad's apple cheeks. "I fell asleep in the back loft, sir. It be the only dry spot about on a night such as this."

"Do you have a name?"

"Aye, sir. Jimmy."

"How old are you, Jimmy?"

"Ten, sir."

Bloody hell. The boy should be at home in bed at this hour, asleep under the watchful eyes of his parents, not catering to a bunch of drunken swines on a damp night.

Lucien eyed the lad's bare feet and shabby clothing, both a glaring reminder of how miserable being poor could be. So many children had to work to feed themselves and help support their families; common necessities were luxuries. Lucien saw glimpses of the youth he had once been in the boy staring at him, and he didn't like the feeling.

"Please don't tell nobody," Jimmy beseeched. "I promise it won't never happen again."

Lucien couldn't bring himself to reprimand the boy. He knew young Jimmy would be out of a job if his employer got wind of his falling asleep. The loss of even those meager wagers could be devastating to his family.

Lucien understood that daily struggle for survival, having grown up in London's rookery amid squalid misery, being taught about life by beggars and prostitutes, how to survive by hawkers, scavengers, and swindlers. It was something that stayed in a man's blood and forever tainted him.

"I've got a job for you," Lucien said.

The boy eyed him warily and took a hesitant step back. "Wot kind of job?"

Lucien knew what Jimmy thought he was proposing: some men found young boys to their liking. The very thought made bile rise in his throat.

"Give my horse some extra oats tonight." He pointed to Sire's stall. "He's had a long day." Lucien pulled out a pound note and handed it to the boy, who gaped at it bug-eyed.

"Thank ee, sir! I'll take care of 'im right an' proper, I will."

Lucien thought to tell the lad to purchase some shoes, but doubted he would. So he simply nodded and turned to go. Then he stopped, a pair of green eyes flashing in his mind.

Looking over his shoulder, he said, "Have you seen anyone strange around here this evening?"

Jimmy canted his head. "Strange, sir?"

Lucien didn't know why he was reluctant to ask the real question, which was if the lad had seen a woman masquerading in men's clothing.

"Never mind." She was best forgotten, anyway.

Lucien headed toward the tavern, where the feeble glow of lamplight shone through the grimy windowpanes, the dregs of humanity within drowning themselves in ale and gin. He knew their type well. It was the life he was accustomed to. The life he had never managed to escape.

He stepped through the door. A cloud of smoke huddled against the rafters, the beams darkened with age, the smell of cheap liquor a familiar one. He needed a drink. He needed a woman. And he prayed to God that tonight he wouldn't need anything more than that.

He sat down at a table in the far corner, his back to the wall as his gaze scanned the motley crowd. A plump barmaid sauntered toward him, ample breasts, ample hips, and lust in her eyes.

"Wot can I get ee, luv?"

"Bottle of whiskey."

"Plan on 'avin' y'rself a good time, do y'?"

"As good as possible."

"Alone?" Her query was as subtle as the rock the impertinent little thief had hit him with.

"Hopefully not." He couldn't bear another night of solitude.

She smiled seductively. "I get off at two."

Hopefully, he'd get off soon thereafter. "Two it is."

Giving him a promising look over her shoulder, she walked away to get his order.

Lucien leaned his head back against the wall and closed his eyes. Why hadn't he just hired another governess for his ward instead of coming here himself? Probably, he thought wryly, because the last two women had up and quit, both referring to Lady Francine Fitz Hugh as a completely incorrigible chit who would never aspire to being a true lady. Hopeless, in other words.

Just what he needed; some willful brat who would give him more headaches than he already had. How the hell old was she anyway? He couldn't remember if George had told him. Fitz had always called her his little Fancy, an angel, he claimed. Clearly the man had been too blind to see his sister for the pain in the rump she was.

The barmaid returned with his bottle and a passably clean glass. She leaned over his shoulder to pour his drink, her mountainous breasts pressing suggestively against him. Normally that would have been enough to stir him, and yet it didn't. He couldn't help wishing that he hadn't lost the lass from the stables. Clearly he had contracted a brain fever.

"Y' are a big hunk o' man. Probably built like a stallion." She shot a glance at his groin. "Ten minutes and Sugar'll give y' the ride of y'r life." With that promise, she sashayed to the next table.

The first shot of rot gut hit Lucien's palate like a rock rolling down his throat. But it would soon do the trick, benumb his brain, and that was all that mattered.

He took another belt and caught the barmaid's summons, a promise of promiscuous sex in her eyes as she waved to him from the stairs leading to the chambers above, clearly in a hurry to fall into bed and do the deed.

Lucien contemplated an excuse—a growing peculiarity for a man who had always thoroughly enjoyed women. Perhaps that was why he couldn't banish the image of the fiery head-basher. She had stirred him, and he had needed to know if the feelings she aroused would carry him through, or if that veil of numbness would descend once again.

Yet the thought of being alone, knowing what awaited him in the hours after midnight when his soul was restless, motivated him to his feet and across the pockmarked floor-boards. Grabbing the barmaid by the hand, he pulled her up the stairs.

"Y' like it rough, do y'?" She scraped her nails across his back and purred in her coarse voice, "So do I."

At the top of the stairs, the barmaid shoved him up against the wall, her hand cupping his groin as her mouth found his, perhaps expecting him to consummate the act in the hallway.

Lucien took hold of her wrists and backed her up a step. Her eyes were nearly feral with lust. "Patience, dear girl. My room is right down there."

He guided her toward the last door on the left, wondering if he could summon a properly enthusiastic response when his body balked at being used against its will.

He was contemplating his options when a flash of movement caught the corner of his eye, drawing his gaze to a partially opened door at the end of the corridor where he spotted a familiar breeches-clad leg, heard a familiar warning, then a familiar thud. A grim smile curved his lips.

"Stay here," he ordered the barmaid as he moved to investigate, his restlessness forgotten as he contemplated the reckoning one little thief was soon to have.